The Dirty Dozen

Weston Raske

Copyright © *Weston Raske,* 2023
All Rights Reserved

This book is subject to the condition that no part of this book is to be reproduced, transmitted in any form or means; electronic or mechanical, stored in a retrieval system, photocopied, recorded, scanned, or otherwise. Any of these actions require the proper written permission of the author.

Contents

Dedication / Acknowledgements 1

About the Author 2

Chapter 1 3

Chapter 2 9

Chapter 3 15

Chapter 4 19

Chapter 5 29

Chapter 6 33

Chapter 7 39

Chapter 8 48

Chapter 9 57

Chapter 10 64

Chapter 11 75

Chapter 12 87

Chapter 13 94

Chapter 14 102

Chapter 15 107

Chapter 16 120

Chapter 17 127

Chapter 18 134

Chapter 19 143

Chapter 20 155

Chapter 21 164

Chapter 22 174

Chapter 23 182

Chapter 24 192

Chapter 25 200

Chapter 26 211

Chapter 27 220

Chapter 28 229

Chapter 29 238

Chapter 30 249

Chapter 31 265

Dedication / Acknowledgements

I dedicate this book to my loving wife, Judy, who never wavered in her support and hardly batted an eye when, out the blue, I suddenly said I was going to write a novel. I told her when we first married 29 years ago that "someday" I'd like to write a book. It has always been in the back of my mind. Well, during those long days of pandemic lockdown, 'someday' arrived and I sat down and began outlining the story and characters you are about to embark on a grand adventure with.

Since this is my first time writing a book, all I can say for sure is that what follows is the type of novel I like to read when I just need to relax and escape reality for a bit. It seemed a logical place from which to start.

As the book slowly began to take shape, I found I could rely on a small group of family and friends who read along week by week as the project progressed, and offered feedback from their varied perspectives which greatly encouraged me and made a huge contribution to the final product. Special thanks in this regard go to my big brother Dan Raske, my son Matthew Raske, my lifetime friend Tim Harpur, his daughter Rachel Harpur, and my parents, Arthur and Ramona Raske who collectively performed this sounding board role and convinced me that the project was worth seeing through.

And finally, a huge thanks to the great team at Amazon Pro Hub who did all the hard work behind the scenes that goes into taking a raw manuscript and turning it into a published book. From masterful book cover artwork to professional editing, formatting, and skillful marketing, they covered all the bases and were pleasant and easy to work with all along the way.

About the Author

Weston Raske was born in Calgary, Alberta (Canada), though his family moved to St. John's, Newfoundland and Labrador, when he was just two years old, and he has lived there ever since.

He graduated with a Bachelor of Commerce Honours (Co-operative) degree from Memorial University of Newfoundland in 1992 and went on to earn his Chartered Professional Accountant (CPA) designation in 1995. For the first half of his career, Weston worked in public accounting with firms such as Ernst and Young and Grant Thornton. Since 2011, he has worked as a senior manager in finance and accounting for Vision33, a private company with a global reach in delivering information technology solutions for both private and public organizations.

Weston married the love of his life, Judy, in 1994, and together they have raised two children. His daughter, Leanne, is currently following in her father's footsteps, having earned a CPA designation, and working in public accounting. His son, Matthew recently graduated with a law degree from Dalhousie University in Halifax, Nova Scotia.

Weston has wide and varied interests with a love of the outdoors, various sports, classic cars such, as his 1965 Mustang coupe, and cruising around on his motorcycle.

Chapter 1

Tanchon, North Korea

Song Hee peered anxiously ahead into the inky gloom from the bridge of the dilapidated fishing trawler as it entered North Korean waters off the port town of Tanchon. Hardly for the first time, he contemplated the questionable wisdom of his plan. He lived a dangerous life, and he knew it. Reveled in it, in fact. But he hadn't made it successfully to his thirty-seventh birthday the previous week by taking unnecessary risks.

As they slowly chugged towards the shore, he signaled the captain to bear slightly starboard, and to slow even further to trawling speed. Two days earlier, Song Hee had paid the South Korean fishing captain handsomely to take him aboard his nondescript vessel and sail out with a dozen other similar fishing trawlers to the fishing grounds, only to slip away earlier that day for the risky night foray into North Korean waters.

As the trawler slowed, the light swell took hold of the vessel, causing it to wallow noticeably. Song Hee braced himself against the wall and trained his night vision goggles on a dark shadow that had begun to take shape as it approached from shore. Soon, he was able to make out the sharp lines of a North Korean Navy gunship. Trailing behind it, he could also make out another vessel, much like their own fishing trawler. Even in the gloom, he could tell that it appeared even more decrepit than his own - dented and scarred with long gashes of rust. He signaled for the engines to be cut, made his way to the deck, and took a powerful LED flashlight from his pocket. Holding it aloft, he pointed it towards the North Korean gunship and flashed 3 times quickly followed by one sustained flash.

After a moment's pause, the gunship reciprocated the pre-arranged signal. Song Hee exhaled in relief, and the hammering in his chest slowed ever so slightly. He had heard all the horror stories of people who entered North Korea, never to be heard from again. That being said, the regime was always desperate for hard currency and had developed a reputation in the underworld for being a reliable partner when cash was on the table.

And cash **was** on the table in a big way tonight. The North Koreans had plenty of what Song Hee's patron was after. And it seemed to Song Hee that the shadowy group that hired him for the mission had plenty of cash – indeed, a good chunk of it was required to convince him to take on this mission. He didn't know who they were or what their business was. Nor did he care. He was paid handsomely to do the job, and he intended to carry it out. In the meantime, he kept his eyes trained on the approaching vessels until they slid alongside.

The fishing captain left the bridge and threw a line and rope ladder over the starboard rail to the gunship. Crossing to the port side, he hurled a second line to the approaching fishing trawler, which was quickly secured to the other side, sandwiching their trawler between the two North Korean vessels.

Four North Korean soldiers scrambled up the rope ladder, automatic weapons slung loosely over their shoulders, landed lightly on the trawler's deck, and approached Song Hee. Two held him tightly while a third expertly searched him. The captain was waved over and received similar treatment. Song Hee knew better than to carry any weapons and had instructed the captain to carry nothing on his person. The only thing they found, other than his flashlight, was a small electronic device that looked like a hand-held GPS. Having completed his search, the soldier nodded to his commander.

"You have the agreed payment?" questioned the lead North Korean commander.

"Of course!" answered Song Hee quickly. He shuddered to think what would happen if he didn't. These guys did not look like they were in the habit of playing games or tolerating fools. Willing himself to appear calm, he added, "Once I inspect the merchandise and confirm it is what was agreed on, the cash is all yours."

After a brief pause, Song Hee was relieved to see the North Korean commander wave to the crew of the trawler, who began preparing six large 4'x4' wooden crates for transfer to Song Hee's ship. He knew the crates would weigh at least five hundred pounds each and had come prepared with a small crane mounted amidships. With a nervous glance towards the trio of North Korean soldiers with their automatic weapons loosely trained in his direction, Song Hee climbed into the crane and began to maneuver the crates onto his vessel.

Song Hee's crane skills were rudimentary, at best. He had familiarized himself with the controls before sailing, but what had seemed a straightforward task on dry land in broad daylight proved far trickier in the dark as the decks of both vessels lurched randomly with the swell. The transfer of the first four crates went about as well as could be expected, but there had been a few close calls, and Song Hee found himself clenching the controls with a death grip, drenched in a cold sweat. *Four down, two to go,* he thought. Song Hee lifted the fifth crate and was in the process of swinging it over the rail and towards the deck when the trawler suddenly lurched sharply down and to the right. The crate slid through the canvas straps like a greased seal and crashed thunderously to the steel deck. The NK soldiers, who had relaxed and let their attention wander, nearly jumped out of their skin, reflexively bringing their automatic weapons to bear and squeezing off a full magazine of rounds – spraying them in all directions.

From Song Hee's point of view, all hell had broken loose. The sound of automatic weapons fire was deafening. The muzzle flashes blinding. In a panic, he threw himself to the deck behind the crane. He could hear the rounds whizzing past his head as he curled into a fetal position, trying desperately not to soil himself. The South Korean fishing captain panicked and made a run for it, catapulting himself over the rail and into the heaving sea below. His gurgling scream as he hit the water drowned out in the commotion.

And suddenly, it was over as soon as it had begun. The NK commander quickly regained control of the situation, screaming at his men to cease fire. A quick inspection revealed no significant damage. Both fishing trawlers sported a few additional holes and dents but were otherwise spared. The South Korean captain was not so lucky. Peering over the rail, they found his mangled body trapped between the two trawlers, lifeless bulging eyes staring accusingly back towards Song Hee's flashlight. The soldiers retrieved his body, wrapped a heavy length of chain around it, and cast it back into the murky waters, where it slipped quietly into the depths.

After a quick inspection of the goods, it was clear that all the crates were still intact, even the one that had taken a tumble to the deck. Song Hee climbed back into the crane and, to his great relief, completed the transfer of the final crate with no further incident.

Pausing for a moment to collect himself, he climbed out of the crane, reached into his pocket, fished out the small hand-held Geiger counter, and held it towards the North Korean commander, who nodded ever-so-slightly. Song Hee needed to confirm that packed into the wooden crates were lead-lined containers of Caesium-137, known more commonly as *radiocaesium*. The North Koreans' reputation as reliable business partners gave him some confidence that this was the real deal. This initial purchase was a kind of a test transaction – both parties feeling out the other side. If successful, additional larger deals would be forthcoming. The North Koreans had large stores of radiocaesium as a byproduct of their nuclear program, and trading it for hard currency seemed a far superior option than funding costly ways to store it safely.

Song Hee tentatively held the Geiger counter over the first container and grinned to himself when it began chirping softly. The protective lead lining prevented any harmful levels of radiation from seeping out, but the Geiger counter was sensitive enough to confirm the trace levels that he was expecting. After similarly inspecting the other containers, he retrieved a duffle bag from a securely padlocked storage locker below decks and handed it to the NK commander. The North Koreans took their time counting and confirming the authenticity of the US currency. Song Hee was confident the cash was all there and accounted for. He had triple-checked it himself. Many years of hard-earned experience had taught him not to bet his life on someone else's word.

In fact, he was beginning to breathe easier at this point. The loss of the captain was unfortunate, but not critical. He had chosen to participate in this venture of his own accord – and his greed had exacted the ultimate price. In fact, all things considered, the transfer had gone more smoothly than he had dared to hope. He would have to pilot the ship back himself but felt, with luck, he could locate the rest of the fishing fleet on his own and then follow them back to port.

After about ten minutes of intense scrutiny of the duffle bag's contents, the commander gave a curt nod to Song Hee, and the North Koreans disembarked back onto their respective vessels. Song Hee returned to the bridge, only too eager to head his ship east towards international waters and safety. While the North Korean trawler headed back to Tanchon, the gunship fell in behind and escorted them until they reached international waters 12 nautical miles offshore. The North Korean vessel then gunned her engines, executed a tight 180-degree turn, and roared back towards Tanchon. Song Hee, meanwhile, turned the fishing trawler 90 degrees to starboard, steering back south the way they had come.

As the sun slowly tinged the eastern horizon pink, the South Korean fishing fleet appeared out of the gloom, and Song Hee eased the trawler into their midst. Later that day, he kept pace with the fleet as they returned to their home port of Gangneung - just another ordinary fishing trawler amongst many, returning home with its catch after a few days at sea. He waited until nightfall before clumsily docking and unloading his cargo. He had three of his men meet him on the dock, and together, they muscled the crates into a rented truck. Driving to a warehouse nearby, they unloaded the crates, returned the truck and made their way back to the safe house that had been set up for the operation.

News of the missing fishing captain was the subject of much-animated discussion in the community for weeks afterward. Local police interviewed the other fishermen who recalled seeing him steam back into port with them, but none remembered engaging him on the radio or seeing him unload his catch. Without any further leads to go on, the trail grew cold, and the case remained unsolved.

Chapter 2

Undisclosed location near Luxembourg, Belgium

The sun had long set, and the night's darkness had settled deeply on a brisk, moonless evening. The cold wind rustled the leaves of the ancient oak trees that dotted the property. One by one, a dozen dark limousines halted outside the wrought iron gates guarding the perimeter of the property and established their credentials before being ushered through the gates to a large stone mansion that dated back to medieval times. The cars pulled up to the main entrance, dispatched their sole backseat passenger, and disappeared into the night. Once inside, each arrival was subjected to a thorough search, passed through a metal detector, and had their phones and other electronic devices confiscated. With the security check completed, they were ushered into a spacious meeting room and seated around a large oval table.

There were a dozen in all. Seven men. Five women. They represented all walks of life, backgrounds, and ethnicities. Wealth, power, connections, and a passion to save the world from itself were what they had in common. All believed that the activities of mankind were creating irreversible harm to the globe that represented an existential threat to the human race. They were equally convinced that the global response was too slow, too ineffective. Too little, too late. Good intentions and strong words, but relatively little action. It simply was not going to be good enough. The Paris Climate Accord had been a step in the right direction, but it was painfully obvious that targets agreed to were slipping by the wayside – not a hope in hell of being achieved. The US, under the previous administration, had withdrawn outright, and that failure of traditional US leadership had devasting effects on the will of the remaining signatory countries to hold the line.

The bottom line was that too many countries paid lip service to cutting greenhouse gas emissions but failed to live up to their good intentions. Oceans continued to be polluted. Factories continued to belch out harmful emissions, poisoning the air. The world's clean freshwater reserves continued to be depleted. Too many parts of the world were embroiled in endless conflicts or were run by corrupt governments such that concern for the environment could never be a real priority. Short-term survival was necessarily paramount. There was no point in worrying about 50 years from now if your focus and energy were required to survive the next week, month or year. Populations around the world were growing, pressure on the environment relentlessly increasing, and time had all but run out. Mankind was very nearly at the point of no return.

The nervous, hushed chatter ceased abruptly as a large monitor at the front of the room flickered to life, revealing the shadowed silhouette of a woman known only to The Council as Helle. Helle had recruited them one by one to this most urgent cause, and they had come tonight at her bidding. While they each exclusively used an alias assigned to them by Helle, and all communications between the group were heavily encrypted, they knew their fellow conspirators' real identities. It was hard to hide, really, because they were all prominent public figures. Only Helle kept her real identity completely hidden, and it was a heavily debated topic amongst the Council in private.

"Ladies and gentlemen," Helle began in a thick, heavily disguised voice, "Thank you all for coming tonight. As you know, just as the earth is nearing a point of no return from which no action of man can save it, so you have passed your own point of no return. A commitment that will no doubt cost you dearly. You have already made a great financial commitment, and this journey may yet extract a greater price than money can measure. It may cost you everything. But we have a cause that is greater than ourselves. And every great cause requires great sacrifice. I thank you for your service.

"Our planet is dying. The science is clear and irrefutable. If we continue on our current course, our best scientific models predict that oceans will rise to such an extent that land on which 70% of the current world's population lives will be underwater within seventy-five years. Simply building dykes or moving to higher ground will not be an option because, by then, the climate throughout the majority of the inhabited world will be too hot to support human life, arable land needed to feed us will be useless deserts, and the oceans poisoned and lifeless. As a result, all human life is facing certain extinction. Seventy-five years is not a long time. But it is much longer than the five to ten years we have left to reverse course and make the changes necessary to avoid crossing the point of no return; the point at which the damage we have done to our planet is irreversible, and our fate is sealed."

The speaker paused and allowed the gravity of her words to sink in. The silence in the room was deafening. No one dared look anywhere but at the screen – gazing at Helle, afraid even to blink. Satisfied she had their full attention, she continued.

"During the recent pandemic, the rippling global shutdowns and reduced economic activity had a remarkable impact. Even though the respite was relatively brief, our planet showed a remarkable capacity to heal. Water and air qualities showed unmistakable and rapid improvement – far greater than we dared hope to believe was possible. Mountain ranges that had been hidden by smog for decades suddenly reappeared for the first time in memory. These changes were real, unprecedented, and documented through solid science. But sadly, as vaccines and effective treatments became widely available and the pandemic receded, the world's economies have rebounded, factories have begun producing overtime to fill pent-up demand, and we are polluting our environment at a faster pace than ever. We are now pumping carbon dioxide into our atmosphere at levels never seen before and eating into our ozone layer at a record pace. By so doing, we are hastening our own demise in the process. We won the battle against the pandemic but are losing the war for human survival.

"Each of you have been fully briefed on our plan to intervene in global affairs and set this planet on a permanent path to recovery once and for all. The means to achieve this noble end are difficult. Many will not understand at first. Intense sacrifice will be required, and some will die. These are not decisions that are taken lightly, and I commend the courage and fortitude you have each shown to do what is necessary in the circumstance we find ourselves in. I am pleased to report that the first steps of our plan are already underway. We have sourced sufficient radioactive material from North Korea, and I expect to hear a positive report shortly from our man in South Korea, who we have paid generously to take possession of it. As we move forward, I will keep you informed. Each of you has a role to play, and we will only succeed if we work together and each play our part."

Each Council member nodded slightly towards Helle and gently thumped the table to signal their solidarity and commitment, all except for the tall, blonde Icelandic woman at the far end of the table who slowly raised her hand. "Yes, Freyja?" acknowledged Helle.

"There must be a better way," she began nervously. Glancing around the room at each individual seated around the table and then back to Helle, she continued more confidently. "Should this plan succeed, many thousands of innocent people will lose their lives in an instant. Tens of thousands more will be maimed – lives irreversibly harmed. Millions will suffer long-term health effects – enduring pain, anguish, and ultimately dying early deaths, ravaged by disease and early-onset forms of cancer. And yet, despite this devastating human toll, there is no guarantee that it will even have the desired effect of bringing healing to our planet. I understand what you are trying to achieve, but I can no longer be a part of this. The cost is too high and the outcome too uncertain."

"I'm so sorry you feel this way, Freyja," Helle replied evenly, her monotone disguised voice sounding eerily calm and devoid of any emotion whatsoever. "Is there anyone else that feels the same way? Now is the time to speak out. There can be no backing out after this point." There was a long pause. Nobody spoke. Barely breathed. Except for Freyja, they all seemed to find something very interesting on the table directly in front of them, requiring their complete, undivided attention.

"All right then," Helle finally continued. "We cannot ask you to participate if your conscience won't allow it. I thank you, Freyja, for your contributions to our cause, but you must leave the room immediately. Your phone and personal items will be returned to you on the way out. Please. Return home to your country, your life, and your family. But you must never speak of this to anyone."

Freyja nodded briefly, pushed her chair back and stood up. Without another word, she walked toward the door at the far end of the room. Helle watched her turn around and then raised her hand. Immediately, the man who had been sitting next to Freyja stood up, reached inside his blazer, smoothly pulled out a Sig Sauer P229 with a silencer attached, aimed briefly, and fired. The gun coughed surprisingly loudly in the quiet room, and the front of Freyja's head instantly exploded. Her body didn't pitch forward or even fall. It simply collapsed straight down into a tangled heap, like a building slated for demolition when the charges are detonated. The shooter holstered his gun and sat down as if nothing had happened.

Helle waited a few moments until the gasps, stifled screams, and retching sounds died down before speaking again. "Thank you, Nicos. I had hoped it wouldn't come to that but I knew I could count on you if it became necessary. As for the rest of you, I'm truly sorry you had to see that. It was necessary to ensure all of us are fully committed to seeing this through. You know we could not take the risk of letting her walk out and expose us all. Saving our planet will cost many more lives, but it need not be yours. Freyja's death will be staged as a tragic accident. As far as the world knows, she will go missing on her voyage back to Iceland and presumed drowned at sea. Now… unless anyone has any further objection, it's time to get to work."

Chapter 3

CIA Headquarters. Langley, VA

It had already been a long day, and yet it was only 2:00 pm. Greg Miller, a junior analyst with the Central Intelligence Agency, rubbed his eyes wearily and scrolled through the photos one more time. He was assigned to a team tasked with monitoring the North Korean nuclear program and had spent several months now poring over satellite photos taken of the Nyongbyon Nuclear Research Center, one of North Korea's prime nuclear facilities.

The facility was known to be responsible for producing fissile materials for North Korea's nuclear weapons program, operating a 5 MWe nuclear reactor, recovering usable uranium and plutonium from spent fuel, and storing dangerous radioactive byproducts in a large underground facility carved into the side of a nearby mountain.

It was his job to write a report every day comparing photos of successive satellite passes over the facility – noting in detail what was different from the photo before, how many vehicles, and what types, were parked by each building; for example, Greg had an eye for detail and freely admitted to being 'a little OCD'. Everything had a place, and before he completed each report, he needed to see everything neatly accounted for.

But... everything was not neatly accounted for, and it bothered him. Alarmed? No, that wasn't it. Annoyed? Yes! It annoyed him that a rail car was missing, preventing him from completing his report. He couldn't care less what the bloody North Koreans were up to. Sure, they ran a sophisticated nuclear facility producing fissionable material that ended up in nukes aimed at his country, and no doubt that was someone's problem. But not his. At least not today. His problem was that they had done something unexpected, and now he couldn't account for a rail car that had vanished overnight.

The North Koreans used 4 specially designed and constructed rail cars to collect spent fuel and other radioactive material from various locations on the compound and transport them to the long-term storage site 10 miles north of the facility. It was one of these rail cars that had disappeared. The movement of the cars around the compound and trips made to the storage area under the mountain was routinely monitored and logged – giving the Americans a fairly good idea of the activity levels of the facility. Different rail cars were designed for different types of containers, and so, depending on which cars were in transit, they were able to glean intelligence on what kind of activities were currently taking place.

So where was the missing car? He knew it was the one designed to carry specialized lead-lined crates of radiocaesium. It had been there the day before, parked in plain sight. Hadn't moved in 2 weeks. But it was not there today. And it hadn't made the trip to the storage facility to the north either. He had checked and re-checked the time-stamped photos and was not able to locate it either in transit or parked at the storage facility. So, it had made a trip somewhere… but where?

Greg tapped on his keyboard, pulling in additional enhanced satellite photos and broadening his search area to a 50-mile radius around the compound. Zooming and scrolling, he spent hours searching all the train tracks that connected with the Nyongbyon compound, which was a struggle because the North Koreans used a lot of trains… and one car looked pretty much like another from an overhead satellite view – even with the best satellites in the world that the CIA had at its disposal.

It was several hours past his quitting time when he finally found his rail car. Strangely, it was attached to a long train of cars headed east toward the coast. Greg downloaded a few more photos and confirmed that his rail car was currently parked in Tanchon, a port city on the east coast of the Korean Peninsula. He breathed a sigh of relief and updated his daily report with the pertinent details. Shutting down his computer, he grabbed his coat, relieved to be headed home for a long overdue supper.

By noon the next day, Greg's report had advanced through several layers of review as senior analysts in the Asian division prepared their daily briefing notes for the Deputy Chief of Asian Operations, Rod Stringer. Most of the mundane details had been stripped out along the way, but the North Korean radiocaesium rail car making its way to Tanchon was deemed notable enough to be retained.

As Rod scanned the briefing, it caught his eye, and he rubbed his temples as he thought about it. *Tanchon? There were no known nuclear facilities there of any kind. Why would they send the car there? Were they picking up radiocaesium and bringing it back to Nyongbyon? That would make the most sense, as there was at least a known storage site for radioactive materials there. But why would there be any radiocaesium in Tanchon, to begin with? Or were they transporting radiocaesium from Nyongbyon to Tanchon? That also didn't seem logical on the face of it.*

The more he pondered it, the less he liked it. *Was it possible they were putting it on a ship? Perhaps they were running out of storage room at Nyongbyon? That hardly seemed likely. They could just dig deeper or tunnel further under the mountain. Surely that would be an easier solution than shipping it by rail to the coast to put it on a boat to go… where? And to who? For what purpose?* An involuntary shudder passed through him as the worst-case scenario flitted across his mind. *They wouldn't. Would they?*

He would order further scrutiny of the port, but truth be told, all they had were satellite photos which he doubted would tell them anything further. What he really needed was boots on the ground. But human intelligence (HUMINT) was in short supply everywhere these days and was currently non-existent in North Korea. He thought harder. He had an idea. At some level, he knew he probably shouldn't. It would never receive official sanction. But given what could potentially be at stake, what choice did he have? And what was the saying? 'Better to ask forgiveness than permission.' And 'Better safe than sorry'. Both comforting bits of wisdom seemed to apply here. He picked up his secure phone and placed a call to an old friend.

Chapter 4

St. John's, Newfoundland, Canada

Blake Zane laughed as he squinted into the late afternoon sun. The glancing rays danced on the waves, littering its surface with millions of glittering diamonds. *Dauntless* and her crew had just completed a full battery of sea trials, and the luxury mega yacht had passed them all with flying colors. His wife Katherine - or Kat, as nearly everyone called her - stood close with her arm around him, and had just whispered something in his ear, mischievous green eyes flashing.

Blake was casually dressed in a navy golf shirt and khaki shorts. Now in his early thirties, he could still easily pass for someone much younger. Tousled light brown hair, pushed up in the front by his mirrored aviator sunglasses perched jauntily on his forehead, completed his relaxed look. Standing just over five foot and eleven inches with a medium, athletic build, Blake did not tend to stand out in a crowd, although, with his ruggedly boyish good looks, he had often been told he could pass as Tom Cruise's doppelganger.

Kat was somewhat tall for a woman, nearly as tall as her husband, and taller if she wore heels. A classic blonde-haired, green-eyed beauty, she still had the taut, athletic build of the competitive swimmer she had been in her college days. Today, her blonde hair was neatly tied back, and she was wearing a loose-fitting white summer dress that reached nearly to her knees, gathered jauntily at the waist with a rope belt.

Dauntless was just rounding the tip of Cape Spear, the most easterly point in North America, and Blake pointed her bow towards The Narrows, which marked the entrance to St. John's harbor. Kat had grown up in St. John's, and her parents and much of her family still lived there. Although Kat had moved away years ago to pursue a swimming scholarship at Boston College, she still regarded St. John's as home and was thrilled to be returning for a visit.

As they glided across Freshwater Bay towards the harbor entrance, Blake turned the controls over to the First Mate, Matt Granger, and reflected on the journey that had brought him and Kat to this point. Only five years earlier, they sold their tech company and related intellectual property for a princely sum. Blake had started the company shortly after high school, using his incredibly gifted mind to develop algorithms that the National Security Agency (NSA) found particularly helpful to mine useful nuggets of intelligence out of the reams of data they collected from communication intercepts around the world.

A few years later, Blake met Kat in an online chatroom full of computer geeks discussing quantum computing. Shortly after graduating summa cum laude with a computer science degree, Kat moved from Boston to Duluth, Minnesota to join Blake's company. Blake could always make Kat laugh. Kat brightened every room she entered, and it wasn't long before they realized they were spending every moment together and could never imagine it any other way. They were married in St. John's just one year later. Kat's large Newfoundland family warmed to Blake quickly – especially after discovering he was a standout high school hockey star and the first American they had met who could skate like a native. Blake also charmed them with his genial personality and sharp wit. Coming from a rather small family himself, he embraced the warmth that exuded from Kat's family and, indeed, found the local culture, history, and scenery of Canada's easternmost province utterly charming. No matter how busy things got, they always found time to make several visits a year 'home' to Newfoundland.

Blake and Kat were more than just marriage partners. They were simply partners in everything, 50/50. They owned and ran the company together. They worked on major projects together. They played beer league hockey on the same team together and even swam together to keep in shape. They made major decisions together, and having desired to start a family, they wept together when they learned that having a biological child of their own would remain forever out of their reach.

Meanwhile, their business enterprise was highly successful. The licensing agreements for their intellectual property with the US government continued to expand. The initial contract with the National Security Agency (NSA) grew in scope and complexity. Within a few years, they also developed and licensed key algorithms to the Central Intelligence Agency (CIA) to help them parse valuable intelligence from the massive amounts of data they collected globally. In addition, Kat consulted with leading tech firms and various friendly governments around the world in her specialized fields of quantum computing and 3D printing.

Having achieved financial independence by their late twenties, however, they began to grow restless and spent many evenings discussing if spending their lives furthering computer science was what they really wanted. Blake had begun dabbling in the exciting (but somewhat frightening) field of artificial intelligence, mulling over with Kat the possibilities of combining the technologies of AI with quantum computing.

In the end, they went in another direction altogether. Having wisely retained full rights to all intellectual property they had developed, and with their tech embedded deeply into the computer systems of both the NSA and CIA, they were able to extract a princely sum from the US government for ownership of the code. In addition, they had tweaked some of their algorithms and licensed them to the upstart internet company, Google, some years previously. At the time, Google was just one of several companies struggling for supremacy in the internet search engine field. Aided by Blake and Kat's algorithms, they were able to improve their search engine dramatically, and the rest, as they say, was history. When offered the chance to purchase the full rights to the technology buried deep in their servers, Google jumped at the opportunity, and Blake and Kat would never have to worry about money ever again.

With their financial independence firmly established, they threw themselves wholeheartedly into their new venture – the Clean World Foundation. The mission and core concept of the Foundation was to identify and fund worthy projects around the globe that promoted clean oceans, clean energy, and clean fresh water. The Foundation insisted on overseeing any projects funded and on utilizing locals as much as possible to carry them out. The project proponents were retained as special advisors and on-site project managers. The Foundation prioritized projects located in 'third world' countries where clean oceans, clean energy, and clean fresh water were often necessary afterthoughts.

One of the immediate challenges they ran into was being forced into the spotlight as the face of the Foundation. Up until this point, their professional lives had been spent behind the scenes, attracting almost zero public attention. Now, to attract attention and funding to their worthy cause, they had to learn the delicate art of schmoozing and rubbing shoulders with wealthy patrons at gala fundraising events. Of course, they contributed handsomely to the Foundation themselves, but they recognized that to truly make a global difference over the long haul, the Foundation needed to raise serious capital on an ongoing basis.

From the outset, they wanted to be personally involved, not just in fundraising, but in actively overseeing the projects.. To do that, they would require maximum mobility while continuing to be fully connected to the outside world. Like a rock band that traveled from gig to gig in an RV. Or an executive running his business from the back of a limousine. But what would give them that kind of mobility and connectivity on a global scale? A yacht!! And not just any yacht.

A full ocean-going mega yacht that would serve as their permanent home, taking them to any part of the world they wished to go while never leaving home. And thus, the concept of *Dauntless* was born.

She quickly progressed from an ambitious concept to detailed plans and drawings – eventually taking shape as an ultra-modern 125-meter all-black mega yacht. They worked together on an overall design concept and basic specs. They envisioned 6 decks in total - 4 above water and 2 below. Kat took responsibility for interior design layout and decor – something she soon found she had a natural affinity for. Blake busied himself with designing more technical aspects of the ship's systems – propulsion, controls, 'toys', and weapons systems.

Yes, weapons systems. Knowing they would be operating much of the time in pirate-infested waters overseeing projects in war-torn third-world countries, they realized their luxury yacht would make a conspicuous target for any and all bad actors in the area. Drawing on their top security clearances and US government and military contacts, they were able to source sophisticated, modern US Navy military technology. Completely hidden from view in sealed hatches, *Dauntless* carried a state-of-the-art 30mm naval cannon and four Aegis missile batteries capable of anti-missile, anti-aircraft, and anti-ship duties. Blake also built in 2 torpedo tubes with the ability to carry up to eight Mark 48 torpedoes and four decoy defensive 'noisemakers' to draw away incoming torpedoes.

The jet-black exterior of *Dauntless* was not just ultra-modern and sleek, it was also radar stealthy. Using clever angles and special 'nano black' paint, *Dauntless* was able to minimize her radar profile. Blake also designed active radar stealth technology that could read incoming radar signals and absorb them without reflecting them back to the source. When explaining the technology, he would compare it to noise-canceling headphones. To avoid becoming a shipping hazard, most of the time, the system would amplify and rebroadcast the incoming radar signals to give off a normal radar signature for a vessel of her size. However, when stealth was required, she could pass for a small fishing vessel on even the most sophisticated military-grade radar. In addition, her exterior skin was strengthened with Kevlar and other space-age composite materials easily capable of repelling small-arms fire. Anything short of an incoming missile or torpedo would bounce off *Dauntless* like a pebble off a window.

Being the flagship of the Clean World Foundation, it was important that *Dauntless* be a carbon-neutral design, and much thought was given to her unique propulsion system. In the end, Blake and Kat decided on a nuclear/electric system powering waterjets. It was one of only a handful of private or commercial vessels in the world with a nuclear powerplant, and installed in a 125-meter vessel, the smallest nuclear-powered ship in the world. The reactor energized a turbine, which generated electricity to power the water jets. The ship would be able to run for at least 5 years before needing to 'refuel' with fresh fissionable fuel rods inserted into its reactor core. In addition, its powerful waterjets, combined with hydrofoils, could propel *Dauntless* to a top speed of up to seventy knots in calm seas. No other vessel in the world of her size could approach that speed on the open seas. The electric motors also gave her uncanny stealth – operating in virtual silence at speeds up to twenty knots. Cruising any faster, the sound of her hull breaking the water would give her away.

The water jet propulsion system had two other significant advantages. Minimal moving parts contributed to a high level of reliability and minimal maintenance. And 360-degree multiple swiveled power nozzles gave *Dauntless* ultimate maneuverability. The three jets at the stern provided forward propulsion, while 3 jets on each of her starboard and port sides and a single bow-mounted jet allowed for ease of docking maneuvers and the ability, in combination with the ship's computers and GPS technology, to hold a stationary position no matter how rough the seas or strong the currents.

As impressive as her weapons and propulsion systems were, the real strength of *Dauntless'* capabilities lay in her electronic brain. Blake and Kat concentrated their talent and energies on building and designing the most capable and secure computer system they could conceive of. Together, they commissioned and installed what could be best described as a 'super-computer', which ran sophisticated software that operated all the ship's systems through touchscreens. Navigation, engineering, weapons, and creature comforts... all could be accessed and run not only from the bridge or 'command center' located just behind the bridge, but from any one of numerous touch screens stationed throughout all decks of the ship. Blake even built in voice-command controls, which could identify authorized voice prints of the ship's crew anywhere on board.

Dauntless' functional capabilities were rounded out by her impressive array of 'toys', as Blake liked to refer to them. Mark Hernandez oversaw all the toys – making sure they were ready to rock and roll at a moment's notice and able to operate and perform routine maintenance on all of them. Mark's toys included several aerial drones, 2 manned submersibles, and several unmanned submersibles. At the rear of the ship, on the 'swim deck', she carried an RHIB landing craft and several jet skis. The submersibles were launched from a moon pool on the lowest deck. Fully outfitted dive gear lockers were located both at the moon pool, as well as on the rear swim deck. Blake, Kat, and most of the crew were all fully certified divers.

Dauntless' final toy was a Bell 429 helicopter, which Blake had modified with folding rotors so the entire unit could be lowered below deck and out of sight. Both Blake and Matt were fully certified pilots. Matt was also a certified helicopter mechanic and did all the necessary maintenance and upkeep on the bird.

The recent sea trials had been done over several weeks in every kind of condition the notoriously violent North Atlantic could throw at it. Every system had been given a thorough workout, and with only a few small exceptions, Blake and Kat were extremely pleased – both with the performance of *Dauntless'* systems and with her crew.

Matt was the first crew member Blake had hired on. Matt's background was in the Navy. He began his career as a bridge officer before eventually becoming a helicopter pilot, flying the MH-60 Blackhawk combat helicopter for the Navy Seals. Blake had met him the previous year when he was training for his commercial helicopter pilot's license. Although Matt was his instructor, they quickly became good friends as well. Blake was thrilled when Matt agreed to take on the role of First Mate on *Dauntless*. He was cool under pressure, trained in combat by the best the US military had to offer, an able bridge captain, and a crack helicopter pilot. Ostensibly, his main role was to run the bridge and be the ship's pilot. But during the sea trials, it became apparent to both men that Blake loved 'driving' the yacht and would often take over just for the fun of it. Matt didn't mind. When he wasn't required on the bridge, he made good use of his time preening over the Bell 429, ensuring it was always fully prepped for flight.

In fact, there wasn't anything Blake liked to do better than to be in control of a manned vehicle. It didn't matter whether it was a car, a truck, a motorcycle, a snowmobile, a submersible, a drone, or, most recently, an airplane and helicopter. If it had a motor and required a driver, Blake itched to do it and had a natural affinity for it. He was born with an uncanny ability to communicate with any vehicle, feel its rhythms, and handle its controls with delicate precision until the machine became an extension of his own body. Which was kind of odd in a way, because, at the same time, he hated working on any of them. He academically understood their various systems and what made them run, but for all his smarts in other things, he found he was mechanically clueless. Anytime he had tried wrenching on something, he would find himself getting frustrated at his ineptitude which would inevitably just make a bad situation worse. It was just as well, he thought, because his interest in that line of work was proportionate to his skill level. It was a great relief once he could afford to pay others to keep his 'toys' in good working order.

Blake's reminiscing was interrupted as Matt announced their arrival at the harbor entrance. "There she is boys! The oldest city in North America. I never get tired of this view."

Blake and Kat glanced to their left, taking in Fort Amherst guarding the entrance to the historic harbor. Last active in World War II, it had fallen into ruin, but you could still see the old crumbling gun placements below the modern functioning lighthouse up above.

On the right, they eased past the Queen's Battery, a semi-circle of 19th-century cannons ominously guarding the harbor entrance, and further up still, Cabot Tower stood atop Signal Hill, standing guard over the harbor and city like a solemn stone sentinel. Signal Hill was so named in honor of it, marking the location where Giovanni Marconi received the first transatlantic radio signal in December 1901. In modern times, it served as the historic city's most iconic landmark and welcomed a constant stream of residents and tourists enjoying its renowned views and storied military history going back to the days when the British and French battled for supremacy in the New World.

No sooner had *Dauntless* slipped through The Narrows and into the sheltered deep-water port beyond when Blake's phone chirped softly with the signature ring of an incoming encrypted call. He glanced down and was surprised to see it was from his old friend at the CIA, Rod Stringer. Blake and Kat had worked closely with Rod on several joint projects aimed at extracting pieces of valuable intelligence from reams of data. Rod was the current deputy chief of Asian operations, and they still kept in touch regularly – mostly through their fantasy football pool - but it was rare, indeed, for him to contact Blake on the encrypted line.

"It's Rod Stringer", Blake told Kat, who had cast a cool, inquisitive glance at the offending intrusion. "And he's calling on a secure line."

Chapter 5

Undisclosed location near Luxembourg, Belgium

Several hours after the shooting, the working meeting adjourned, and the Council members dispersed into the night, the line of limousines repeating their earlier parade to the main entrance before exiting the grounds.

Helle leaned back into her chair and rubbed her temples wearily, the incident with the Icelandic woman replaying itself in her head. She hadn't pulled the trigger, but she had killed her in cold blood as surely as if she had. It was unfortunate. She would have preferred to have avoided it. It was messy and created additional complications in covering up the murder. But she had planned for that. And besides, it had served a useful purpose. By making the group witnesses to the murder - and now accomplices through their silence - they were even more fully committed and bonded to their purpose.

An insistent buzzing jolted her back into the present, and she glanced down to see her burner phone lit up with an incoming call. She had been anxiously anticipating an update from the South Korean local gang boss she had hired to make the initial purchase of radioactive material from the North Koreans. He was relatively young, but struck her as capable, smart, and ambitious. Even so, she figured it was a 50/50 proposition that he wouldn't just take the cash and disappear. But she had assured him there would be plenty of more cash to be made if he were successful. And he seemed smart enough to understand that she had the resources and will to hunt him down should he decide to take the money and run. If that weren't enough, there was no guarantee she could trust the North Koreans to hold up their end of the bargain either. Despite the earlier confidence she had expressed to the Council, the truth was the whole operation was flying on little more than a wing and a prayer. But, other than cash, they had little to lose. It wasn't as if you could buy radiocaesium at your local Walmart. Nothing ventured, nothing gained. Or something like that.

She picked up the phone, ensured the encryption and voice synthesizer icons were active, and answered.

"It's done," reported Song Hee. "The six crates are in the warehouse."

Helle exhaled in relief. She appreciated the brevity of the report. All the crucial facts were there, nice and succinct. Not that she took him completely at his word. She had questions.

"Good work, Mr. Hee. Once I verify the material is there and is authentic, you will receive the other 50% of your payment wired to your account."

"Verify?" questioned Song Hee. "How do you plan on doing that? How will I know when you have verified it?"

"As to your first question, it is none of your business," Helle answered evenly. "As for your second question, I really thought you were smarter than that. You will know I have completed my analysis because you will either be significantly richer or significantly deader."

"OK. OK. Fine. But it is the real deal. I am sure of it. The Geiger counter could detect radioactivity even through the lead lining of the containers."

"Any complications I should know about?" inquired Helle.

"Well... yes. The fishing captain I hired to take me on his boat is dead. There was a little panic when one of the crates dropped onto the deck during the transfer. The North Koreans started firing, and the captain panicked and jumped overboard. Unfortunately, he was crushed between the two ships tied together. We retrieved his body, weighed it down with chains and threw it overboard. I had observed him operate the boat and was able to take command of the vessel, find the fleet early the next morning and return to port with them. No one attempted radio contact. I waited until the rest had unloaded their catch before docking. Some of my men met me, and we quickly unloaded the cargo and brought it to the warehouse."

Helle didn't like it. This could bring unwanted attention. "Has he been reported missing? Are the police investigating? Any surveillance cameras on the docks that could have seen you return alone and unload the crates?" The questions came rapid-fire.

"I have my guys out with their ears to the ground. The police have no leads. They are assuming the captain returned with the boat and disappeared afterward. They'll never find the body on the sea floor in North Korean waters. They have been pretty diligent in interviewing the other fishermen, but no one knows anything. The only thing they are sure of is seeing him sailing back to port with the rest of the fleet. And yes, the docks have security cameras, but I had my guys disable the one covering our area before I docked the boat. It was done carefully to appear like an internal short in the wiring. As far as the authorities know, it was just bad luck that the camera went down when it did."

Helle was grudgingly impressed. Song Hee was proving to be the resourceful and thorough man of his reputation. "OK. It sounds like the situation is under control for now. Keep your eyes and ears open, and let me know if anything changes. I've also heard from the North Koreans. They will be ready soon with another shipment. I will send you instructions for the next rendezvous. Can you find a ship?"

"Yes. That won't be a problem. I'm confident I can operate the vessel myself and can take a couple of my guys with me as a crew. Your cash will free up a suitable ship. In fact, I am pretty sure the ship I used the last time is now for sale or lease, and my local reputation for knocking heads when necessary will ensure wagging tongues stay quiet."

Helle considered for a moment and nodded to herself. "Ok. Let's proceed. You have one week to make your arrangements and make it to the rendezvous point for the next pickup. Once you have secured the next shipment, report back to me."

Chapter 6

St. John's, Newfoundland, Canada

Blake thumbed his phone and put it to his ear. "Hey Rod, you old rascal," he exclaimed. "What's up with you? Still anchored to your desk? When are they going to realize you should have retired years ago and throw you out on your ear?"

"Easy, young fella'. Not everyone gets to gallivant around with a pretty young woman in a fancy yacht saving the world. All the same, I guess it's a fine gig if you can get it," Rod laughed. "Where are you, anyway?"

"We just pulled into St. John's, actually," Blake answered. "We've had a busy few weeks running *Dauntless* through her sea trials. I have to say, she performed flawlessly! I think we're all a bit worn down. Kat and I are looking forward to a little downtime here with her family. And the crew is anxious to get acquainted with George Street. They've heard a lot about it from Kat. It's supposed to be the densest 2-block collection of bars, pubs, and restaurants anywhere in the world. And I can tell you from experience, the locals love themselves a good old-fashioned shed party. Best music and dancing I've seen anywhere. Speaking of Kat, say hello to Rod, dear."

Kat leaned over as Blake held out the phone. "Hello Rod!" she chirped. In truth, she was glad to hear from Rod. He and his wife, Mary, would never fail to invite them over for dinner whenever Blake and Kat were in town on business. They were older than her and Blake, but there was a closeness to their bond such that she thought of them as adopted parent figures.

Blake brought the phone back to his ear. "Hey Rod, what's bothering you? You wouldn't be calling on the encrypted line just for a social chat."

"Nope. You got me there, Blake. Can you find somewhere private with Kat and put me on speaker? I've got a proposal I want to discuss with you."

"Sure, just one moment," Blake answered. "Kat… Rod wants to talk to us in private. Let's pop into the war room." Then he turned to Matt. "Guess what Matt… you get to have all the fun docking her. I have to take this call. Be gentle with my girl. You put one scratch or dent in her, and I'll know!"

"Got it covered boss," Matt replied with a grin. "Maybe I'll just get the computer to parallel park her. Don't tell me you paid a billion dollars for this thing, and it doesn't have the self-parking option!" Blake looked over, determined Matt was just pulling his leg, shook his head, and laughed.

The 'war room' was located just off the bridge of the *Dauntless*. It was a combination of a conference room and weapons control room, with an oak table in the center large enough to comfortably seat eight people. On the walls, banks of large video monitors could display anything from TV shows to digital maps and charts to live feeds from aerial drones or submersibles. In essence, it was the nerve center of *Dauntless*. Perhaps its most notable feature was what appeared to be a full-size cockpit – similar to a jet plane or race car simulator. In fact, it could function as such, but its real purpose was to access and operate the considerable offensive and defensive weapons systems of *Dauntless*. It was the creation and private domain of Eric Hansard, *Dauntless*' Chief Weapons Specialist.

Blake and Kat entered the war room, closed the door behind them, and sat at the conference table with the phone on speaker between them.

Kat scooted her chair close and said, "Go ahead, Rod. Whaddya' got for us?"

Rod paused for a moment and cleared his throat. "Well, this is strictly off the record, but I'm in a bit of a situation, and there is something you might be able to help me out with. You'll want to discuss it with your crew, but it can't go any further than that. I know you've all got security clearances, and that's the only reason I can even bring it up. If you're not comfortable with what I'm about to propose, just say so. No hard feelings, I promise."

Blake and Kat shared a knowing glance, and Kat nodded slightly as she spoke. "Sure Rod. We understand. You've got our attention, that's for sure. We're listening."

Rod continued. "So... I read in the news that the Clean World Foundation is funding *Operation Ocean Renewal*, a project aimed at removing plastics and other debris from the Sea of Japan east of the Korean peninsula. Is that correct?"

"That's right," Blake responded. "It's been underway now for a couple weeks and will run for another few months. The initial proposal was put forward by Sonja Larsen. She's Denmark's representative to the European Union and was recently appointed to the European Commission's Climate Action and Energy Portfolio. I have to say, she is a real tour de force on environmental issues and will be pushing for aggressive greenhouse gas reduction targets for member EU countries. We've met with her a few times, and she's been instrumental in getting the project off the ground. She has lined up a dozen vessels that are currently trawling grids in the area for plastics and other pollutant particles. We have targeted collecting a hundred thousand tonnes of plastic waste from the sea and disposing of it safely in lined underground bunkers."

"And based on progress so far, we are actually ahead of our targets," added Kat. "But since when is the CIA interested in plastic pollution in the Sea of Japan?"

"Good point, Kat," admitted Rod. "I know it's an important issue, but it's not the sort of thing that keeps me up at night. Glad you folks got it covered. My concern is something we noticed going on in North Korea. It may be nothing. I certainly hope it's nothing, but I can't assume it's nothing. The bottom line is I need better intel, and as you know, we've got practically zero intelligence assets in North Korea."

Rod then took a few minutes to share with them the observation of the specialized rail car making an unexpected trip to the coast. "I don't really know if they are bringing radioactive material from their nuclear facility to the Tanchon or picking up radioactive material that has been offloaded from a ship and bringing it back to their nuclear facility. Heck, for all I know, they are doing it just to mess with us. But we've never seen this before and can't afford any nasty surprises."

Blake and Kat shared another glance – this time with a mixture of alarm and puzzlement. "Uh… Rod. We're not sure where you are going with this. First of all, we are currently halfway around the world from North Korea. And secondly, if we were standing on the border, there's no way either of us is setting foot in that place. We've heard the stories. They tend to end badly, no?"

"No, no. I'm not asking anyone to penetrate North Korea. Heavens, no. I wouldn't send my worst enemy there, much less my good friends. I was just thinking that now that *Dauntless* has passed her sea trials, maybe you could sail her across the pond and check up on *Operation Ocean Renewal*. Didn't you say you like to be 'hands-on' with your projects? And a good run halfway around the world would be another good test for *Dauntless*. What I'm asking is that while you are poking around the area saving the world, maybe you could keep an eye out for anything suspicious that might tie into radioactive materials being moved around. I know you've got some pretty sophisticated aerial drones that could have a little look-see. Just stay out of North Korean waters, and if you operate any of your drones in their air space, I don't ever want to know."

"Geez, Rod. I don't know," Blake said hesitantly. "I don't think anyone has ever asked me to sail halfway around the world before. And potentially piss off anyone as prickly as the North Koreans. You always seemed like a pretty level-headed guy. You sure you haven't dipped a little too heavily into that bottle of scotch you keep in the bottom drawer?"

Before Rod could respond, Kat piped up. "Tell you what, Rod. Blake and I will discuss it together and with the crew, and we'll get back to you."

"Sounds good guys. Really sorry to interrupt your little vacation. Let me know what you decide." With that, the connection was cut off.

"What do you think, Kat?" inquired Blake.

Kat drummed her fingers on the table for a minute before responding. "We've got fundraising events coming up this fall, starting with Boston, so we need to be back in time for that. It will take a couple weeks to get clear around the world, and another two weeks to get back. That leaves a few weeks we can spend on site if we need to. Obviously, the crew needs a little break, and we do too. Besides, Mom and Dad would never forgive us for pulling into town and leaving right away."

Blake nodded in agreement. "And speaking of the crew, we need to ensure they are OK with this mission. They signed up to crew the *Dauntless* and support Clean World projects, not perform potentially dangerous espionage on behalf of the CIA. As for *Dauntless*, Rod's right. Sailing the globe is what she is designed for. I'm anxious to put her to work."

"All right then," said Kat. "I think we just docked. We better call in the crew before they scatter."

Chapter 7

St. John's, Newfoundland, Canada

Blake got on the ship's intercom and asked everyone to join him and Kat in the war room. One by one, they filed in and took their seats.

First in was Matt, next door on the bridge, who had just finished ensuring *Dauntless* was securely moored. Eric Hansard and Mark Hernandez were next to arrive, *Dauntless'* weapons and toys specialists, respectively. Eric wore his brown hair long and usually in a ponytail, and generally dressed in tattered jeans accompanied by aging t-shirts with cheesy slogans. Today's rumpled t-shirt of choice read, *"Humble and Proud of It."* Mark, on the other hand, was a dark-haired, dark-eyed, handsome Latino who was always dressed to the nines and prided himself on being a charmer with the ladies. Oddly enough, despite their widely different looks and interests, they had struck up the beginnings of a strong friendship over the last few weeks and were laughing together at some inside joke.

Close on their heels, the ship's engineer, Scott (Scotty) MacDuff, strode through the door. Scotty, a crisp red-headed Scotsman, was responsible for running and maintaining the ship's unique propulsion system. He was a no-nonsense, unflappable sort of guy most of the time, but equipped with a dry sense of humor that was razor-sharp on the rare occasion he chose to reveal it. He spoke with a thick Scottish brogue that never failed to fascinate and entertain his shipmates.

The final two crew members to arrive could not have been more opposite in physical appearance. Emily (Doc) Watson was the ship's medic. Before joining *Dauntless*, she ran the emergency department of Abbot Northwestern Hospital in Minneapolis. Barely 5'2", she was a classic blue-eyed blonde that turned heads wherever she went. Inside her petite frame, however, beat the heart of a lion. She never turned down a challenge and had earned the nickname 'Energizer Bunny' at the hospital, where she was known to routinely put in 36-hour shifts without ever slowing down.

Last in was Barry Galveston, the ship's chef. He had stopped to grab a plate of sandwiches and a selection of cold beverages, which he placed at the center of the table before seating himself. Barry, or 'Biff' as everyone had called him since grade school, was a walking physical spectacle. A mountain of a man. He was every bit of 6'10" and 350 lbs., although he kept his exact dimensions to himself. He was also the only black crew member. Biff possessed unnatural strength, which itself was a mystery, as he was never seen in the ship's gym. Although large, he was anything but soft. He carried his weight in a massive barrel chest with arms the size of a normal man's thighs. And for a big man, he moved with unnatural speed and grace. He probably could have made a fortune in the NFL terrorizing the opposing team's quarterback, but his first love was food, and he had dedicated his life to it. Blake and Kat had found him heading up the kitchen of their favorite upscale restaurant in downtown Minneapolis and had no trouble convincing him to leave that for a position on *Dauntless*.

Once everyone was seated, Blake began. "First off, Kat and I want to congratulate all of you on your work the past few weeks putting *Dauntless* through her paces. Mother Nature threw everything she could at you and our ship, and you both passed with flying colors. We couldn't be more pleased with the results. You have all earned a nice little bonus and some time off." Blake raised his glass. "To *Dauntless* and her crew. May the wind be ever in her favor." Around the table, the crew murmured, "To *Dauntless*", and the room was filled with the sound of glasses clinking in response to the toast.

Once things had quieted back down, Kat spoke. "I know we planned to spend a full week here in St. John's, but something has just come up that we need to discuss with all of you. Blake and I have talked it over and are willing to entertain the idea, but only if it is 100%

unanimous with you guys. And to ensure everyone is free to exercise their vote without pressure, your vote will be tallied via anonymous ballot. Blake… please tell them about the phone call we had with Rod."

Everyone listened intently as Blake explained Rod Stringer's request. He stressed that the primary mission would be to support and oversee *Operation Ocean Renewal* and that they had no intention whatsoever of encroaching on North Korean territorial waters or airspace. When he finished, he opened it up for questions.

Matt Granger spoke first. "The only question I have is when do we leave? I enjoy time off as much as the next guy, but I have to say, I love the sound of this!"

Blake smiled, hardly surprised. "Well… time is of the essence. Kat and I agree if we do this, we need to cut our visit here short. We would sail in 36 hours."

"Supposing we go, how long are we planning to stay on-site over there?" asked Doc Watson. "Don't you have commitments back in the States this fall?"

"Yes, good question. Even with *Dauntless'* speed, it's a 4-week round trip minimum. So, the longest we foresee being on station is about 2 weeks," answered Kat.

There were no other questions, so Kat distributed six small squares of paper and asked them to mark a 'Y' if they were willing to take on the mission or an 'N' to oppose. "Does anyone need more time to make up their mind? "Heads around the table shook in unison. "In that case, it's time to vote." Kate grabbed an empty glass, waited until everyone had marked their paper, and then walked around the table collecting the ballots in the glass. "If you will, please just wait a minute. Blake and I will leave the room, tally the ballots, and report back shortly."

Blake and Kat exited the war room to the bridge and closed the door behind them. Together, they unfolded the squares of paper. All six were clearly marked 'Y'. One also included a goofy happy face for good measure. Blake was pretty sure that would be Matt's ballot. "I guess that's it then," remarked Blake. "We once again work for the CIA."

"Yeah. I guess it's the sort of place where you can check out, but you can never leave," Kat chuckled. "You inform the crew." I'll contact Mom and Dad and tell them we've arrived, but we're not staying long."

North Atlantic – east of the Grand Banks

Following her brief pit stop in St. John's, *Dauntless* was underway again shortly after dawn, racing east across the North Atlantic into the rising sun. During their abbreviated stopover in St. John's, Blake and Kat had enjoyed a brief visit with Kat's parents while the crew enjoyed some of the local cuisine and culture. Eric and Mark, in particular, looked a little worse for the wear, having spent a couple of late nights on George Street. They had managed to get themselves 'screeched in', a local tradition inflicted on visitors involving kissing a codfish and downing a shot of 'Newfie Screech' rum. By doing so, they were now deemed honorary Newfoundlanders – and even had matching t-shirts to prove it. Scotty had rented a car and explored around on his own. Doc Watson and Biff spent much of their time walking the colorful, historic, downtown core, drawing plenty of glances from the locals at the incongruous pair - the giant black man with the tiny blonde.

On this August day, the seas were relatively calm – about the only time of year when the normally tempestuous North Atlantic allowed for calm seas - and Scotty and Matt had *Dauntless* taking advantage, running at speeds up to forty knots. Mega-yachts are not generally known for their prowess in the open seas. Their billionaire owners generally prefer to fly to meet them while they are docked in port and letting the crew sail them from place to place, wallowing at relatively slow speeds while consuming massive amounts of fuel. *Dauntless* was cut from a different cloth altogether. At higher celerity and rising out of the water on her hydrofoils, she was a magnificent sight to behold as she overtook more pedestrian ocean traffic on the busy shipping route. Matt was keeping a close eye on things, but *Dauntless'* computers did most of the work, navigating by GPS and using radar to detect and keep clear of any vessel traffic they came across. With her unique nuclear-electric jet propulsion technology, she was nearly silent and vibration free, the only sound being that of her hull breaking through the waves.

After a vigorous workout in the onboard gym on Deck 4, Blake toweled off and headed down one deck to check in with Matt on the bridge. Satisfied things were well in hand, Blake continued down to Deck 2, where he found Kat in their private quarters. "Hey dear," he said as he gave her a quick nuzzle and kiss on the back of her neck. "Why don't we give Sonja a call and let her know we're on the way over to the Sea of Japan to see how *Operation Ocean Renewal* is doing? Perhaps we can arrange to meet up with her on the way. I was thinking we could hop on the helicopter as we approach the Strait of Gibraltar and meet up in Seville. We'll rejoin *Dauntless* after she has passed through the Strait and into the Mediterranean."

"Great idea, Blake," Kat responded. "Scotty tells me he is aiming at a 72-hour Atlantic crossing. That's pretty quick for a boat, but still should give her enough time to make the necessary arrangements to meet us. I'll shoot her a text." Kat retrieved her phone and tapped out a quick message. Within a few minutes, her phone chirped and lit up. "She says that sounds like a wonderful idea. She will rearrange her schedule and meet us at the Barcelo Sevilla Renacimiento in Seville. According to Sonja, it's a lovely little hotel right on the Canal Sevilla-

Bonanza. She'll provide us an update on the project and some suggestions on how we can help out once we get there."

"Fantastic," replied Blake. "Seems like we've spent our whole lives land-locked in the middle of the continent, and I'm so looking forward to getting out and exploring the world. Can you check with the Spanish authorities and see what paperwork is required to land our helicopter in Seville and be let out in the town for a few hours?"

"You know? We should have people for that," said Kat with an exaggerated sigh. "I'll get it all in order."

Blake laughed and slapped her shoulder. "That's my girl! Looks like I *do* have a person for that sort of thing."

"Humph," Kat grunted and shot him a dirty glance as he cleverly retreated from the room. "You can do the honors next time!" she grumped.

The next few days passed quickly, and as *Dauntless* approached the Strait of Gibraltar, Blake and Kat climbed aboard the Bell 429. It was pouring rain, so they boarded belowdecks as Mark opened the hatch above them and operated the elevator to smoothly raise the helicopter onto the pad located just back from the bow on the main deck. Blake quickly worked through the pre-flight checklist, unfurled the rotors, and warmed up the engines. A few minutes later, he smoothly lifted the chopper into the air and hovered briefly above *Dauntless* before swinging slightly north towards the Spanish mainland for their rendezvous with Sonja.

The weather conditions improved steadily, clouds giving away to clear skies as they flew inland. The approach and landing at the Seville Airport, located northeast of the city, went smoothly, and after a brief delay checking in with Spanish border services, they found themselves back outside, hailing a cab in the sweltering heat.

Fortunately, the cab was equipped with air-conditioning and as the driver made his way to the hotel, Blake and Kat were captivated by the history of the city that dated all the way back to Roman times. Things that were older than a few decades were considered 'old' in Blake's hometown in Duluth, Minnesota. And even in St. John's, which billed herself as 'the oldest city in North America', history was measured in a few short centuries. In Europe, documented history and Western civilization dated back thousands of years, and they both found the difference in time scales fascinating.

Soon enough, they were crossing the modern Puente de la Barqueta bridge across the Canal Sevilla-Bonanza and pulled under the portico of the beautiful white slab-stone hotel where they had arranged to meet Sonja. They entered and made their way to a rear patio ringed by palm trees and bordering on a beautifully finished slate pool. Perfectly manicured grass that would not look out of place on a professional golf course completed the aesthetic. Sonja was already there waiting for them, jauntily perched on a tall bar stool/table combination, nursing a fancy tropical drink served out of a pineapple. She looked icy cool in a form-fitting, blindingly white sleeveless dress, matching wide-brimmed hat, and large aviator-style sunglasses. She smiled as she saw them approach and lightly jumped down, giving both a brief welcoming hug and a double cheek brush.

"Thank you so much for taking the trouble to come all the way down here to see us," gushed Kat. "It is so good to see you again! My goodness, you look fabulous! And congratulations on your appointment to the EU's Climate Action and Energy portfolio. I hear you have already submitted a proposal for aggressive new greenhouse gas emission targets. If anyone can push them through, I know it's you."

Sonja smiled broadly at the welcome. "It's something I feel really strongly about, for sure. I'm hopeful that if the EU can show leadership in this area, it will encourage the rest of the world to follow suit."

All three seated themselves, and after exchanging further pleasantries and small talk, the conversation turned to the business at hand. Sonja brought them up to date on *Operation Ocean Renewal*, describing in detail the vessels involved, the design of the seines utilized to trap debris, the sonar technology built into the seines to help them avoid unintentional trapping of marine life, and the barges where the refuse was offloaded. Even the weather had been cooperating. Kat asked about the level of cooperation they had received from neighboring countries and was pleased to hear they had permits to operate in the territorial waters of South Korea, China, Japan, and even Russia. North Korea had not even responded to their messages, and all ships involved in the operation had been warned to steer clear.

"That's great to hear, Sonja," beamed Blake. "You're probably wondering why we are traipsing halfway around the world to stop in on a project going so smoothly. In truth, it's as much about further testing of *Dauntless* and training for the crew as it is about checking in on the project. Since we took delivery of her a couple months ago, we've been anxious to get some experience under our belts and see the world. We had a small window before Clean World's autumn fundraising season gets underway back stateside, and so we decided to make the best of it. The crew, as good as they are shaping up to be, are still pretty green and learning to function as a team, so this little 'road trip' is a great way for everyone to get more comfortable with each other and with their new roles."

"Well, I'm just glad you are able to fit us in," Sonja smiled. "It sounds like you guys have done an incredible job designing *Dauntless* and bringing her to life. I'll definitely have to get a full tour sometime. But tell me, is it true that *Dauntless* has teeth?" Sonja asked with a wink. "I've heard she's well-armed. Have you gotten to blow anything up as part of your testing?"

"Well… I can't go into details," Blake responded hesitantly. "But yes, we anticipate operating in some rough areas of the world, and so we've taken certain security precautions. I expect we'll be able to give as good as we get if pirates want to take a run at us. But our first and best defense is speed. I'm doubtful we will come across anything that can outrun us."

Kat laughed out loud at that. "That's not how I heard you played hockey growing up. Running from a fight?! Didn't you lead the league in penalty minutes one year?"

Just then, Sonja's phone buzzed. She looked down, frowned, and then excused herself. "One moment, I really need to take this call." As she gracefully made her way back inside, Blake glanced down at his watch, pausing momentarily to admire the yellow-dial Breitling Super Ocean he was wearing for this trip. Blake owned a small collection of quality watches, but this one was his current favorite. "We really need to get going anyway. I'd say *Dauntless* is through the Strait of Gibraltar by now and racing away from us. If we aren't in the air within the hour, I doubt we'll have enough fuel to catch her."

Kat nodded. "When Sonja returns, we'll say our goodbyes and be on our way."

Sonja rejoined them after a few minutes, and Blake and Kat explained their need to get going. They both laughed at her exaggerated frown and pouty face in response. Exchanging brief hugs once again, Blake and Kat headed toward the exit. As they walked away, Blake called back over his shoulder. "We'll be in touch again in a couple weeks to give you an update. Again, thanks for making the effort to come down here. And best of luck with your new EU portfolio. Go get 'em, Tiger!!" Sonja grinned, gave them a final wave, and returned to the table. Her smile slowly faded, and long after they left, she lingered, lost in thought.

Chapter 8

Sea of Japan, 30 miles east of the Korean Peninsula

Just fourteen days after leaving port in St. John's, *Dauntless* entered the Sea of Japan. It was a long journey of approximately 13,500 miles, meaning *Dauntless* had averaged 35 knots for the entire journey – a monumental feat – and Blake was incredibly pleased with his ship. After crossing the Atlantic, they traversed the Mediterranean, through the historic Suez Canal and into the vast expanse of the Indian Ocean, passing south of Sri Lanka, before threading the Malacca Strait between Singapore and Malaysia, and finally turning northeast across the South China Sea, east of Taiwan, and then up into the Sea of Japan.

Along the way, Biff had kept the galley humming, impressing them all with his culinary skills. Blake and Matt had organized various daily drills to further their training and ensure the crew, the ship, and her various systems were fully prepared for whatever awaited them over the next few weeks. The Indian Ocean had been flat calm, and Scotty had authorized several sustained runs at *Dauntless*' top speed of 70 knots. During periods when the ship was traveling at slower speeds, Mark took advantage, cycling through launching and retrieving his various aerial drones. When *Dauntless* was running full out, the drones could not even keep up.

The pollution problem in the Sea of Japan is a real and growing concern. While Japan has a reputation for being one of the cleanest societies in the world, its beaches and shorelines are among the world's most polluted, with plastics and other trash washing up regularly. Blake had recently read that Japan disposes well over 100,000 tons of seaside trash annually. The problem is that China and Korea, on the eastern side of the Sea, are among the world's greatest contributors to ocean trash. The prevailing ocean currents tend to deposit the entire region's trash production on Japan's western-facing coastline. *Operation Ocean Renewal's* goal was to trawl the waters in between and intercept the trash before it could reach Japan.

And garbage-strewn beaches creating an eyesore for residents and tourists alike is hardly the worst of the trouble caused by the mess. Beyond the awful aesthetics, the massive negative impact of biodegrading plastics on marine life and up through the food chain is still not fully understood.

Blake and Kat understood that the only way to solve the global problem permanently was to demonstrate an economically viable and eco-friendly use of recovered plastics. Anything else was merely treating the symptoms of the disease. To that end, The Clean World Foundation had put out a request for proposals to convert waste and recovered plastics into clean-burning fuel. Several promising proposals were currently being analyzed by the Foundation as prospects for funding.

The first order of business was to meet up with one of the large trawlers engaged in towing a large seine along a pre-mapped grid. Matt, Kat, and Blake stood together on the bridge of *Dauntless* as she made her approach, and all were impressed by the size of the seine the vessel was pulling. In fact, 'seine' did not really convey the right mental image of what they could now see with their own eyes. It was, in fact, a massive 1,000-foot-long water-borne garbage collector that trailed behind, extending down through the water column, scooping up plastics and other trash. An ingenious system strained the trash from the water and cycled it into a large containment area via a conveyor belt system. Once full, it would make its way to a barge stationed nearby and run the loading system in reverse to offload before returning to resume its grid. A steady parade of towed barges was required to support the operation. It reminded Blake and Kat of the stream of dump trucks filled by snowblowers as they cleared the streets after a winter snowstorm.

"Tell you what, Matt," said Blake. "Get Captain Margrave on the radio. Kat and I will take the RHIB over to meet him and get the grand tour of the operation. Then get a message to the crew to be in the war room in two hours. I want to talk to everyone about our other purpose for being here."

"We'll be here, boss," answered Matt with a sarcastic smile. "No doubt I love garbage collecting as much as the next guy, but if I had to choose between that and doing some good old-fashioned espionage, I think I know what I'd rather be doing."

Blake and Kat both laughed at that. "Careful what you wish for there, Matt," winked Kat. "You might just get a little more excitement than you bargained for."

True to their word, Blake and Kat were back on board 2 hours later and found the rest of the crew in the war room tucking into a fine lunch consisting of seafood chowder and Montreal smoked-meat sandwiches. Biff was smiling broadly, observing his shipmates relish his creation. Eric was wearing another of his goofy t-shirts. This one featured a picture of a hammer with the caption, *"This is not a drill."* Blake smiled in spite of himself.

"It's obvious that *Operation Ocean Renewal* is in fine hands with Captain Margrave and his cohorts," began Kat. "It's one thing to read about, but seeing it in action was amazing. We will be meeting some of the other ships' captains as well as observing the offloading process at one of the barges nearby over the next couple of days. But meanwhile, we want to get on with doing some general surveillance looking for any kind of suspicious activity."

Doc Watson spoke for all of them, asking, "Suspicious activity… what exactly would that look like?"

"Good question, Doc, and the answer is that we won't know it until we see it. Essentially, Rod is worried that the North Koreans may be shipping radioactive material out of Tanchon for unknown purposes and, even more worrying, to unknown parties. So, I think we start by monitoring shipping traffic in the area. Most ship traffic follows established patterns. Commercial container ships and oil tankers follow pre-planned and verifiable routes and schedules. With our drones, we can identify them and ensure they are where they should be. Fishing boats have home ports and traditional fishing grounds. They tend to follow the fish, and we should find them loosely grouped. Obviously, there is a bit more variability to their routes, but Kat has done some background research on the voyage over here, and that will help us identify any anomalous behavior."

Turning to Mark, Blake continued. "Mark, I want you to get your drones in the air immediately and check out any ship traffic you see. Get in close enough to see the ship's identification number and pass it along to Kat, along with the coordinates of the ship's position. She will be able to determine if the ship is where it should be or not. We are looking for a needle in a haystack here, and we aren't even sure there is a needle. To increase our odds, concentrate your search in the waters adjacent to North Korea. But make sure you keep your birds outside the 12-mile international boundary! Eric, you work with Mark monitoring the camera footage from the drones. The rest of you can maintain your normal duties but stay alert and rested. If we find something or trouble arises, we may need to react fast. Matt, you man the bridge and put *Dauntless* on a north-by-northwest heading, generally following the drones. Any questions?" There were none, and with that, the meeting was over.

Mark immediately launched all 3 drones, each equipped with sophisticated cameras, infrared, and night vision capabilities. Once in flight, he returned to the war room with the camera footage up on the wall-mounted screens. Meanwhile, Eric climbed into the 'weapons cockpit' and donned a pair of virtual reality (VR) goggles to view the drone footage from a first-person perspective.

"Hey Mark, once you spot a ship, assign me controls for the nearest drone, and I'll bring it in for a flyby and identification, and then pass it on to Kat to check it out."

Kat reappeared, coffee in hand, and set up at her computer station. Soon all three settled into an effective routine. Mark would spot a ship at a distance, Eric would assume the controls of that drone and zoom in close for a definitive ID, and then Kat would check it out on her computer and confirm its legitimacy. Hours passed, and dozens of ships were checked out without anything appearing out of the ordinary. Mark was moving the drones steadily north and west until the sun slipped beneath the horizon. They overflew several dozen small fishing trawlers, and after specifically identifying several of them, Kat determined that they all originated from Gangneung, South Korea, and were congregated on a common fishing ground for that time of year.

Mark pressed further north and west, generally relying on his visual camera to pick up the running lights of any ships in the area. Occasionally however, he would cycle through his night vision and infrared cameras, and that was when he spotted what appeared to be another fishing trawler with no running lights, steaming on a northwest heading from the main group. "Eric, I've got a lone vessel, all blacked out, heading northwest from the fishing fleet we passed over earlier. You've got control of the #2 drone to take us in for a closer look."

"Copy that Mark," answered Eric. He adjusted his VR goggles and danced his fingers over the controls as he guided the drone in for a closer view. Switching to infrared, he could see three clear heat signatures – all huddled together on the darkened bridge. Switching back to the night vision camera, he noted that it was clearly a fishing trawler, and its wake indicated it was moving in a straight line to the northwest. *So,* he thought, *obviously not fishing. Definitely has a specific destination in mind. And based on its current heading and speed, it will be inside North Korean waters within an hour.* He maneuvered the drone even closer, zoomed in his night vision camera, and read out the ship's ID number to Kat, who quickly confirmed it to be a fishing trawler out of Gangneung that seemed to have strayed far from the fishing grounds where the remainder of the fleet was located.

"Back up a safe distance and stay on her, Eric," commanded Kat. "I'm bringing Blake in on this."

Blake strode into the war room a minute later. "What's up? You guys find something?"

"Hard to say for sure, dear," replied Kat. "We've got a South Korean fishing trawler out of Gangneung maintaining a steady course north and west towards North Korean waters. She doesn't appear to be fishing, and the rest of her fleet is well to the southeast on their established fishing grounds. We are tracking her with one of our drones, and we are currently about 20 knots south of her position, matching her speed and heading."

"If she were to maintain her current course heading, what would be the nearest port when she enters North Korean waters?" asked Blake.

Kat had already checked that and answered instantly. "Tanchon".

Blake's eyes went wide. "Holy crap!!" he gasped. "This could be it! You guys keep a close eye, and I want updates every 10 minutes. I'll have Matt shut off all our lights and put on a burst of speed to close the gap 3 knots. Full stealth mode. If she enters North Korean waters, we need to round everyone up and decide what we are going to do about it."

Over the next 45 minutes, *Dauntless* closed within 3 knots as the South Korean fishing trawler approached the North Korean territorial waters off Tanchon. Mark and Eric kept an eye on her at all times. Never once did any of the three onboard leave the bridge. Neither did the vessel they were tracking deviate at all from her heading. As Blake had requested, they updated him every 10 minutes. Scotty and Matt remained in close communication as *Dauntless* raced through the dark. As the fishing vessel they were tracking approached the international boundary with North Korea, it slowed noticeably, but maintained her heading. The entirety of the crew had now gathered in the war room to watch.

"30 seconds and she will cross the boundary," announced Matt. "10 seconds". Everyone held their breath. "She is now in North Korean waters."

"Return two of the drones immediately to *Dauntless*. The third, I want stationed 1,000 feet outside North Korean airspace and continue to keep eyes on that trawler," commanded Blake.

"Roger that," Matt answered. "I have our bird hovering at 500 feet elevation, 1,000 feet east of North Korean airspace. 2 birds incoming. Both will be retrieved within 5 minutes."

"OK. Now we wait and watch," Blake replied, tension creeping into his voice. As the minutes crept by, all eyes were glued to the monitor showing the feed from the hovering drone. Mark adjusted the zoom to keep the trawler in view, but as she moved farther away, the image grew increasingly indistinct. Suddenly, the night vision camera picked up 3 quick flashes of light followed by one long one that appeared to come from the trawler and directed towards the shore. Before anyone could comment, they saw, even more clearly, an identical light signal returning from the direction of the mainland. Out of the gloom, behind the reciprocating light signal, a lone North Korean patrol boat appeared - heading directly towards the South Korean fishing trawler.

Both vessels had switched off all running lights as they approached each other.

"Is this the best view you have, Mark?" asked Kat. "Clearly, we need to see what this rendezvous is about."

Mark fiddled vainly for a minute with the controls. "This is the best we can get from here," he admitted.

"OK. I know I said we weren't going to enter North Korea," said Blake. "But I think we really need to see what is going on here. I propose we move in to get a better view. I want the drone kept in the air overhead but remain with *Dauntless*. In the dark and with our low radar profile, we should be able to stay hidden. If we think we've raised suspicion, we'll quickly retrieve the drone and high-tail it out of here."

"OK boss," replied Matt. "I'm with you."

Blake glanced at Kat, who nodded. He then glanced around the room, looking into each pair of eyes. "Are we all agreed?" Heads nodded in unison. "Ok then. Eric, I want you to man your weapons station. Keep the weapons hatches closed, but if we need to defend ourselves, I need you ready."

"Aye, aye, sir," answered the normally informal Eric. He immediately climbed into his cockpit and donned his VR goggles.

"Mark, keep that drone directly over *Dauntless*, her eyes trained on those vessels. I want to see exactly what they are up to."

"You got it, captain," answered Mark immediately.

"Scotty, I need you to be ready to give us full power, and then some." McDuff nodded curtly and turned on his heel to man his station.

"Kat, you stay with Matt and I on the bridge. Biff, go and secure everything in the galley. If things get rough or we maneuver aggressively, we don't want the wine glasses falling about. Doc, stay on the comms, secure your sick bay, and then work together with Biff to ensure the rest of the ship is secure and ready for action." Blake then turned to Matt. "I may regret saying this, but take us in. Keep us at 10 knots, close to 1,500 feet and let's see what these guys are up to."

"Aye, aye, Captain," answered Matt as he advanced the throttles. *Dauntless* responded immediately, her dark hulk easing forward soundlessly.

Chapter 9

Tanchon, North Korea

This was Song Hee's fourth trip to Tanchon, and while the hair on the back of his neck still rose every time he entered North Korean waters, there was something of a familiar routine about the whole process that made it slightly less terrifying. The last two encounters had gone much smoother than the first, and there was a certain amount of trust that had developed between the two sides. Even better, he had been told that tonight's rendezvous would be the last, and he was in for a big payday.

He smiled to himself as he thought about how surprised he would be if someone had told him a few weeks ago he would be a 'fisherman'. To keep up appearances, he figured it best to make some effort to fish and be seen offloading his catch. The two men with him had some prior experience as deckhands and were familiar with handling the gear. No doubt they were, by far, the most inept fishing boat in the fleet, but Song Hee figured it was kind of like operating one of his restaurants that served primarily to launder his drug money. It didn't really have to be very good to do the job. Just modestly operational for appearances only.

Song Hee hefted his night vision binoculars to his eyes and scanned the dark waters ahead. A few minutes later, he spotted the North Korean gunship headed towards them and the rendezvous location. It seemed the North Koreans decided they could use the gunship to ferry the radiocaesium containers, as he hadn't seen the old fishing trawler since the first exchange. Stepping out onto the deck, he exchanged the now-familiar prearranged light signals as they slowed. The seas were calm tonight, and there was no drama whatsoever as they rendezvoused and tied up together. Song Hee was anxious to get this over with and found his nerves a bit on edge. He had that strange feeling that he was being watched somehow and kept scanning in all directions with his night-vision binoculars, trying to shake it. Seeing nothing, he shook it off and concentrated on the job at hand.

The NK soldiers – always the same group – had grown more at ease with each meeting. They no longer bothered to board Song Hee's ship. Song Hee was operating the crane and had five of the containers transferred over to his vessel when he noticed something amiss. Over on the gunship, the NK commander was becoming quite animated, his voice rising and his arms waving. As he released the container that he was transferring to the deck, one of the NK soldiers gave him a throat-slash signal to cease operations.

Song Hee climbed out of his cab and made his way back to the bridge where his two crewmen had remained. "What's going on?" he demanded.

"From what we overheard, it seems like the North Koreans have picked up something on their radar to the east. I've been looking at our radar, but I'm not picking up much. Every now and then, I'm getting a small return that might indicate a small fishing boat or something. Their radar is probably a lot better, and they seem concerned."

A moment later, the NK commander boarded and approached the bridge. "We have detected something no more than 500 meters east of our position. It could be a small fishing boat, but it has no running lights. And if it was just a derelict, it would be drifting with the current. But we've been observing it for the last 15 minutes, and it hasn't moved at all. It's steady as a rock, but there are no shoals in that location. It's probably nothing, but we are going to untie and check it out. Hold tight until I return and give the all-clear."

Dauntless

Matt and Kat manned the bridge while Blake, Eric, and Mark gathered in the war room. It was deathly quiet, and all three were breathlessly watching the drone footage on the large monitors. They observed the two ships as they pulled alongside and tied up together. One man left the bridge of the South Korean fishing trawler, climbed into a small deck-mounted crane, and began to deftly transfer several bulky crates from the gunship to the fishing trawler.

Blake was the first to break the silence. "Mark, make sure you get some good close-up shots of those crates. Rod will be anxious to identify the cargo being exchanged. He might be able to tell if that's the radioactive material he was worried about."

After the crane operator had roughly half of the crates transferred, there was a pause in the action. A lone figure left the gunship, scrambled aboard the fishing trawler and approached the crane. Moments later, the man returned to the gunship, the crane operator returned to the bridge of his trawler, and a couple of men from the gunship untied the two boats.

Eric spoke up, alarmed. "Blake!! I think we've got a problem!! They've only transferred about half of the containers, and the gunship is underway and coming around in our direction. Do you think they're on to us?"

"We've seen what we need to see, and I agree that we may have worn out our welcome. Time to exit, stage left," responded Blake. "Get that bird back immediately and open the weapons hatches. We don't fire first, but if that gunship gets frisky, I want to be sure we fire last."

"Roger that Cap'n. Drone is already inbound. Bringing all weapons online and at the ready… now."

Blake turned on his heel and reentered the bridge where Matt and Kat had overheard the whole thing. "No sudden moves, Matt, but get us turned south and headed perpendicular to the gunship's approach angle. If they direct fire this way, we can turn up the jets and get out of the firing line. Whatever they think they are coming out to look at, they won't be expecting something that can move like *Dauntless*."

"Already on it, boss," replied Matt.

Blake activated the ship-wide coms. "Battle stations, battle stations!! We've got a North Korean gunship headed our way with unknown intentions. We are taking evasive action but need to be prepared for all eventualities. Hang tight everyone. This is the real deal."

Matt eased *Dauntless* south, keeping her speed just under 10 knots, barely rippling the calm, dark water. The massive hulk of the super-yacht slipped through the water like a shadow, silent and invisible against the inky black sky and water.

NK Gunship

The NK commander nosed his craft towards the indistinct radar return, keeping his night-vision binoculars trained in that direction but seeing nothing. Glancing down at the radar screen, he noted that the mystery object was now on the move to the south… and definitely moving faster than any drifting derelict. With one quick stride, he stepped to the control panel and switched on his powerful searchlight, sweeping it forward and to the right in the direction of the suspect vessel.

The bright beam of light shot out, and as it began arcing to the right, it picked up a hulking black outline. It was so unexpected that for several long moments, he could not understand what his eyes were trying to tell him. This was no small fishing boat. It appeared to be something out of a nightmare – a huge, dark behemoth.

He gasped, disbelieving his eyes for a moment, but quickly regained his senses. "Fire, fire, fire!!" he screamed. Seconds later, the heavy machine gun roared to life, tracers lighting up the night sky. He desperately wanted to unleash his anti-ship missiles on the offending vessel, but for some unknown reason, he couldn't get a radar lock on the target.

And then… it was gone. One moment the searchlight had the helpless target dead to rights, and the next, it was gone, the gun still firing blindly into the dark.

Dauntless

The moment the NK gunship activated its searchlight and caught them in its glare, Matt shoved the throttles forward so hard, they banged against the stops with a noticeable clank. He counted to 5 and then threw *Dauntless* into a tight turn to port, while still accelerating like a runaway train. Blake and Kat were thrown by the centrifugal force of the turn and grabbed onto whatever they could find to maintain their balance. *Dauntless* had taken some direct fire, but Blake was confident that the armored exterior was up to the task. He made a split-second decision – knowing it was really the only option he had at this point. He took a deep breath, thumbed his com, and spoke calmly.

"Eric!! You got that gunship locked in?"

"Yes sir. Locked and loaded," came the prompt reply.

"OK. We've only got a few seconds before they pick us up again with their searchlight. Hit 'em with two anti-ship missiles. Then light 'em up with the cannon. We have got to finish them before they have a chance to report in!"

Blake had barely finished speaking when two missiles shot out simultaneously and streaked in the direction of the gunship. They had barely launched when the roar of *Dauntless'* 30 mm cannon filled the room, firing deadly armor-piercing, explosive shells at a rate of 200 rounds/minute. Fully computer-controlled firing solutions ensured that despite Matt's continued aggressive maneuvering, the shells found their target with deadly accuracy. Within seconds, the NK gunship was literally shredded into bits of scrap metal from the overwhelming fire she had taken from the missiles and cannon.

"Mark… you got eyes?"

"Yes sir. She's done for!! That was some shooting, Eric!!"

"Anyone abandon ship?" Blake wanted to know.

"No sir. I don't see how anyone could have survived."

Blake didn't really know what to feel. Venturing into North Korean waters was a massive risk, and now it had extracted a huge price – costing lives and no doubt triggering an international incident. On the other hand, he felt the exhilaration of victory and pride in his crew for handling themselves so well in the heat of the moment. The decision to sink the gunship quickly and decisively in a way that precluded the survival of her crew was his and his alone. The gravity of that choice, though, would weigh heavily on him once the shock had worn off.

"Good work Eric. Masterful shooting!"

"Matt, get us out of here. I want every ounce of speed you can squeeze out of *Dauntless*. I want us witnessed so far south of here by first light that no one could reasonably conclude we might possibly have had anything to do with the sinking of that gunship," instructed Blake.

Song Hee was stunned. It had all happened so fast. He had witnessed the hulking *Dauntless* caught dead-to-rights in the searchlight's glare. It was so unreal – so utterly shocking - that it took a few moments for it to register that he was looking at a giant, black mega-yacht lurking at close range. He was even more stunned when, just as the gunship opened fire, the massive yacht vanished into thin air just as suddenly as it had first appeared. It seemed utterly impossible. But then, moments later, he had witnessed the devastating counterattack that literally lifted the gunship almost out of the water and exploded it into jagged metal fragments that quickly sank out of sight. There were no survivors, of that he was sure.

Forcing himself to think, he sprang into action. It was time to get out of Dodge. The North Koreans would no doubt be on-site, in force, very soon. He had no intention of being anywhere in the vicinity when they showed up. Not to mention that the invisible black yacht might decide to make his little trawler its next meal! He had no idea where it had come from or where it went, and so he decided to set a straight course back to Gangneung. He swung his trawler to the southwest and got underway. A short time later, he was back in international waters, and there was no further sign of the mystery yacht. In fact, his pulse was almost back to normal when it occurred to him that he had yet to report the night's events to his shadowy boss. That was going to be unpleasant… no doubt putting his much-anticipated payday at risk. But money is no good to dead men, and he figured, all in all, it was pretty fortunate he was still on the sunny side of the sod.

Chapter 10

Matt and Scotty worked together for the next 8 hours to keep *Dauntless* amain hurtling south, giving a wide berth to any ship traffic they encountered along the way, the dark moonless night providing cover, and the calm seas enabling a sustained top-speed run. By dawn, *Dauntless* would be far away, off the south coast of South Korea. As dawn approached, Matt steered in the direction of a large container ship, passing well to the west of her and then turning north again to cross her path. He radioed greetings to its captain as they passed. There would no doubt be an investigation into the violent sinking of the North Korean patrol vessel, and he wanted to establish an alibi that *Dauntless* was seen mere hours later hundreds of miles south of the sinking and on a northerly course ***towards*** the area.

Meanwhile, Blake and Kat called Rod Stringer on the secure line to fill him in on what had taken place. While the sinking of the North Korean patrol vessel had not yet hit the mainstream media, Rod had already been briefed on it. In the absence of any better intelligence, North Korea naturally assumed South Korea was to blame, and both Koreas were on heightened alert and headed down a dangerous escalation path.

Rod was having a hard time absorbing it. "That was you??!! You attacked a North Korean military vessel in their own territorial waters?? That's an act of war!! North Korea is on the verge of launching a retaliatory missile strike against South Korea which could well lead to an all-out war. The President is on the phone with China's President right now, trying to convince him it wasn't South Korea, and we have no idea who it was. We're hoping China will rein North Korea in long enough for the incident to be investigated and cooler heads to prevail. You promised to stay clear of North Korean territory!"

Blake and Kat let Rod vent until he eventually began to run out of steam, allowing Blake to respond. "I made a judgment call to enter North Korean waters in order to observe what appeared to be suspicious activity that may be related to what you asked us to keep an eye out for. And for the record, they fired first without any warning whatsoever. I made the decision at that point to engage them with overwhelming force in order to keep our identity and mission a secret. We are well out of the area and have an airtight alibi, so if you can keep North Korea from retaliating, we should be good. Oh… and we sent over some footage we took of them transferring material to the South Korean fishing trawler. Did you have a chance to look at that?"

"Indeed. I am 90% sure it is *radiocaesium* which confirms that they are shipping it out of the country to unknown parties and for unknown purposes. We didn't have any satellites overhead at the time, so we don't know where the fishing trawler went. Do you guys have any way to track it?"

"Yes", Kat replied. "We have the vessel's ID number. It's a fishing boat based in Gangneung. I've run a search on it and found that just 3 weeks ago, its owner went missing. He had returned from a fishing trip with the fleet and hasn't been seen since. The vessel was subsequently deregistered and listed as sold by his estate but hasn't been re-registered, so it isn't clear who owns it now. But we can head over to Gangneung, have a look around, and ask some questions."

"Yes, I'm ok with that", Rod responded after a pause. "In fact, I've got an agent on the ground there who you can work with. Her name is Wei Lei. She can provide proper ID papers, etc., but it would be best if you can impersonate a South Korean national."

Blake assured Rod that Kat was an expert in disguises, and she would get to work immediately on transforming herself into a South Korean woman and send a photo over for purposes of preparing a fake South Korean passport and ID. After a few more minutes of conversation to finalize the details of the meet, both sides exchanged farewells and the call was terminated.

Once Song Hee reached the relative safety of international waters, he turned the helm over to one of his crewmembers and retreated to his quarters to make the dreaded call to report the disaster that had unfolded so unexpectedly. He didn't beat about the bush. Just stated his observations, such as they were, and that he was fairly certain he had made a clean exit and would be returning to port with the fleet later that day.

To his surprise, the news was received calmly on the other end. "I will look into it. In the meantime, continue as you have planned and let me know when the material is safely in the warehouse. We now have all we need, and you will be paid in full. In the meantime, keep an eye out down at the docks and let me know if you catch wind of anyone poking around asking questions. Anyone hanging around down there that doesn't belong… I want to know."

Kat emerged from the 'Beauty Parlor' on Deck 4 a few hours later, completely transformed into a South Korean native, complete with jet-black hair, toned skin, and a brand-new face with Asian contours. Blake couldn't believe his eyes. If he didn't know better, he would have assumed they had a guest on board. The face was fake. Kat had created it with her 3D printer from a stock image she found on the internet. Some light make-up, a casual turtleneck, jeans, and tennis shoes completed her outfit. She had sent a picture of her new self to Rod Stringer, who was having a South Korean passport and identity created in the name of Ji-Woo that Wei Lei would give her when they rendezvoused.

As *Dauntless* cruised about 3 miles offshore, Blake and Kat launched the RHIB from the swim deck and headed ashore. Blake pointed the craft towards the main working port of Jumunjin, located north of the city center. As they entered the harbor, they spotted a figure with a bright red hat on a nearby pier who returned their wave and tied up nearby.

"Be careful, Kat, I mean it," cautioned Blake. "Whoever took delivery of that radioactive material got away clean and are likely operating in this area. They will be on heightened alert. You need to blend in. Any outsider snooping around is certain to draw their attention, and I doubt they are nice people. Stay in touch on the coms. *Dauntless* will be stationed about five miles offshore, and I'll have Mark keep an eye out with the drones."

Kat embraced him, holding him tight while exchanging a quick kiss. "Roger that, dear. We'll wander around, do some shopping just for show, and make a few discreet inquiries amongst the fishermen. Hopefully, we'll just look like a couple of local girls flirting with the cute deckhands. If that fishing trawler was sold recently, the other fisherman will know something about it and will be tripping over themselves to share the gossip with a couple cute girls." With that, she grasped the nearby rope ladder and scrambled up to meet her new friend, Wei Lei.

After an hour or so perusing the nearby fish market and shops – just in case anyone was watching them – Wei Lei and 'Ji-Woo' made their way down to the working pier, where they found the fishing fleet tied up and a number of fishermen milling about, tending to their gear and performing maintenance on their boats.

A few minutes later, Kat nudged Wei Lei and pointed to a decrepit-looking trawler at the end of a nearby floating dock. "That's her," she exclaimed excitedly but keeping her voice low. "That's the boat we tracked into North Korean waters and observed taking possession of the radioactive materials."

"OK then," responded Wei Lei. "Let's see if anyone knows anything about who's operating her." They approached a couple of young guys doing some painting on a nearby boat, and Wei Lei launched into conversation, gesturing broadly and giggling as she engaged them in conversation. Kat nodded along and smiled brightly, not having the faintest clue what was being discussed. After a few minutes, Wei Lei clapped Kat on the back and laughed loudly. Kat did the same as Wei Lei linked arms and pivoted to walk away. Kat followed along, chancing a quick turn, winking, and waving at the guys who now looked even less interested in painting than they had been a few minutes before."

"So?" asked Kat when they were a safe distance away, "What did they say?"

"They didn't have much to say about who was operating the boat. If they know, they aren't saying. But they did confirm that the fisherman that owned and operated the boat had gone missing a few weeks ago after a routine fishing trip. They swear they know nothing about it or who the new guys are that have been operating the boat. Of course, the story of the missing fisherman had been all over the local news, but we hadn't really thought much of it. Of course, now that you have confirmed that this is the same boat you observed in North Korean waters… well, that puts things in a whole new light!"

Kat thought for a bit. "Did the missing fisherman have a wife or family?"

"Yes, I believe I remember reading that he left a widow. No kids though", answered Wei after a short pause.

"Well then… let's pay her a visit and see what we can learn from her. We can pose as investigators into his disappearance, following up on the case. Was he hanging around with anyone new? Did he have any enemies? In hindsight, was there anything at all different in his demeanor or behavior prior to his disappearance? And she can also tell us who she sold the boat to."

Wei Lei nodded in agreement. "I'll contact my office and request they produce some proper credentials for our cover. In the meantime, I know a great place nearby we can grab a coffee, and you can update your folks on our progress."

Song Hee had stationed two of his men at a table outside a small bar down by the docks with instructions to report any new faces they came across. After a few weeks of working with Song Hee as fishermen and deckhands, they had met most of the other fishermen, or at least recognized them. The other fishermen knew that they ran with a gang that was known for their ruthlessness. In fact, most of them figured the disappearance of their friend a few weeks ago was somehow tied to this gang – a belief that was only reinforced when Song Hee had taken over the operations of his trawler.

It was easy work for the two thugs. Getting paid to enjoy free drinks and warm sunshine was a fine gig, as far as they were concerned. It wasn't long before the two young women caught their eye as they ambled across the street from the shopping district towards the more industrial fishing docks. You didn't see such a sight down on the wharf too often. The conversation they engaged in with the two deckhands seemed innocent enough, and before long, they were waving goodbye and had disappeared.

At first, they were inclined to dismiss it, but Song Hee had been insistent. *Anything* out of the ordinary was to be reported. "What do you think?" asked the taller of the two as he put down the binoculars.

His buddy thought for a moment before responding. "Before we call Song Hee, let's go over and ask those guys what that was all about. If it was just their girlfriends dropping by to say 'hello', then we don't want to waste his time. Those girls looked a little too classy for those fellas, though, so I definitely think we ought to check it out."

As the two deckhands saw Song Hee's henchmen approach, they straightened up and eyed them apprehensively. The less contact they had with those guys, the better, as far as they were concerned. They had little desire to disappear like the unfortunate fisherman a few weeks previous.

The conversation was brief. Song Hee's men just wanted to know if the two women were familiar to them and what they talked about. The deckhands admitted they asked about Song Hee's trawler and if they knew anything about who was sailing her. They hastily added they had told them they knew nothing about who had been operating her since her previous owner had gone missing.

"That's it? And then they left?".

"That's it, we swear. Never saw them before, and we know better than to stick our noses in your business."

"OK. If they come around again, let us know. And keep your mouths shut if you know what's good for you." And with that, Song Hee's men turned and left.

As soon as they were out of earshot, they reported the morning's events to their boss, who immediately picked up his encrypted burner phone.

Helle answered right away. "Yes Mr. Hee?"

Helle listened in silence as Song Hee told her about the two women down on the docks asking about the fishing trawler and who was operating it. She immediately sensed trouble, and there was no doubt in her mind that there was a connection to the black mega-yacht that had appeared like a demonic phantom, blown up the North Korean gunship, and disappeared. As unlikely as it seemed, someone appeared to be closing in on their operation, and she needed to act.

"Listen closely", she hissed. "I bet their next step is to talk to that bloody captain's widow. It's the only lead they have and our biggest vulnerability. Set up an ambush near her house, and when those women show up, you grab them and bring them to the warehouse. I expect they'll be there sooner rather than later."

The widow lived on the outskirts of town in a wooded, hilly area. A small twisting one-lane driveway snaked its way through the trees from a rural highway about a quarter of a mile to her house. Within an hour, Song Hee had dispatched two teams of 3 men to cover each side of the driveway where it met the highway. One of his guys was dispatched to scout the driveway and soon radioed in that there was a rental car parked at the house.

As soon as the local police credentials were ready, Wei Lei and Kat returned to Wei's rental car, picked up the fake badges, and headed directly out to the widow's house. While nursing her coffee, Kat had updated Blake on the morning's activities and their plan to visit the widow. Blake, in turn, assured them that Mark was following their every move, tracking them from overhead with one of his trusty drones.

After a 30-minute drive that took them out of the city, they followed the narrow winding driveway up a steep wooded hill until they came to a modest bungalow. A small, pale woman answered their knock, her eyes glancing furtively from one to the other. She was probably no older than forty, but she appeared tired and listless. Even though it was getting towards midday, she was still dressed in pajamas covered loosely with a tattered bathrobe. Wei Lei introduced themselves as new investigators assigned to the case of her missing husband and asked if it was all right if they could come in and go over all of it again, apologizing in advance for asking some of the same questions and assuring the woman it was standard procedure to confirm key information.

As before, Kat stayed silent, unable to follow the conversation. She pretended to take notes as the conversation went on, figuring it was better than appearing completely useless. Suddenly, Blake's voice came through her earbud. "Kat… you've got trouble. We've got visuals on two cars stationed on each side of the driveway, with at least 3 guys in each car. One guy got out and walked up the driveway to the house before turning around and heading back out. We're pretty sure you are being followed."

Kat clicked her mic twice to indicate she had heard and understood. She tapped Wei Lei on the shoulder and nodded her head towards the door, indicating it was time to go.

Wei clued up the conversation, and the widow showed the two women to the door. Kat quickly filled her in on Blake's warning. Wei Lei informed Kat that the woman didn't know any reason why her husband would disappear. He wasn't perfect, but he had no enemies as far as she knew, and their life together was peaceful. However, it wasn't long after his disappearance that a man had showed up and paid cash for his boat… way more than it was worth. No bill of sale. No paperwork. She didn't even know his name. And he insisted that was the way he wanted it.

Wei Lei accelerated down the driveway, taking the turns as fast as she dared. The plan was simple. Leave quickly and catch whoever was watching by surprise. But it didn't work out that way. No sooner had they reached the highway, when a large sedan smashed into the front passenger side. Almost simultaneously, another large sedan violently struck the driver's door, neatly pinning the small rental car between them. Both women were momentarily stunned from the impacts. Kat recovered her senses first and was able to push her door open and climb out. Wei Lei opened her eyes and tried her door, but it was jammed tight against the other vehicle.

Six tough-looking young Korean men poured out of the two attacking vehicles and formed a loose circle around the rental vehicle, and began inching towards Kat, slowly but surely closing the trap they had set. Kat was about to make a run for it when the nearest guy pulled a handgun and gestured for her to place her hands on her head while another broke formation and circled behind her. Kat glared at the man in front of her and slowly complied. The guy behind her grabbed her arms roughly, pulling them down behind her back, preparing to cuff her wrists. The man with the gun grinned lewdly and stepped close, his rank breath wrinkling Kat's nose in disgust.

Channeling her anger, frustration, and years of martial arts training, Kat exploded into action, snapping her head back viciously. She was rewarded with the satisfying crack of her skull, making solid contact with her assailant's nose, shattering it. The man yelled and went down hard, clutching at his face, which was already spurting bright red blood. Nearly simultaneously, she shifted her weight and kicked her right leg upward with all her might - catching the gunman cleanly in the crotch. He screamed and collapsed like a felled log, gun clattering across the pavement. He lay there curled into the fetal position and vomited. Kat had only a moment to relish the carnage she had caused when a shot rang out. Glancing back at the four guys still surrounding her, she saw a second gunman, who had fired a warning shot into the air, slowly level his gun until it was pointing directly at her head.

"One more sudden move, and it will be your last," he snarled in Korean. "Now get on the ground, face-down and put your hands behind your back!" Kat wasn't exactly sure what he said, but his tone and body language were perfectly clear. She decided that she had probably pushed her luck far enough and slowly complied. Two of the other gang members reached into the car and roughly yanked Wei Lei out and onto the ground next to Kat. Both women were frisked and had their phones and communications gear removed before being blindfolded and flex-cuffed. Kat was shoved into one car and Wei Lei into the other.

Kat wasn't scared or even intimidated. Instead, she nursed a white-hot rage, stoking it like a blacksmith stokes his forge. Controlled, but intense. Every sense heightened. Ready to explode into action when the moment was right. She also took some satisfaction that she had put two of those creeps in the hospital - and allowed herself a small smile.

She knew three things. Firstly, her captors would eventually mess up. And when they did, she would be sure not to miss her opportunity. Secondly, she had time. They could have killed her already but had not. More likely, they needed information. And the longer she held out from giving them what they wanted, the more time she had. And finally, she knew that somewhere overhead, the unseen *Dauntless* drone had captured the entire scene. And there was no doubt in her mind that Blake and the trusty crew of *Dauntless* would respond. Whoever was behind this had just stuck their hand into a hornet's nest. They just didn't know it yet.

Chapter 11

Back aboard *Dauntless*, Blake and the rest of the crew had watched the attack and kidnapping from afar, frustrated beyond measure at their inability to do anything in that moment to help. Mark used the drone to track the two vehicles holding the women back into town and into an industrial area, where they observed the two prisoners being dragged roughly into a non-descript warehouse.

The color had drained from Blake's face, and no one dared speak or even look directly at him. He clenched and unclenched his fists repeatedly as he stared at the warehouse where the women were now in the hands of an enemy they knew so little about.

Scotty was the first to break the silence, his thick Scottish brogue somehow soothing. "Well now mate, your wee young lass gave those bampots quite the skelpin'. Good on 'er. They'll be ruing the day they ever tangled with the likes of her."

Blake smiled despite himself. "She did what now?"

Emily spoke up. "I think what Scotty is trying to say is that Kat gave those jerks all they could handle and more. Two of them are out of commission for quite a while, I would think. But beyond that, rest assured we're going to get them back, Blake. I know I speak for all of us when I say we are here for you one hundred percent. Whatever it takes. Just say the word."

"Thanks Doc. I really appreciate that." He looked around the room and saw heads nodding at Emily's words. "They not only kidnapped Kat, they've also got a US government asset in Wei Lei. Let me call Rod and see what he plans to do about it." Blake left the room and closed the door behind him. The conversation was evidently short as Blake returned minutes later. They could tell by the grim look on his face that it had not gone well. He sat down and took a deep breath before speaking. "The bottom line is that Rod can't do anything. Certainly not soon enough to suit me. He will alert the local authorities but can't give them anything specific without alerting them to the fact that the US is operating covertly in their back yard. He can only tell them that Wei Lei, a US embassy employee in Seoul, is missing and was last heard from on a weekend shopping excursion in Gangneung. He was also absolutely clear that we were not to take matters into our own hands."

"So we're just going to sit here and do nothing?" Matt asked incredulously.

Blake turned his head slowly, leveled his gaze directly into Matt's eyes and measured his words carefully. "I said no such thing. We are going to put a plan together in the next 30 minutes to rescue those girls. And an hour after that, Kat will be safely back on board. You can take that to the bank!"

After a 45-minute ride – a ride which Kat was pretty sure took many extra turns to confuse her sense of direction – the car shuddered to a stop, and she was pulled out and alternately shoved and dragged into what seemed to be an oversized garage or warehouse. She was pushed down forcefully onto a hard concrete floor as a garage door clanked its way shut behind her. Moments later, Wei was shoved down next to her, and their blindfolds were removed.

Both women blinked as their eyes adjusted to the gloomy interior. They found themselves in some sort of run-down corrugated metal warehouse. It was dimly lit with a sparse number of dusty hanging fluorescent lights. Craning her neck further, Kat could also see a mezzanine level, housing cramped offices running the length of the side wall behind her. Everything seemed to be covered in a thick layer of dust, except for a stack of twenty-five to thirty large wooden crates at their back. She twisted around for a better look and recognized them as the same crates she had seen being offloaded from the North Korean gunship.

The four men who had brought them in stepped back as a fifth man made his way down the stairs from the mezzanine level, and strode over to stand in front of them. He raised his arm and struck Kat hard across the right side of her face, the sound of the slap echoing off the metal interior walls. Kat's cheek turned crimson, but instead of crying out, she surprised Song Hee by glaring back at him. "You will regret that," she hissed, the white-hot ember of anger inside her flaring into an intense flame. "You think you're a big man, slapping a handcuffed woman while surrounded by your armed buddies? You're nothing but a pathetic little worm," she growled, spitting on his shoes to emphasize her point.

Song Hee was shocked. No one had spoken to him like that in a long time. He was accustomed to his victims cowering in fear and pleading for their lives. He was sorely tempted to cave in a few of her ribs with a good kick but stopped himself just in time – remembering that he was not in charge of this operation. Looking closer at Kat, he noticed something odd about her chin. It was like his slap had dislodged her skin somehow – leaving a piece of flesh hanging off. He reached down and grasped it, giving it a hard tug. If he was shocked at Kat's fiery demeanor a moment before, he was doubly shocked now. Instead of a Korean woman sitting in front of him, he was suddenly confronted by a Caucasian woman.

"Well, well, well. What have we here?" Song Hee sneered. "Maybe I should rip the face off your friend here too! It certainly would give me great pleasure after the trouble you two have caused me."

Wei Lei shrank back, as Kat answered, "Sorry to disappoint once again, but I'm the only one in disguise here. My friend here is a police officer just doing some routine follow-up on a missing fisherman. I am a police officer in the United States over here on a police exchange program. I wanted to accompany her to visit the fisherman's wife, and we both felt it would make her more comfortable if I appeared to be a local."

"It's true, boss," one of the men nearby said. We found their badges when we searched them.

Song Hee felt a cold chill. *Plainclothes police?* he wondered. He had paid handsomely for the local cops to look the other way for the benefit of his illicit drug operation, but there was no way they would ignore the kidnapping and roughing up of their fellow officers! He pulled out his phone, snapped a few pictures of his captives, and stalked away.

Moments later, up in one of the warehouse offices, he placed a call. Helle listened as he brought her up to speed, including his finding that the women were local police officers. "Show me the pictures you took of them," she demanded. When the pictures appeared on her phone, she stifled a gasp. She **knew** the Caucasian woman. *Replace those dark brown eyes with bright green eyes and the dark hair with blonde hair, and it was **her**. Definitely!* If she could alter her appearance with a rubber face, she could certainly come up with some colored contacts and hair dye. "That white woman is no police officer. I doubt the other one is either. Those are fake badges. But I must tell you, Mr. Hee, you should take no solace in that fact. They have powerful friends who have now become your powerful adversaries. I will call you back shortly with further instructions. In the meantime, step up your security to the highest level possible and be ready to move when I call back. You have an hour or so, meanwhile, to find out what you can from them. I've heard you can be very persuasive. Try not to disappoint!"

Thirty minutes later, Blake and his team had a plan. It was, by necessity, a rudimentary plan, rooted more in desperation than in solid intelligence. But they had a few things working in their favor. They knew precisely where Kat and Wei were being held. They would know if, when, and where the captors moved them. And finally, Mark was able to gather good site intelligence, zooming the drone in close to identify four armed guards, one stationed on each corner of the building, and four security cameras covering all four sides of the structure.

That was the good news. The bad news was that they had no idea how many bad guys were inside the building, where Kat and Wei were being held, or any idea of the interior layout. They had to assume it was mostly open space and, based on the fire escape door and a set of stairs on one exterior side wall, it appeared to contain a mezzanine level.

The rescue party would consist of Blake, Matt, and Biff. Scotty would remain with *Dauntless* and man the bridge. Mark would be the eyes of the operation, flying at least two drones and staying in constant comms contact with the rescue party. Eric would be standing by on weapons because… well because you just never know. Emily would prepare the sick bay for emergency treatment of any potential injuries sustained on the mission.

The sun was setting as the three climbed into the RHIB and set off on the ten-minute ride to shore. They had selected a small public beach with a finger pier at the far end to tie up. It was nearly deserted, with the last few beachgoers packing up to leave when they arrived. No one took notice of the three men as they pulled up and disembarked. The first step of the plan was to acquire a vehicle for temporary use… preferably a large one that could carry five people as well as their gear. Matt took out his phone and called a local cab company – specifying they needed a large SUV or van. Minutes later, a large older-model Ford Expedition showed up. Blake opened the passenger door, leaned in, and spoke to the driver. "You speak English?" he asked. The man nodded. "Great. How much is your vehicle worth?"

The man's eyes widened in surprise. "Uhh... It's not for sale," he stuttered, with a wary glance over Blake's shoulder at the giant black man on the curb.

Blake straightened up and looked the truck over. "I'd say $10,000 tops. Here's the deal. We need to borrow it for an hour. I'll give you $10,000 cash right now. You wait here, and I'll give you another $5,000 when we return with the vehicle. If we don't show up, buy yourself another vehicle. If we do, you keep the truck with a bonus $15,000 in your pocket."

Blake handed him an envelope of cash, and after a quick verification of its contents, the man climbed out, leaving the keys in the ignition. The three men threw their bags in the back, climbed in, and drove off, leaving the cabbie staring after them.

Song Hee was getting nowhere fast with the two women. Wei Lei stuck to her story of being a local beat cop out investigating the case of the missing fisherman. Kat stuck to her story of being a police officer from Minnesota participating in a police exchange program. He yelled. He threatened. Enticed them with the prospect of cold bottled water. At one point, he produced a stun gun. Leering at Kat, he threatened Wei Lei with it. Kat bit her lip but said nothing. Wei Lei's eyes bulged in fear as Song Hee brought it closer and closer. "Last chance. Neither of you have anything to say?" he snarled. When both women stayed silent, he jabbed Wei Lei just under her rib cage, sending 30,000 volts surging into her body. She went instantly rigid, her eyes bulging grotesquely and limbs straining against the cuffs. When Song Hee retracted the weapon, she screamed and collapsed to the cement floor.

Kat reflexively lunged towards Song Hee, but still being cuffed, he easily sidestepped her and applied his weapon to Kat's ribcage. Over and over, he mercilessly electrocuted both women, even as his hardened men shrank back in aversion. To his disgust, neither woman budged, sticking to their story between screams of agony and begging him to call the local police station to confirm their credentials. Song Hee wasn't quite ready to take that chance. On the off chance they were telling the truth, there was no way in the world he wanted to be connected to their kidnapping. Instead, he ordered a close eye be kept on them and stomped back up to his office to ponder his options and wait for the woman to call him back with instructions.

Blake drove, forcing himself to stay calm and obey the traffic rules, while Matt rode shotgun, using his phone to navigate and provide directions. Mark confirmed through their earpieces that the women were still being held at the warehouse. "How many vehicles are currently parked out front?" Matt inquired.

"Three," answered Mark immediately. "2 large sedans – the same ones used in the kidnapping, and a large white Toyota pick-up truck."

Soon they found themselves entering a large industrial park in the city's southwest quadrant. Dusk had given way to night, which would work to their advantage. Some of the more modern-looking buildings were brightly lit, but Mark had reported that the target warehouse was older and, except for a lone streetlight out front, was dark. Blake turned onto the street and headed towards the building. "That's it, there on the left, just ahead," he stated. "Eyes sharp and stick to the plan." He pulled into the adjacent building's parking lot, parked with the nose facing toward the street, and killed the engine and the lights. "Showtime," he said.

Blake and Matt got out and quickly disappeared into the gloom. Biff waited three minutes before heaving himself out and slamming the door loudly behind him. If his enormous size made him stand out at home, it had an exponential effect in this South Korean town. As he lumbered down the road and into the parking lot of the old warehouse, both guards, stationed at each front corner, stared incredulously at the giant coming towards them, left their respective positions, and began to converge on the intruder.

Before either of them could speak, Biff called out in a friendly voice. "Hey fella's, my truck broke down back there, and my cell phone is dead. Can one of you call a tow truck for me?" As he spoke, he continued walking towards them, narrowing the gap.

The two Korean gangsters glanced at each other, unsure how to respond. In heavily accented English, one of them said, "You'd better move along, mister. If you know what's good for you." As he spoke, he pulled a handgun, pointed it in Biff's general direction, and then waved it to indicate that Biff needed to turn around. It turned out to be the last act of his young life.

Blake had used Biff's distraction to slip up undetected behind him, throw one arm around his body, and use his other arm to slit his throat from ear to ear. Biff closed the gap swiftly to the second guard, moving quicker than any man his size had any right to do, and wrapped his thick, long arms around him. The man struggled to reach for his gun and tried to shout, but Biff squeezed hard, pinning his arms to his side. All that came out of the man's open mouth was a gasp of exhaled air from his compressed lungs. Biff tightened his grip inexorably, and the man's face began to turn purple, his eyes bulging out. Biff squeezed even harder and felt the satisfying snap of a few ribs. He continued squeezing with all his considerable might for another minute until it was all over.

Blake took out a .22 rifle with a silencer attached and disabled both cameras on the front corners of the building. "You ready, Matt?" he whispered.

"Roger that, boss. Both guards and cameras are down at the rear of the building. I'll meet you at the bottom of the fire escape."

Blake nodded to Biff. "Good work. Slash the tires of all three vehicles out front and then go back to our vehicle and be ready to scoot. Matt and I will be there shortly with Kat and Wei Lei." With that, he ran down the side of the warehouse towards the fire escape.

Song Hee still hadn't heard back from Helle and decided to head back downstairs for a second round of interrogation. While he hesitated to kill or even seriously harm them, he decided a little more stun gun therapy wouldn't hurt. In his experience, even the toughest break down eventually. As he made his way down the corridor and past the security office, he glanced at the monitors and was shocked to find them all blank. He quickly radioed his four sentries posted outside the warehouse. No one responded. He screamed, "We're under attack!!" at the four men below. The words had no sooner left his lips when the fire escape door twenty feet down the hall exploded inwards.

As soon as the fire escape door was blown, Blake and Matt lobbed in three 'flash-bang' grenades, followed by three tear-gas grenades. They waited for a few seconds and then poured through the door, wearing protective masks and cradling automatic weapons with laser sights at the ready. Song Hee had flung himself into the security office and crawled under the desk, holding his shirt over his mouth and nose for relief from the tear gas. He was momentarily deafened and blinded by the 'flash-bang' grenades – helpless to do anything but stay put until his senses returned.

Matt and Blake crawled to the railing and looked down below. "Kat… you there?" called Blake.

"Over here," came the answer immediately. "By the stack of crates! Wei Lei is here with me. Careful. There's four bad guys down here somewhere, and their boss is upstairs."

Blake turned to Matt, "Cover me. I'll grab the girls and go out the front. Once I'm out, you go back down the fire escape, and we'll meet up back at the vehicle." With Matt providing overwatch, Blake prioritized speed over caution and hurtled down the stairs, hitting the concrete floor at the bottom with a thud. One of Hee's men popped up and winged a shot in Blake's direction but was quickly driven back under cover by Matt's prompt return fire. Blake spotted Kat and Wei Lei crouching in front of the stack of crates, quickly ran over, and sliced through the plastic cuffs. Both women were gagging and choking on the tear gas. Blake reached out and grabbed their hands, saying, "I've got you. Time to go home."

Song Hee's hearing and sight slowly returned, but he soon found himself overwhelmed with the tear gas. He cautiously poked his head out from under the desk, exited the fire escape, and descended the stairs to ground level. Making his way to the front of the building, he was soon joined by his four remaining men. It was clear the attackers were gone and had taken the women with them. It was also clear that he wouldn't be pursuing them in any of the three vehicles parked out front—all with ruined tires sitting sadly on their rims. Silence settled over the group of dejected men when they all heard a vehicle engine start-up at the adjacent building. Song Hee perked up immediately. "That's them. It's gotta be. Quick… we've still got the pickup in the warehouse and a score to settle. Let's go!!"

Biff was mightily relieved to see Blake and the two women heading for the truck, with Matt right on their heels. He started the engine and, as soon as everyone was on board, gunned it. The old Expedition bogged down momentarily before finding its footing and lurching forward. Seconds later, they were headed out of the industrial park and back towards the beach. Kat glanced behind her. "I hate to say this, but we're not out of the woods yet," she announced grimly.

"I slashed the tires of all three vehicles out front. You sure we're being followed?" questioned Biff.

"I'm sure. They had another white pickup stashed in the warehouse, and I'm pretty sure that's the one coming after us," Kat replied. Moments later, shots rang out, and the back window was shattered as bullets whizzed past their heads.

"Everyone down," yelled Blake. "Biff... Go!! Matt... guide him back to the beach, but you'll have to take evasive action on the way. I'll try and keep them pinned down." With that, Blake grabbed his automatic weapon, rolled down the window and leaned out, aiming a stream of slugs back at the white pickup, hoping to keep the shooters at bay long enough to form a better plan.

Matt guided Biff towards the coast, taking a zigzag route to keep their pursuers at bay. As they worked their way through the city, traffic became a little thicker – sometimes a boon, providing cover, and sometimes a curse... slowing their progress and allowing their pursuers to catch up.

Blake pressed his comm and said, "Mark. Eric. You guys there?"

"We're here boss," they chimed in together. "Seems like you're in a spot of trouble," added Mark.

"Listen carefully. We are headed for the coast, where there is a road that will take us in a relatively straight line to the beach where the RHIB is tied up. The problem is, once we are on that road, they will be able to close in and use their superior firepower to finish us. When I give the word, I need *Dauntless* to take out the pursuing vehicle. Can you do that?"

"Nothing to it, boss. Just say the word," Eric smiled. "Mark has that pickup painted with the targeting laser, and I can drop an exploding shell or five right on their heads anytime you say."

Following Matt's clear, accurate directions, Biff managed to keep just far enough out of range of their pursuers to reach the coastal highway about a mile south of the beach where the RHIB was waiting. As soon as their attackers pulled onto the highway behind them, Blake keyed his mic. "Fire!"

Dauntless was lying 3 miles offshore, near the edge of her 30mm cannon range. Blake began counting aloud. "One Mississippi, two Mississippi, three Mississippi, four Mississippi, five Mississippi." A heartbeat later, the white pickup disappeared in a dozen blinding flashes and a cloud of smoke.

Eric's voice came through the comms loud and clear. "Like shooting fish in a barrel. Should be clear sailing ahead. We'll be expecting you shortly. *Dauntless* out"

They found the taxi driver waiting for his vehicle in the parking lot. Blake apologized for the damage caused, and instead of giving him an additional $5,000, he handed him an envelope with an additional $10,000. Wei Lei had called ahead for a cab to meet her. She and Kat shared a quick hug and a promise to keep in touch, and she was off. The others climbed aboard the RHIB and lost no time getting back to *Dauntless*.

Chapter 12

They hadn't gone far when Blake's cell phone chirped to indicate an incoming call. Blake winced when he saw it was from Rod Stringer. He picked it up and answered, "Hello Rod", after which he never said another word for nearly two minutes as Rod lit into him about the 'blatant attack perpetrated on South Korean sovereign territory.' Once again, the President was on the phone with his South Korean counterpart, urging restraint. Naturally, the South Koreans had assumed North Korea was responsible, likely in retaliation for the loss of their patrol boat, for which they blamed South Korea. Even worse, according to the latest briefing Rod had received, the shelling had struck a civilian pick-up truck on a public road, killing three men and injuring two others. The South Korean navy had been activated and was scrambling to intercept the offending vessel. If, as Rod strongly suspected, *Dauntless* was involved, they had 'better get the hell out of Dodge'!!

Blake waited for Rod to run out of steam before attempting to respond, his anger growing. "Are you finished? You greenlighted the mission, and when things went sideways, you completely dropped the ball. Did you really think I was going to stand by and do nothing? Oh… and not that you asked, but yes, we successfully rescued Kat and your girl, Wei Lei. They're a little banged up but will be fine. Wei Lei is on her way back to the US embassy in Seoul, and I'm sure you'll hear from her soon. And those 5 guys in the truck we shredded? They were no innocent Sunday-school teachers, and as far as I'm concerned, they got what was coming to them. Best we can tell, they belonged to a local organized crime gang that were responsible for the kidnapping and were also in possession of the radioactive material acquired from the North Koreans. Also, just so you know, at the time of their demise, they were doing their level best to kill us! We iced four more of them guarding the warehouse where they were holding the women. I won't lose a minute's sleep over them either. So, pardon me for putting myself and my crew in harm's way while you sit comfortably in your office, second-guessing everything I do in the field. I suggest you handle your business keeping the Koreans from escalating this into a full-blown regional conflict, and I'll handle my business just fine."

Rod was silent for a beat, considering what Blake had said. When he spoke again, it was in a subdued tone. "OK, you have a point. If I were in your shoes and they had Mary, I'd probably have done the same thing. But… you must get out of there pronto. You can't let the South Korean Navy catch you. And you can't fire at them!!"

"As soon as we get back on *Dauntless*, we'll be out of here," Blake promised. "I like our chances of making a clean getaway."

"Ok. Godspeed. We'll talk again soon," Rod promised as he ended the call.

The RHIB was no sooner winched aboard when *Dauntless* surged forward, her three powerful stern jets shooting a rooster tail of white water a full 300 feet behind her. Blake and Matt hurried to the bridge, where they found a worried-looking Scotty at the helm. "We've got a wee bit of trouble, I'm afraid sir. We've detected what appears to be an Incheon Class frigate headed our way, dispatched from their Donghae naval base just 20 miles down the coast. A couple helicopters have just launched as well."

"Thanks Scotty. I just heard the same from Rod Stringer a few minutes ago," Blake replied. "Matt and I will take over from here. Good work. Hey… can you ask Emily to take Kat to the sick bay and check her out? She says she's fine, but I'll feel better hearing it from Doc."

Matt stepped to the helm and glanced down. Given the conditions, *Dauntless'* current max speed was 60 knots which meant they would reach the relative safety of international waters in just under eight minutes. "Hey boss, that frigate will never get near us. We've got a twenty-mile head start on them. The helicopters are a bigger concern. They are likely Sikorsky SH-60 Seahawks which have a top speed of about 170 miles per hour. With our head start, I estimate we'll reach international waters ahead of them with about 3 minutes to spare."

"OK. Pedal to the metal," Blake replied tersely. "Every second counts. Once we reach international waters, continue full speed ahead for 2 minutes. Then we come to a full stop, spin around 180 degrees to face the shore, and turn on minimal lighting just to show someone is home. When those helicopters spot us, I want them to see an innocent toy of the filthy rich, peacefully anchored for the night."

"Sounds good, Cap'n," nodded Matt. "But we do have one other thing to worry about. We have no way of knowing if they have any submarines in the area. We might be radar-stealthy, but at this speed, the cavitation from our jets will sound like a herd of stampeding elephants to a hunter sub. Not only that, it's likely they have fixed underwater hydrophone arrays that are busily recording the sound of our escape."

Blake just smiled. "Well... nothing we can do about a submarine, so no point in worrying about it. And as for any sounds they pick up on their hydrophones... well, they already know something fired 30mm naval shells onto their sovereign territory, but they have never heard the sound of *Dauntless* at full bore, so it will just be one more unsolved mystery for them to puzzle over. Now... get us out of here. I'm going to check on Kat."

Twenty minutes later, *Dauntless* was lying fifteen miles offshore with the minimum required outward running lights and a few of her portholes emanating soft interior lighting. The calm of the night was broken only by the intermittent sound of two helicopters flying precise search grids and a South Korean Navy frigate, which raced past them off their starboard bow about two miles to the south.

Song Hee emerged from the wrecked pickup miraculously unscathed. Three of his men were killed instantly in the barrage. Another was critically injured and was dependent on the skill of a surgical team racing to save his life. Song Hee had flung himself out of the moving vehicle the moment he determined they were under attack, suffering only a painful separated shoulder when he hit the ground, and a host of accompanying cuts, scrapes, and bruises. He looked and felt awful but would be fully functional in a few days.

With her disguised voice, it was difficult to judge Helle's reaction, but she didn't seem too surprised at the turn of events. After all, she had warned him that his captives had powerful friends. Song Hee believed in his men, and they were good, but they couldn't be expected to go up against highly-trained and better-equipped special forces. He wasn't in the mood for a lecture in any case. In one hour, he had lost seven of his men – eight if he counted the guy fighting for his life. And two others were out of commission for a while, thanks to Kat. That was nearly his entire organization wiped out in the blink of an eye. Rival gangs would be looking to take advantage of his temporary weakness, and it would take all his considerable skill and cunning to survive this setback and rebuild.

After her call with Song Hee, Helle immediately convened an emergency virtual meeting of the Council. "Thank you for adjusting your schedules to attend," she began. "There have been some concerning recent developments you all need to be aware of that require some adjustments to our plan." With that, she brought them up to speed on the dramatic interruption of the final transfer of radiocaesium, the subsequent investigation and interference in Gangneung, and finally, the kidnapping and subsequent escape of the two women.

"Song Hee has survived and can still be useful to us, but most of his men have been killed or are out of action. Furthermore, the location of our radiocaesium cache has been compromised, and we need to take steps to move it as soon as possible to a new secure location."

"Do we know the identity of the person or organization who is behind this interference?" asked one of the attendees.

Helle paused. "I have reason to believe it is The Clean World Foundation." There was a collective gasp as this stunning revelation sank in. "More specifically, Blake and Katherine Zane operating from their flagship mega-yacht, *Dauntless*," she continued. "In fact, it was Katherine Zane in disguise that Song Hee detained. She was working with another woman claiming to be a local police officer, but I have not been able to confirm that. We have two immediate problems. First, we need to move the radioactive material."

"I believe I can help with that," a gravelly voice offered.

"Go ahead, Nicos. You have already proven your loyalty and dedication to the cause. We are eager to hear your idea," Helle answered.

"As you all know, I own Cirillo Shipping Inc., one of the largest container shipping companies in the world. I can divert one of my ships to Gangneung and pick up the radiocaesium within the next couple of days."

"Thank you, Nicos. That will work out well," Helle responded. "Please do so with all possible haste. I will make the necessary arrangements with Song Hee. He is down on manpower but should be able to assist with this task. I will also speak to him about joining our team full-time and sailing with your ship to watch over our precious cargo. Now on to our second problem. What to do about Blake and Katherine and their interference in our operation."

Several ideas were debated among the Council members. In the end, it was decided that Helle would get in touch with her North Korean contact and inform him that she had solid intelligence that it was *Dauntless* that attacked and sank their naval patrol vessel. They felt confident that North Korea would be keen to retaliate and send a message that North Korea was fully capable of defending its sovereign territory and would not stand for willful intrusion and military attacks on its naval assets.

South Korean naval search activities continued well into the night, but by dawn, things seemed to have quieted down. The frigate and helicopters had returned to base, and Rod confirmed that the South Koreans had found nothing to either confirm or allay their suspicions that the North Koreans were involved. In any case, while *Dauntless* had been spotted at anchor, no one suspected her of being involved in the altercation.

Kat underwent a thorough medical examination and had received a clean bill of health by Emily. The only visible signs of damage were a bruised cheek and a 'shiner' on her right eye – courtesy of Song Hee's slap.

Following a well-deserved sleep and a fine breakfast of scrambled eggs, bacon, and assorted fruit courtesy of Biff, Blake assembled the full crew in the War Room to debrief and plan their next move. Everyone smiled when Eric strolled into the room, his tattered t-shirt of the day captioned, "In my defense, I was left unsupervised."

Kat brought everyone up to speed on her Gangneung adventure, skipping lightly over being subjected to the business end of Song Hee's taser, and profusely thanked the crew, particularly Matt and Biff, for everything they did to ensure her speedy and safe return. The fact that her disguise had been compromised was discussed as well, but the consensus was that it seemed unlikely that Kat's real identity had been compromised. After all, what was the chance any of those gangbangers had any interest or connection to environmental issues and The Clean World Foundation?

The discussion then turned to the next steps as the realization sank in that they had not really learned any more about who they were up against or what their intentions were. Blake pointed out that now that their hiding spot for the crates holding radioactive material had been exposed, they would no doubt move quickly to transport the cargo to a new, secure location.

Kat let out a chuckle. "Did I leave out the fact that I managed to place a miniature GPS tracker on one of the crates?" She opened her laptop, tapped a few keys and then showed it around the room. "See that blinking blue triangle? That's their stash of nastiness which we can now follow wherever it goes."

Chapter 13

Tartus, Syria

The trio of dusty Jeeps, each towing a sizable empty utility trailer, crawled in rag-tag formation across the dark and rocky terrain. They had set out earlier that evening from Tartus – a modern, picturesque Syrian town on the coast of the Mediterranean. The lead Jeep was driven by Achmed, a former low-level ISIS commander, and after an arduous 3-hour journey inland, they were now approaching their destination outside the small town of Al Sukhnah located in Homs Province. Achmed coasted to a stop and killed the headlights. The following two Jeeps did the same.

Achmed was a single child, born and raised in Tartus by hard-working entrepreneur parents who made and sold leather goods from a stand in a small open market. Tartus had always been a popular Syrian vacation spot. It also boasted a small Russian naval base, and the market was frequented by locals, well-heeled vacationers, and Russian sailors. Achmed's family eked out a reasonable living, but they all worked fourteen hours a day to stay marginally above the poverty line. Achmed's father produced most of the goods, tanning hides, cutting out templates, and stitching together the various wares. From the time he was 7 years old, Achmed would split his time between school, helping out in the workshop on weeknights, with his weekends spent ferrying inventory to the market stall and working the market patrons to lure them to the stall to make an unplanned, unnecessary purchase.

By the time Achmed was nineteen, he was tired of the constant grind - hopeless and disillusioned. Late at night, he turned to the internet and was soon attracted to the slick propaganda of the new Islamic State (ISIS), which had sprouted from the ashes of Al Qaeda in Iraq. ISIS recruiters offered hope. Hope of purpose. Hope of economic security. Hope of respect, authority and power. Hope of eternal paradise in the next life, if not in this one. Though by day, Achmed continued to work hard in the family business, by night, he was quickly becoming radicalized. One night, together with three of his similarly radicalized buddies, they stole a car belonging to one of their parents and fled to Raqqua, where they pledged undying allegiance to ISIS and its revered leader, Abu Bakr al-Baghdadi.

The initial training and indoctrination were brutal. The new recruits were subjected to physically exhausting training interspersed with intense indoctrination sessions. Even during the short periods in which they were allowed to sleep, the mesmerizing jihadi music – *Nasheeds* – was played incessantly, featuring stark Arabic chants that formed the soundtrack of militant Islamic extremism. The music was interspersed periodically with sermons featuring vehement messages of hate towards Jews and infidels and calling on all 'true Muslims' to exact righteous vengeance on Allah's enemies. By day, they were forced to watch and participate in extreme punishments meted out to the locals for minor infringements of *Sharia* law – rules and laws that were regularly updated in increasingly restrictive announcements posted in and around the city. Executions by beheading, hanging, and shooting were common and often took place in the town square or patches of dirt and grass that had, until recently, served as soccer pitches for the local kids.

Within a few months, Achmed and his fellow recruits were fully acclimatized to their new way of life. What was shocking at first had quickly become 'normal'. They wore their black uniforms and facemasks proudly, strutting around town brandishing powerful automatic weapons, terrorizing the local population, and exploiting the obeisance of the local townspeople. The pay was steady and good. Not that they really had to use it to make purchases. Anything they wanted could be taken by force from whoever had it. The new Achmed quickly grew unrecognizable from his former self. The pleasant, sociable, hard-working boy his parents had raised was gone – forever erased in just a few short months.

But what goes around comes around. You live by the sword, you die by the sword. You reap what you sow. These cliches are old for a reason. It's because they are tried and proven true by millennia of violent human experience.

Due to its unique combination of slick propaganda, effective organization, and sheer brutality, ISIS rose quickly to power and, at its height, occupied or controlled vast amounts of territory inside the borders of the supposedly sovereign states of Iraq and Syria – The Caliphate. But in so doing, it had created many powerful enemies which began to push back slowly but surely. Over the next two years, in a bitter, devastating military conflict, ISIS lost 95% of the territory it once held. The Caliphate dream was shattered.

Life for Achmed, who had been promoted to the rank of a local commander in charge of about one hundred men, grew increasingly desperate. The regular pay cheques became irregular and finally stopped altogether. Food and ammunition became scarce. Eventually, there was nothing left to even steal from the locals. Local dogs and cats disappeared into the bellies of he and his men. But that misery was nothing compared to the terror inflicted by the constant barrage of missile strikes from stalking Western warplanes and exploding artillery shells lobbed in from the infidel enemy that encircled his position. Worst of all were the drone strikes. The invisible American drones were a constant threat, and they quickly learned that any attempt at electronic communication would draw them like flies to honey. It was hopeless. Cut off from all supplies and contact with the outside world, Achmed's men melted away. Many were killed in action. Those fortunate enough to avoid a horrible mutilating death simply donned civilian clothes – some even disguised as women – and made a break for it. Eventually, Achmed was forced to do the same. He had no food, no water, no ammunition, no fighters, and no purpose left to fight for. It was time to run or time to die. He chose to run. He found a local widow with two small boys, forced them at gunpoint into a rundown Toyota pickup, and managed to convince the infidel soldiers at the checkpoint that they were a civilian family fleeing the destruction. It was touch and go, but, in the end, the truck was waved through, and Achmed was able to return to Tartus to try and pick up the pieces of his life.

He found return to civilian life to be even harder than his adjustment to life as an ISIS militant. If he found the routine of the family business uninspiring before, it was unbearably dull now. He longed for the power and affluence he had briefly enjoyed. His grieved parents were afraid of this unfamiliar, churlish man who had replaced their good-natured boy.

But then, one day, the sullen and brooding Achmed had an idea. A brilliant idea. A way out of the dead-end life he despised but nearly resigned to. ISIS had developed expertise in explosives and built several large manufacturing facilities to produce its own homemade explosive product on an industrial scale. One such facility was located in Homs Province. After the final defeat of ISIS in early 2019, active operations ceased, but there remained a sizable cache of explosives on-site, along with various other bomb-making materials and components. The entire stock had fallen into the hands of a local militia leader named Hasim, who, himself, was a former ISIS commander that Achmed knew well from his days in Raqqua. Achmed arranged to meet with Hasim, who was only too eager to hear Achmed's pitch to convert a chunk of his illicit inventory into cash.

Following the meeting, the two former comrades reached a handshake understanding, and Achmed immediately went to work to find a buyer. He engaged the services of another friend, who had formerly worked with ISIS' sophisticated technology division, to advertise his product on the dark web. Months went by with nary a nibble before, finally, he was contacted by a mysterious disembodied voice—Helle.

She needed to procure a massive amount of explosives, along with detonators, timers, wiring, fuses, and casings. And she was willing to pay handsomely. Achmed immediately got in touch with Hasim and worked out a deal. From the driver's seat of the Jeep, he allowed himself a small smile at the 100% markup he had worked out for himself on the resale of the material to the mysterious woman and whatever outfit she represented. Having demanded half the money upfront in Bitcoin, he had what he needed to make the purchase. The remaining 50% of the agreed sale price would be received once the buyer took possession. That second payment would be all profit. This one deal would make him a made man. He would once again enjoy all that life had to offer – wealth, power, and respect!

Achmed climbed out of the lead Jeep, and the other 5 men gathered around. "Ok brothers, we do not have far to go now. If Allah smiles upon us, we will be returning this way in an hour or so with the goods we came for. Let's review the plan." He glanced at his watch. "We need to arrive precisely at 2:00 am. So, we wait here for 30 minutes, and then we cover the final two kilometers to the small industrial site just north of Al Sukhnah, where the goods are stored. When we get there, everyone exit the vehicles, and Hasim's men will approach. They will make sure we are unarmed and search us for any electronic devices. It's ok. I know Hasim, and he stands to make a lot of money from this deal, so just stay calm. Once everything is loaded and ready to go, I will settle up with Hasim, and we will be on our way."

The men nodded. A few lit up cigarettes to pass the time and calm their nerves. Soon enough, it was time, and the Jeeps resumed their laborious crawl through the desert and up into the hills to the north of the town. Achmed found a small track and turned to the right, bumping along it until he came to a number of Quonset huts loosely surrounding a construction trailer. He came to a stop, blinked the lights, killed the engine, and slowly climbed out – hands outstretched. The other men followed suit.

A dozen of Hasim's men jogged out from around one of the Quonset huts and quickly patted down the visitors. With the search complete, Achmed was led toward the construction trailer. A large, swarthy man stepped out as Achmed approached. *"As salamu alaikum wa rahmatullah wa barakatuhu* (may the mercy, peace and blessings of Allah be upon you). It is good to see you, my brother."

Achmed smiled broadly and shook the man's outstretched hand vigorously. *"Wa alaikum salam wa rahmatullah wa barakatuhu* (and may the peace mercy and blessings of Allah be upon you). Allah be praised, my brother! It is good to see you again too!"

Hasim led Achmed to one of the nearby Quonset huts, ushered him inside, and flicked on the lights. Achmed was impressed with how well-organized everything was. Drums of the manufactured explosives were stacked neatly against the walls. Sturdy metal shelving units housed electrical components, timers, fuses, and shaped charges. "What you see here is just a fraction of what I have," said Hasim with a sweeping gesture. "When it became inevitable the Caliphate would fall, Baghdadi himself sent me, and my men, on a mission to secure this site and await further orders. Of course, no further orders ever came. I can use some of this stuff in my line of work, but there is way more here than I could ever use in a lifetime, so I am happy to sell on the open market what I cannot use."

Hasim gripped Achmed's shoulder and turned him until they locked eyes before continuing. "But I have one concern, brother. I do not wish for any of this to end up in the hands of my enemies. Our country has many competing forces, as you know. There are official Syrian government military forces with which I am aligned. Then there are Iranian-backed Shia militias, militant Sunni militias and terrorist groups, not to mention the American-backed Kurdish Syrian Democratic Forces. I must have your word that this material will not end up in the hands of any of these groups."

Achmed nodded pensively. "I understand, my friend. As Allah is my witness, my buyer is not planning to use any of this in the region. My instructions are to store it at a secure location in Tartus, where a ship will be sent to pick it up. It was paramount to them that they would be able to pick up the merchandise at a commercial port. I do not know their ultimate purpose, but I am confident that all of this will soon be sailing west across the Mediterranean."

Hasim nodded, satisfied with Achmed's assurances, and gestured towards the front garage door, where the order was already neatly laid out. "Everything you asked for is there. Go have a look."

Achmed carefully looked over the goods, marking the items off against a list he pulled out of his shirt pocket. "It's all there, Hasim. Let's get it loaded up." Thirty minutes later, under the watchful eyes of Hasim and Achmed, the trailers were securely loaded and covered with heavy tarps. Achmed's men stood alongside the Jeeps while Achmed and Hasim returned to the trailer. Achmed sat down at Hasim's computer, logged into his Bitcoin account, transferred the agreed payment, and logged back out. Hasim then sat down and verified the Bitcoin payment had been received into his account.

"I guess that concludes our business for this evening," Hasim beamed. "Go in peace, my brother, and may the blessings of Allah be upon you".

Achmed extended his hand. "*As-salamu alaikum* (Peace be upon you)."

With that, he climbed into his Jeep, his men followed suit, and the little caravan bumped their way back down the track. They arrived back in Tartus a few hours later, attracting little attention as they made their way through the deserted pre-dawn streets. Achmed led them down to the waterfront and pulled up to a nondescript, corrugated metal storage shed located at the base of a large finger pier lined with massive container cranes. One by one, they backed through the garage door and deposited their explosives-laden trailers. Achmed winched the door closed, and the Jeeps dispersed into the darkness.

Achmed took out his phone and placed a short call. "It's done," he said.

"Wait for further instructions," answered the familiar, disguised voice of Helle. "We will have a ship pick up the package next week. Once it is safely loaded, you will receive the other half of your payment."

Chapter 14

European Union Headquarters, Brussels Belgium

Sonja Larson was about to make the biggest speech in her life and wanted it to be perfect...needed it to be perfect. She had the same feeling she had as a little girl on her first roller coaster as it crested the top of that first steep climb. The years of hard work - like that slow, clanking climb - had finally paid off when she was selected to be her country's representative to the European Union. She felt like she had peaked when she was named to the Commission and appointed Chair of the Climate Action and Energy portfolio.

Now, in a few short minutes, she would be unveiling a hugely ambitious plan for the EU member countries seeking aggressive new reduction targets for greenhouse gas emissions. She could almost sense the momentum of that roller coaster beginning to shift, like when the lead car crests the hill and tips down the steep slope on the other side, pulling the remainder of the train along with them. If she could just pull this off, she was sure that gravity – which had seemingly fought her tooth and nail every step of the way – would finally become her ally, fueling dramatic and rapid change in the way the world was responding to this unfolding crisis.

Indeed, the whole planet could be viewed using the same metaphor – quickly approaching the point of no return. Centuries of human activity had created a situation that was about to unleash climate change on a scale that would lead to human extinction. The last few decades of measured, observable change were like the roller coaster cresting the top and looking down the abyss on the other side. The pace of change that followed would accelerate and be unstoppable. Time for delay and half measures had run out.

Since World War II, much of the world had looked to America for leadership. But America could no longer be counted on as a leader on the world stage. Deeply divided and increasingly inward-focused, she had too many problems of her own to provide effective international leadership on important shared national issues. Even though the current administration had shown renewed interest in environmental issues - such as rejoining the Paris Agreement - it could just as easily withdraw again following the next election cycle.

Besides, America was addicted more than ever to fossil fuels. It was now, by far, the world's largest oil-producing country in the world, at nearly 20 million barrels a day. Saudi Arabia, in second place, produced less than 12 million barrels a day. If that weren't bad enough, the United States also led the world in oil consumption – consuming even more than it produced. Sonja was shocked to discover that the US consumed fifty percent more oil than China even though China had four times the population. On a per capita basis, that works out to the average American citizen accounting for eight times the fossil fuel consumption compared to the average Chinese citizen. Counting on America to lead the world in a shift away from fossil fuels towards alternative energy solutions was like asking the family drunk to guard the beer cooler at a beach outing.

It was clear to Sonja, and many of her EU colleagues, that it was high time for the EU to assume the mantle of leadership vacated by the United States. *The world would either follow or it wouldn't. Either way, it is the last chance for humanity.* Her pensive thoughts were interrupted by a knock on her office door. Her lead speechwriter, Maria, looked in and announced, "It's time, Sonja."

"Thanks Maria. I'll be with you momentarily."

After a brief pause, Sonja closed her laptop, pushed her chair back, and stood up. *Go time,* she thought to herself. Exiting the office, she joined Maria, and they walked together to the EU Commission chamber. The other Commission members were already assembled, and they rose as one and applauded as Sonja entered the room and took her position behind the podium on the dais at the front of the room. Maria took a seat with the other aides at the back of the room underneath the large teleprompter screen. It was a big moment for her as well. She had worked together with Sonja on this speech for the last three weeks, and she shared Sonja's conviction that the world was at a critical crossroads—one of those seemingly innocuous decisions that turn out to have the most profound impact on the future.

Sonja cleared her throat and began. "Ladies and gentlemen, distinguished members of the European Commission, thank you for confirming me six weeks ago as the Commission's Chair of the Climate Action and Energy portfolio. I do not take your confidence in me for granted, and I have worked diligently to present a proposal to you today that will represent a major step forward in the global fight against the existential threat of radical climate change. A painful step, no doubt, but one long overdue as the European Union takes a critical step forward in leading the world on a new path and towards a new and brighter future."

The familiar words of the speech, so passionately delivered by Sonja, rolled over Maria like a comforting breeze. She knew every word by heart. Hung on every word. Together, they had practiced for hours, agonizing over every inflection, nuance, and gesture - writing and rewriting key parts of the speech as they struggled to bring into sharp focus the story that the reams of data and scientific evidence were telling. The story that so much of the world seemed to have no time, energy, or appetite to understand. It felt like they were in a burning building filled with occupants they could not wake despite their best efforts.

As Sonja continued, Maria glanced around the room. She was encouraged to note that the Commission members were paying close attention. Some nodded along. Others were taking studious notes.

When Sonja got to the part of her speech where she detailed the new greenhouse gas reduction targets in the proposal, a few pulled out their mobile phones and tapped out urgent messages. The Paris Agreement, which the EU had signed on to, called for a reduction of greenhouse gas emissions by at least forty percent by 2030 compared to 1990. Under Sonja's proposal, the reduction target was increased to sixty percent by 2030, and then another twenty percent by 2040. By taking this unilateral action, they hoped that the EU would be able to pressure other major greenhouse-gas producers to follow suit.

Maria snapped back to attention as Sonja concluded her presentation. "And so, ladies and gentlemen, the time to lead is now! The time to act is now! Delay, half-measures, lip service, and excuses will only serve to seal our fate. There is much to do and little time to do it in. Thank you."

The Commission members rose once again to their feet and applauded vigorously as Sonja stepped off the dais and took her place at the table. Over the next few hours, the Commission voted to accept a resolution Sonja's office had drafted in advance, recommending the plan to their respective member states. They then set a date the following month to meet again and vote on the adoption of the plan itself.

Sonja and Maria left the room and walked back to their office suite together. Maria was positively bubbling with excitement. "You had them eating out of your hand!" she bubbled excitedly. "You were absolutely brilliant!"

"Thanks Maria. Today was a good day – an important step towards real progress and I agree it went about as well as could be expected. I feel hopeful, for the first time in a long time, that an aggressive plan like this might actually be adopted by the EU. You have played a key role in today's success, and I want to personally thank you for your contribution. However, we can expect some strong headwinds as the Commission members bring this back to their individual governments for consideration. It's not the individual support of Commission members we need. It's the support of the democratically elected governments they represent. And the economic cost will be just too high for some to stomach."

Sonja continued. "America still poses a massive threat to whatever progress the EU makes. I just can't see the United States being convinced to join in without a massive jolt to their thinking. In the short term, their continued reliance on relatively cheap, domestically produced fossil fuels will give them an economic advantage that will make it impossible for the EU to convince other key countries to follow us and change course. We need other large oil-consuming countries like China, India, Japan and Russia to agree to similar greenhouse gas emission reductions. But if the United States resists, it is unlikely that these other key countries will be motivated to fall in line either. Worse, that will make it impossible for the EU countries to stick to their pledge, and we will be back to square one, out of time, and doomed to failure. The EU needs to lead, but it still needs the United States to follow suit to turn the tide in our favor."

Chapter 15

Undisclosed location near Luxembourg, Belgium

Helle had been working her way through elaborate protocols now for two days, trying to reestablish communication with the North Koreans. You didn't just pick up a phone and call someone's direct line. There were ways to let them know you wanted to talk, and eventually – maybe – they would reach out to you.

She was relieved when her secure 'burner' phone finally chirped, and the familiar gruff voice came across the line. "Our business is concluded, is it not? We have lost a ship and good men. Dear Leader was extremely displeased, which puts our careers, our livelihoods, our freedom, and even our lives in extreme peril. We are not interested in doing any more business with you. We must never speak again. Any attempt to do so will end badly for both of us. Goodbye!"

"Wait!" Helle interjected quickly. "I can help you."

"You have one minute before I terminate this call," the man replied.

"I know who is responsible for the attack and sinking of your ship!"

The man on the other end chuckled derisively. "Of course you know who is responsible. So do we. So does the whole world. We will make the ROK dogs pay for this blatant and unprovoked attack on our sovereign territory. And we don't need your help to do it."

"Really? Is that what you think? Or is that just a convenient scapegoat to sell to your Supreme Leader in hopes of saving your skin? What possible motivation would the South Koreans have to risk all-out war by taking a potshot at a small naval patrol boat? And any retaliation by North Korea carries the same risk of all-out war – a conflict that would likely destroy both countries and risk further regional escalation by drawing in superpowers like China and America. What if I told you that my man who was there that night got a good look at the ship that sank your patrol vessel? What if I told you it wasn't the South Koreans? What if I told you it was a privately-owned civilian vessel that you could act against without the risk of starting World War III?"

The North Korean was silent for a few moments as he pondered what Helle had said. "All right. Go on. You've got my attention."

"My guy described the vessel as a large, dark yacht. At least one hundred meters long. But one that could move extremely quickly," Helle began.

"A large, black yacht!?" interrupted the North Korean. "I don't think so. This conversation is over."

"No Wait! Hear me out. There is a large black yacht currently operating in the Sea of Japan. It is named *Dauntless* and is owned and operated by *The Clean World Foundation*. And get this… It is rumored to be armed to the teeth, possessing extraordinary capabilities far beyond those associated with luxury mega-yachts."

"OK. Let's assume, for argument's sake, you are right. What possible motivation would this environmental organization have to send their vessel into our waters? Are they secretly an arm of the South Korean military or their National Intelligence Service?"

"Good question," admitted Helle. "I'm not sure they are affiliated with any particular government's military or intelligence agencies, and I don't know what motive they may have had for being where they were. But what I can tell you is that Katherine Zane, a co-founder of the *Clean World Foundation,* is currently aboard *Dauntless.* Furthermore, my guy captured her less than 36 hours later, impersonating a South Korean police officer while investigating the disappearance of a South Korean fishing captain whose vessel we were using to conduct the rendezvous that night. Commandos from *Dauntless* overpowered my men in recovering her, and the ship provided covering fire in their subsequent escape."

"The ROK is blaming us for that attack!! That was *Dauntless?*" the North Korean asked incredulously.

Helle continued. "I don't see how it could be anyone else. I'm not going to tell you how to conduct your business, but this ship is causing everyone a lot of grief and has inflicted great loss of face on the Democratic People's Republic of Korea. Not to mention their reckless endangerment of your country's sovereignty and security. It's time for some payback, don't you think?"

The man on the other end of the phone cleared his throat and then spoke. "It is not what I think that matters. But I will pass your information on to my superiors. We will not speak again, but I assure you my country appreciates you bringing this information forward and will take appropriate action."

With that, the connection was cut off. Helle allowed a slow smile to spread across her face. Blake and Katherine didn't know it yet. But they were the walking dead. The days of them interfering in her operation were numbered. She was sure of that. North Korea would take care of business.

Dauntless – Sea of Japan

With Kat safely back on board and not much else to do but monitor the tracking device she had placed on the radiocaesium crate, everyone agreed it was time to get back to *Clean World Foundation* business and *Operation Ocean Renewal*. *Dauntless* spent the next two days visiting several other trawler captains and catching up on the project's progress. They also made a point to visit one of the massive barges to observe the offloading process of the plastic and ocean refuse. Kat and Emily donned protective orange suits and gloves and boarded the barge to get an up-close-and-personal look at what had been cleansed from the ocean. They were particularly interested in collateral damage to the marine environment and were pleased to find that measures put in place to protect marine life and habitat were proving effective.

They briefly put into the South Korean port of Busan for resupply. The long voyage to the Sea of Japan and flurry of activity on arrival had seriously depleted their stock of dairy products and fresh fruits and vegetables – something Biff was growing increasingly concerned about. *Dauntless* could run on her nuclear fuel for years, but perishable food items and fresh water ran out much quicker. And she still needed to take care of mundane tasks like discharging her sewage and gray water tanks. Legally they could discharge raw sewage at distances greater than three miles from shore, but Blake and Kat insisted that the flagship for the Clean World Foundation would do no such thing.

It was, overall, a pleasant and relaxing couple of days for the crew, who were still settling into their normal work routines. There was always lots to do to keep *Dauntless* in the state of readiness demanded by Blake and Kat. Mark and Eric worked together to reload the gun magazine and missile launchers – cleaning, lubricating and running diagnostics to ensure they were all operating within spec. They then checked and rechecked the dive gear, drones, submersibles, and RHIB, ensuring oxygen tanks were full, batteries were charged, and fuel tanks topped up. Scotty ran through reams of checklists ensuring *Dauntless'* reactor was running optimally, and all components of the propulsion system were properly maintained. Together, he and Matt went over every inch of the exterior, repairing some minor damage caused by the raking fire of the North Korean gunship and repainting the damaged skin with the special black paint that helped reflect radar.

Emily insisted everyone receive regular medical checkups and used the 'downtime' to cycle the entire crew through her sickbay. Biff's waking hours were evenly divided three ways - prepping ingredients for a meal, cooking a meal, or cleaning up from a meal - and he seemed to take equal enjoyment from all three.

And the crate of radiocaesium with the tracking device attached stayed put.

Sang-O II (Shark) Class Submarine, Sea of Japan

The commander of North Korea's most modern class of attack sub couldn't decide if the butterflies in his stomach were brought on by eager anticipation of the mission at hand or fear of failure. A bit of both, he eventually concluded. He had left port twenty-four hours earlier and was approaching the expected position of the luxury mega-yacht, *Dauntless*, based on the most recent transmission he had received. Never in the history of his country had a naval commander been given orders to attack and sink a civilian vessel operating peacefully in international waters. He had read and reread the order several times to be sure. He was also warned that this yacht was not the soft target it seemed and to proceed with extreme caution, using every advantage his stealthy, lethal submarine possessed. Stay silent and undetected. Stay submerged. Get close. Use the element of surprise. No use of active sonar, which could alert his target.

He picked up his microphone and pressed the 'transmit' button. "Periscope depth." The plan was to bring his sub close enough to the surface to communicate back to base and receive the precise current location and bearing of his target. Several minutes later, the sub leveled out at a depth of ten meters – close enough to the surface for their VLF radio to receive and transmit. He nodded to the radio operator, who immediately donned his headphones.

A minute later, they had the information they needed. *Dauntless* was only 5 knots to their south, bearing 270 degrees at only 8 knots. He quickly plotted a course that would place his sub directly in the path of their target. Once on station, they would sit silently, allow their prey to pass by, and then launch their deadly salvo of Russian-made Type 53 torpedoes from behind. It wasn't sporting. But it would be lethal. "45-degree turn to port. Bring us to a new bearing of 135 degrees. Descend to 30 meters and maintain speed of 7 knots." He glanced at his watch. They should be in position in just 45 minutes. It didn't matter that *Dauntless* was invisible to radar. It wouldn't help her that she didn't use conventional propellors for propulsion. His Type 53 torpedoes used a ship's wake to home in on its target, generally following an S-type pattern from one side of the wake to the other, the variations narrowing with the wake pattern as it closed on its hapless victim. He would launch from a range of 2,000 feet, enough distance to avoid damage to his own vessel from the shock waves of the explosions, but still point-blank, can't-miss range for his weapons. *Dauntless* and her crew would never know what hit them.

Dauntless – Sea of Japan

It was 3:00 am, and most of the crew were sound asleep. Matt was in command on the bridge, accompanied this night by the 'energizer bunny' Emily, who loved the night shift – no doubt a holdover from her ER doctor days where she had first earned the moniker. *Dauntless* was trundling along at just under ten knots, almost due east towards Japan, aiming to rendezvous the next morning with another *Operation Ocean Renewal* trawler. It was a calm night with partly cloudy skies, and both Matt and Emily were nursing a coffee while engaging in quiet conversation.

The still of the night was suddenly shattered as loud warning claxons erupted throughout the ship, causing them both to nearly jump out of their skin. Simultaneously, the autopilot kicked in, throttling up to full power and throwing *Dauntless* into a sharp, sweeping, starboard turn. Matt and Emily were thrown to the floor as the ship's synthesized voice chimed in. "Warning! Incoming torpedo. Impact in 55 seconds. Warning! Incoming torpedo. Impact in 50 seconds."

Matt managed to lurch to his feet and rushed to the controls, grimly thankful that while her crew might sleep, *Dauntless* did not. Her hydrophone receivers constantly monitored the noisy sea surrounding them, and her computers were programmed to detect and react to threats such as incoming torpedoes. Matt could instantly see on his display screen four incoming torpedoes approaching from their stern at a range of less than 2,000 feet, closing at a speed of 55 knots.

The ship's computers had also determined that there was a 90% probability that these were Russian Type 53 wake-chasing torpedoes – which explained the sharp turn the autopilot had executed. The torpedoes wouldn't know *Dauntless* had changed course until they got to the location the ship had been just prior to making the turn. In other words, they couldn't just alter their current trajectory to shorten the distance to the target. The additional time would work in *Dauntless'* favor as she would continue to accelerate to a top speed that exceeded that of the chasing torpedoes.

Dauntless surged forward like a sprinter leaving the blocks and, within a minute, had reached a velocity that exceeded that of the chasing torpedoes, leaving them further and further behind with no chance to close the gap. Matt tapped on the screen and switched off the warning claxons.

Emily had also picked herself up, made her way over to Matt's side, and stared at the screen. "Someone fired on us?" she stammered breathlessly. "Is that four torpedoes chasing us?" Her mouth opened as if to say more, but snapped shut, her eyes continuing to stare at the screen.

"Appears so," replied Matt, who was still in shock himself. "No way those torpedoes are going to catch us now, so we are in the clear. The question is, what do we do about it?"

Just then, Blake rushed onto the bridge, followed closely by Kat – both looking slightly ridiculous with tousled hair and baggy pajamas. "What the blazes, Matt!" roared Blake. "Did someone fire on us?"

"'Fraid so, boss," answered Matt calmly, pointing to the blinking red icons on the screen in front of him. "We've got four fish giving chase. If it wasn't for your fancy computerized threat detection system, they would have blown us to smithereens. As it is, however, we were able to get up to speed and outrun them. I was just saying to Emily, the question now is, how do you want to respond?"

The rest of the crew were now staggering in, rubbing their eyes. Matt brought everyone up to date on the situation and then turned to Blake. "Over to you sir. Your wish is our command."

While Matt was addressing the crew, Blake had reached an important conclusion. But it was Kat that spoke up first. "We are a civilian vessel minding our own business in international waters. This unilateral, unprovoked attack is simply outrageous, and we are perfectly in our rights to defend ourselves. We simply cannot stand by and let the perpetrator go free to carry on and attack us again at their time and choosing."

"I was just about to say the same thing, dear," Blake smiled. "Time to do a little midnight sub-hunting."

Sang-O II (Shark) Class Submarine, Sea of Japan

The sub-commander ordered all four torpedoes to be fired at point-blank range. It was the first time he had ever fired live torpedoes at a real target, and even though it was an innocent civilian target with no chance to defend itself, he couldn't help but feel the thrill of the kill course through him. Looking around at the crew, he could see they were feeling the same surge of adrenalin as the torpedoes released with a whoosh of compressed air and immediately began closing on their target.

All eyes turned towards the screen showing the four torpedoes as small green triangles began to close rapidly on the large red triangle representing the target. But almost as suddenly, the closing rate began to slow noticeably. The weapons officer spoke up, "Sir, the target is coming around to starboard and increasing speed. Now at 20 knots… 30 knots… 40 knots… 50 knots… 58 knots."

"That is not possible!!" roared the commander.

But yet, it was. Everyone could see the green triangles continuing straight, even as the target raced off at right angles. By the time the torpedoes made the turn to follow, the target was racing away - impossibly increasing the gap. It just didn't make sense. No ship of that size could react that fast. Turn that quickly. Reach those speeds. Much less a lumbering mega-yacht toy of a billionaire playboy. He slammed his fist against the bulkhead in frustration.

His chief weapons officer spoke up, "Commander, the torpedoes have run out of fuel and exploded." The green triangles on the screen blinked briefly and disappeared. "All four tubes are reloaded and ready to fire on your command."

As the commander pondered his next move, the weapons officer waved his arm and began speaking excitedly, "Target is slowing. Target is slowing. Target… has disappeared. I have lost contact with the target. Last known position, dead ahead at a range of 2 nautical miles."

The commander made up his mind. "It appears they have lost their engines and are dead in the water. Proceed on course towards their position at 5 knots, and let me know if you pick up anything at all on passive sonar. We will close to within 500 feet of their last known position, and if we haven't picked them up by then, we'll ping them with our active sonar. We won't miss again."

The sub crept forward, her diesel-electric engines making barely a whisper as she stalked her prey once again. Fifteen minutes went by when the silence was abruptly broken by the unmistakable sound of active sonar pinging. And it wasn't coming from them!

Dauntless – Sea of Japan

Once the chasing torpedoes had run out of fuel and exploded harmlessly, Blake had Matt bring *Dauntless* to a halt and turn to face their opponent. He expected that the attacking sub would have followed along behind the torpedoes, probably wondering how they had managed to evade them and close in for a second shot. Blake didn't intend to disappoint them. But he did intend to deliver a nasty surprise of his own. After all, as the old saying goes, the best defense is a good offense.

"Now we sit here quietly and wait. If I'm right, that sub is proceeding directly towards us, but has no idea exactly where we are, and with us sitting still in the water, we are effectively invisible to them. Of course, we can't hear them either, as I expect they are keeping their speed down and operating as stealthily as possible." Blake glanced down and checked his Omega Seamaster dive watch, twisting the dive bezel to mark the time as he spoke. "Let's give them 15 minutes. If they don't start pinging us, we'll start pinging them. Eric, get both torpedo tubes ready to fire. As soon as we have a lock on that target, I want both fish in the water."

Eric nodded, "Understood, sir." And with that, he stepped into the war room, settled into his weapons station, and donned his headphones.

"Excuse me, Blake." Scotty had been quiet up until now. "Once active sonar comes into play, no matter who employs it first, both sides will be able to pinpoint the other's position. Won't they fire on us as well?"

"Of course they will," Blake responded. "And we'll be ready. We evaded them once, and we'll do it again."

Scotty nodded thoughtfully. "I have an idea." He approached Blake and whispered something to him that the others couldn't make out.

"Brilliant, Scotty! I think that just might work. Head down and make your preparations. You'll need to be ready to go the instant I give the word."

The others looked around, confused, as Scotty hurried off the bridge. "You'll see shortly," Blake promised them before glancing down at his watch again. "Ok, ten more minutes and then we start pinging."

Time crawled by. It occurred to Blake that submarine warfare was like World Series baseball. It isn't the action that provides the thrill. It's the suspense. Finally, it was time. With a final glance at his wrist, he spoke. "Eric, crank up the active sonar and see if you can paint that sub."

Eric nodded and tapped on his screen and closed his eyes as he listened intently. A moment later, he announced, "Got her. Dead ahead. Bearing seven degrees at five knots. Range one thousand feet. We have a firing solution."

"Fire two torpedoes," Blake commanded.

Eric was ready. "Two torpedoes away. Time to target – thirty seconds." Then, a beat later, he exclaimed excitedly, "Wait sir… I am picking up two incoming torpedoes. They've fired on us again! Now three. Make that four. We've got four incoming!!"

Blake tapped the intercom, "Now Scotty!! Go!!" Glancing around the room, he continued, "Scotty had the great idea to put the RHIB in the water and send it racing away from *Dauntless* to draw away those wake-homing enemy torpedoes. We just need to sit still and ensure they pick up on the obvious target we've created for them. Hold her steady Matt. I want those incoming fish to see just one wake… the RHIB's!! And Eric… Make ours count!!"

Mark's jaw worked up and down like he desperately wanted to say something. In the end, nothing came out, but it was plain that he was having trouble coming to terms with the idea of his beloved RHIB playing the role of sacrificial lamb to the incoming enemy torpedoes.

All eyes turned to the nearest screen to watch the action. As hoped, the attacking torpedoes picked up the wake of the fleeing RHIB and turned away from *Dauntless* to chase the decoy. Meanwhile, *Dauntless'* torpedoes homed in relentlessly on the enemy sub, which was now maneuvering aggressively to evade the threat. "Hey Eric, based on the sound signature of that sub, can you ID it?" asked Blake.

"Yes sir. The computer positively identifies it as a Sang-O II class North Korean sub," answered Eric. "But it won't be for long. Ten more seconds, and it will be scrap metal headed for the ocean floor."

Everyone continued to stare intently at the screen as the final seconds wound down, and the green triangles representing their torpedoes relentlessly closed the gap with the North Korean sub represented by a large red triangle. As the gap disappeared, all eyes turned towards Eric, who was once again listening intently with his eyes closed. A few moments later, he opened his eyes and somberly confirmed the grim truth.

"Target destroyed."

And a few seconds later, the RHIB blew up in spectacular fashion behind them, four massive explosions ricocheting across the water.

Chapter 16

Gangneung, South Korea

It had been nearly a week since he narrowly escaped death. Song Hee had recovered to the point where he was functional but was still a bit of a mess. His separated shoulder was stiff and painful, but he had discarded the sling. The rest of his body still ached from the pounding it had taken in his desperate dive from the truck, and the numerous scrapes and bruises he had suffered bouncing along the rocky shoulder were only now beginning to fade. He knew it could have been far worse. It was a miracle that he had escaped the shrapnel from the exploding shells that tore up his men.

One day, he would return to his hometown and rebuild his little criminal empire. But for now, Helle had convinced him to take a lucrative break and accompany the contraband on its journey to the West. He had rented a boom truck and forklift and spent two full days transporting the radiocaesium crates – two at a time – from the warehouse down to the commercial shipping port and loading them into the two 20-foot shipping containers that Helle had arranged. The shipping manifest indicated the goods contained in the crates were chemicals used in the manufacture of fertilizer – normal commercial goods that wouldn't be likely to raise any eyebrows. He still didn't know much about the broader plan, only that the ship would arrive today to load the containers and set sail for Tartus, Syria, where they would be picking up a third container that he was to keep an eye on.

Song Hee sat low in his truck and gazed out to sea as the sun grew low in the sky behind him. Before long, a large container ship appeared on the horizon as it made its way into port. *Zeus* was a giant, measuring just under 1,300 feet in length, with a width of 190 feet. Painted a dark green, her deck was stacked high with standard twenty-foot shipping containers. Song Hee had read up on the vessel. As one of the largest of this class of freighter in the world, she could carry over 19,000 such containers at one time. It was owned by a Greek company, Cirillo Shipping Inc., which had a worldwide fleet of approximately six hundred ships – not all of them the size of *Zeus*, but still, the large shipping company formed a vital cog in the global supply chain. Song Hee was assured that, while Cirillo's ships did not normally frequent Gangneung, *Zeus* would be dropping off and picking up at least a hundred other containers. It would be unheard of for such a large freighter to be diverted into a port to pick up such a small load.

The large ship made its way cautiously into the relatively small harbor and, with the help of a couple of harbor tugs, was eventually wedged tightly against the pier. Song Hee could not recall ever seeing such a large freighter – especially in his hometown. The ship towered over the small pier, and the shipping crates stacked atop its enormous flat decks were piled at least twenty high. It reminded him of the ship that had gotten itself wedged sideways across the Suez Canal the previous year. Once *Zeus* was secured, the three large gantry cranes on the pier swung into action, offloading targeted containers and depositing them gently onto the waiting terminal tractors to be quickly whisked away into the nearby storage yard.

The sun had set by now, and the container port was lit up brightly by its array of light towers. Song Hee started his truck and returned it to the nearby rental yard before approaching the pier on foot. Helle had provided him with proper ID to board *Zeus* as its newest crewmember, and the captain had been given orders to give him broad leeway to ensure the cargo on his two containers were kept secure and monitor all activity on the bridge. Song Hee had been given the direct mobile number of the CEO of the company, Nicos Papadakis, and if anyone aboard *Zeus*, including the captain himself, gave him any trouble, he was to use it. He chuckled to himself as he thought about the irony of his current situation. Five weeks ago, he had never set foot on a ship of any kind. It was a meteoric career progression – as he assumed the role of de facto captain on one of the largest mega merchant ships in the world.

By the time he had made his way through security and onto the dock towards the massive ship, the loading process had reversed, and the 3 giant cranes were busy plucking shipping crates from the terminal tractors and loading them onto the ship. Somewhere in there were the two containers he was interested in, and soon enough, he would know exactly where they were. He took a deep breath and started up the gangplank to begin his new career.

Dauntless, Sea of Japan

While most of the crew returned to their quarters for the remainder of the night, Blake and Kat had one more task to complete before hitting the hay. Leaving Matt and Emily on the bridge, they stepped into the war room, closed the door, and called Rod Stringer.

When Rod picked up, Blake winked at Kat and spoke in a cheerful tone. "Hello Rod. Hope you're having a great day!"

Rod groaned. "I was up until now. Something tells me that's about to change. I highly doubt you'd be calling me with good news when it's the middle of the night in your time zone."

"Not at all," Kat chimed in. "I'm sure you'll be happy to hear we are whittling away at the North Korean navy. We're pretty sure they can cross a Sang-O II (Shark) Class submarine off their list of active-duty vessels."

"What?! Are you trying to start World War III?? We've been using every single diplomatic trick in the book to keep North and South Korea from going to all-out war. And now, thanks to you cowboys, it appears to have been all for naught."

Blake and Kat exchanged a mirthful glance before Blake cut him off. "Now Rod, don't get all worked up. You know it's not good for your blood pressure. The truth is, we were in international waters, peacefully minding our own business, when a North Korean sub conducted a surprise attack on us." Blake went on to describe their narrow escape and the sinking of the sub. "But Uncle Sam will be getting a bill for a new RHIB, and I'll be sending it to your attention—"

"Seriously though," Rod interjected. "This attack has to be retribution for your sinking of their patrol boat... which means they know it wasn't South Korea."

"Our thoughts exactly," agreed Kat. "You can rest assured that all of their hot air about going to war with South Korea is just for show. Provided you keep South Korea in line, there is no real risk of further escalation."

"And they can't very well make a big deal about losing their sub. After all, they initiated the attack on a civilian vessel in international waters. They're just going to have to take this on the chin," added Blake.

"That's the way I see it too guys. Glad y'all are still in one piece. That was too close for comfort! So what now?"

"Well…," answered Blake, "We are continuing our work with *Operation Ocean Renewal* while we monitor the radiocaesium cache for movement. We may have left out that Kat placed a GPS tracker on one of the crates, and when it moves, we'll know and intend to follow it. We still haven't learned much about who is behind this and their intent."

They chatted for a few minutes before ending the call and heading back to their suite. As they left the war room and re-entered the bridge, Blake called out, "Good work tonight, Matt and Emily. You guys ok to keep the rest of your watch?"

"We're good sir," responded Emily with a wink. "I'll make sure Matt here stays awake."

The rest of the night passed uneventfully. The next morning, Biff had served up a hearty breakfast of oatmeal, fresh fruit, yogurt, and strips of ham, and everyone gathered in the ship's main dining room to dig in. Eric's t-shirt of the day read, *"I am Nobody. Nobody is PERFECT. Therefore… I am PERFECT!"*

Mark slapped him on the back with a laugh. "If your shooting wasn't perfect last night, we'd all be out treading water and fending off sharks right now. Instead, we're all here being fattened up by Biff for our next shark encounter." He winked at Biff, who nodded back with a smile. Mark then turned to Blake, pointing an accusing finger. "I didn't appreciate you sacrificing my beloved RHIB last night. I couldn't sleep a wink. I was tormented the rest of the night with visions of her being vaporized by those NK torpedoes." Although he used his best theatrical hurt voice, everyone could see the twinkle in his eyes and knew that, like the rest of them, he was very appreciative of Blake's cool leadership in getting them through a tough scrape.

"Not to worry, Mark. I've already put Uncle Sam on notice that they are going to buy us a new one, and we'll have it delivered to us at sea via chopper. After breakfast, you can go shopping for the best RHIB money can buy and order it. All the bells and whistles. I'll make sure it is delivered within 48 hours."

Mark grinned, nodded, and gave Blake a thumbs-up sign before tucking back into his oatmeal.

Kat spoke up next with some news to share. "The radiocaesium is on the move. Yesterday, I noticed it moved a short distance from the industrial park down to the Jumanjin commercial shipping port. Then overnight, while we were busy fending off North Korean torpedoes, it left Gangneung and appears to be headed in our general direction… south along the east coast of the Korean Peninsula. I cross-referenced its position with a commercial ship-tracking database, and it appears that our cargo has been loaded onto a large containership named *Zeus*, which is owned by Cirillo Shipping Inc."

Blake shot her a raised eyebrow. "I'm sure you've already checked her schedule to see where she is headed. Do share."

"Of course, dear," Kat grinned. "I'm just building suspense. I've gone back and tracked *Zeus*'s schedule for the last six months. She generally operates in the Bay of Bengal, shuttling between major commercial ports in India, Bangladesh, Thailand, and Malaysia. Until this week, she has never been in these waters. In fact, it appears her schedule was amended just a few days ago to make her first stop ever in any South Korean port. It is rather odd."

"It's a pretty big coincidence that her schedule was altered to make a first-time stop in a port over a thousand miles off her regular beat right around the same time Kat was kidnapped snooping around their radiocaesium operation," said Emily thoughtfully.

"Too big a coincidence," Blake agreed, nodding. "Sorry Kat. Where did you say she was headed next?"

"Well, she has a number of stops on her schedule," Kat continued. "Most of them are regular haunts of hers in Malaysia, Thailand, and India. But then something else unusual. She has booked a reservation to transit the Suez Canal en route to a stop in Syria – which is another anomaly. She hasn't been through the Suez Canal anytime in the last year and has never been to Tartus, Syria. In fact, I couldn't find any record of a Cirillo Shipping vessel ever making a stop in Tartus."

Blake slapped the table and looked around the room. "I guess everyone knows what that means. Our mission here in the Sea of Japan is officially over. We'll shadow *Zeus* from a distance as she makes her way west. I'll let Rod know. We'll learn everything we can about Cirillo Shipping and compare notes with what Rod can find. This might be our first big break."

Chapter 17

Dauntless, East China Sea

The next scheduled stop on *Zeus's* schedule was the Port of Tapei on the northwest corner of the island country of Taiwan, roughly a two-day sail south traversing the entirety of the East China Sea. *Dauntless* allowed her a generous head start of a hundred miles and then meandered along behind. Between the tracking device, publicly available ship-tracking systems, and the published schedule of the giant containership, Blake figured it must be the easiest tracking job in the entire history of spycraft.

Blake and Kat required the crew to spend at least eight hours a day on active duty, and although each had their own unique assignments, everyone had to pitch in on general cleaning duties, except Biff, who kept the galley spotless but was otherwise exempted from general ship-cleaning duties. Even Blake and Kat pitched on the mundane shipboard tasks. After all, even luxurious mega-yachts need their toilets cleaned regularly.

Mark took Blake up on his word and ordered a replacement RHIB from a company in Shanghai, complete with twin inboard diesel engines paired with twin jets. It was armed with a front-mounted stabilized, remote-operated, optically guided .50-caliber machine gun. Eric strolled in sporting another of his seemingly endless supply of tattered t-shirts – this one sporting an illustration of a whiskered street panhandler with the caption, "I used to hate facial hair. But it grew on me."

"Reminds me of a porcupine," remarked Eric when Mark showed him the new RHIB order sheet. "If you kick it, there will be consequences. How much does something like that run?"

"If you have to ask, you can't afford it," winked Mark. "Between Blake and Uncle Sam, I don't think it will be an issue. It's being choppered out to us tomorrow morning, along with a technician to go over everything with us. Which is good, because who wants to read the owner's manual, eh?"

"Count me in," Eric responded eagerly. "I'm thinking I may be able to program that thing so I can operate the machine gun remotely from *Dauntless*. That could definitely come in handy. And if we can do that, we might be able to remotely operate the steering and throttle as well. I definitely need to have a chat with that technician tomorrow!"

Kat, who was nearby with her ever-present laptop, couldn't help but overhear the conversation. "Boys and their toys," she sighed, with an exaggerated eye-roll and headshake that prompted a couple of laughs. "Next time we have to rescue you from the bad guys, you'll be singing a different tune," Mark chirped back with a laugh, earning a second eye-roll from Kat.

"Uh oh. That's a major strike-out there. Thought you fancied yourself a lady's man," teased Eric, slapping Mark on the back and walking away. "Let me know when that RHIB arrives!"

Blake convened the crew for supper in the ship's main dining room on the second deck. He waited until Biff served up another of his spectacular signature creations, tonight's offering featuring roasted leg of lamb served with his proprietary garlic and rosemary spice blend. With the meal served, conversation hit a lull as they dug in. Blake turned to Kat. "I know you've been doing quite a bit of research today, seeing what you can find out about Cirillo Shipping Inc. Do you mind bringing us all up to speed on what you've learned?"

Kat shrugged. "Not a whole lot, I'm afraid. Seems pretty straightforward. Cirillo Shipping Inc. is a privately-owned container shipping company. It dates back to the 1960s when a young Greek entrepreneur named George Papadakis acquired a couple small freighters and began operating throughout the Greek Isles. Over the invetervening decades, Cirillo has grown into the largest privately-owned container-shipping company in the world and one of the largest overall. It operates over six hundred ships throughout Asia, India, the Mediterranean, Europe, and the eastern seaboard of North America. George retired about five years ago, and today, his son, Nicos, oversees the multi-billion-dollar enterprise. From what I can tell, the company is run smoothly, keeping its ships properly registered, maintained, and insured. You could say Nicos runs a tight ship." Kat paused and grinned as a collective groan went around the table. "I know, I know. Lame."

"Anything else of note about this Nicos Papadakis fella'?" Matt inquired. "The guy must be a billionaire, and the world is full of temptations for someone like him."

"Nothing sordid, if that's what you mean," Kat answered. "About the only interesting thing I could find out about him is his reputation as a generous philanthropist. The Papadakis family has their own charitable Foundation that is known to support environmental issues – although it is a bit on the extreme side for my tastes. However, it is not inconceivable that our own Clean World Foundation could partner with them someday. If there is anything shady going on, I haven't been able to find it."

"Shady?" interjected Mark. "Diverting a ship over a thousand miles out of its way to a port not properly equipped to accommodate a ship the size of *Zeus* to pick up dangerous North Korean-sourced radioactive contraband is definitely shady! Downright criminal, in fact. It could even be part of a terrorist plot. There is no way I am giving them the benefit of the doubt."

"Well... yes, there is that," chuckled Kat. "We don't know for sure that Cirillo hasn't been duped into thinking this is just a slightly irregular commercial transaction. But we must assume someone high up in the company is in on the scheme."

"What about this scheduled Tartus stop?" Blake asked. "The other ports of call on her schedule you were mentioning - Taiwan, the Philippines, Malaysia, and Sri Lanka are all routine stops for *Zeus*. But the passage through the Suez Canal and the stop in Tartus, Syria, is an odd duck."

Kat nodded. "I was just getting to that. I had our computers run an extensive search through various municipal and commercial records and came up with something interesting. Two weeks ago, Cirillo rented a small storage shed down by the port facilities in Tartus. For a company that deals in massive numbers of modular shipping containers, it just doesn't add up. And also, just like Gangneung, the port isn't a large commercial container port with the type of facilities to economically deal with giant containerships in *Zeus*'s class."

Scotty had been listening intently, stroking his reddish-gray goatee. "Aye, you'd 'ave to be a pure dafty if ya' dinnae think there was something up with 'dis crowd," he offered.

"Couldn't have said it better myself, if I catch your drift," Blake said after a pause. "Kat, keep your ear to the ground on these guys. But I think we are all agreed that we are on to something here. Matt, after dark, go to stealth mode and put on a burst of speed. I want to do a wide loop around Zeus and approach her from the east, crossing her bow at dawn. Mark… once we are within range, launch a drone and let's get a good look at our target."

"You got it boss," answered Matt while Mark nodded and gave a thumbs up.

After dinner, Blake and Kat retired to their private quarters. They had just settled in when Kat's phone lit up. "It's Sonja. Good timing. We should have called to let her know we are leaving the area, and our time on site with *Operation Ocean Renewal* has come to an end, for now."

Kat picked up the call and put it on speaker. "Hello Sonja," she answered brightly. "How good to hear from you. I was just saying to Blake that we owed you a call."

After exchanging pleasantries, the trio chatted about their joint project, and all agreed it was going very well. "We were able to meet with several of the trawler captains as well as tour one of the off-loading barges," Kat offered. "We were very pleased to report minimal impact to marine life and habitat, and overall, we are at least twenty percent ahead of the targets we had set for waste collection. I guess that's good news, but the flip side of that coin is that the ocean is even more polluted here than we thought."

"So, how much longer will you remain on site and continue overseeing the project?" Sonja asked.

Blake tapped Kat on the shoulder and pointed at his chest, indicating he would take this question. "Actually, Sonja, we are just leaving the area now and have already started for home. We felt we had completed what we had come to do. Besides, I'm sure you've heard on the news that tensions are on the rise between North and South Korea. In fact, the US State Department has just issued an advisory that non-essential travel to the Koreas is discouraged. The advisory includes a ban on pleasure craft operating in the Sea of Japan. I know we are here on official *Operation Ocean Renewal* business, but we sure look like a pleasure craft to any inquiring eyes, and we just don't need the hassle. The increased regional tensions have seen all the regional powers step up their naval activity in the area. It's just not a smart place for a luxury yacht like *Dauntless* to be cruising around in at the moment. Besides, as Kat was saying, the project is going as well as could be hoped for, and we think we've accomplished our mission here."

"Yes, I see," Sonja mused. "That makes total sense. Besides, I think you mentioned before that you had some engagements coming up this fall in the US that you needed to be back for. What is your current position, and will it allow you to get home in time?"

Kat shot Blake a look and shook her head slightly. "Oh yes, Sonja. Thanks for asking. We're keeping an eye on the clock, and those meetings aren't in any jeopardy. We're making a beeline for home."

The conversation then turned to Sonja's recent impactful speech at the EU. "I'm really proud of you, Sonja," Kat exclaimed. "It showed real leadership by the EU, and the whole world has taken notice. How has it been received by the individual EU countries? Do you think the EU will adopt the aggressive targets you have recommended?"

"That's the million-dollar question, isn't it?" Sonja replied thoughtfully. "It's not a sure thing. My peers here on the Commission are deeply supportive and are doing what they can to champion the initiative at home, but I'm not going to lie – it is a tough sell. In the end, I think there is a good chance the EU will adopt these targets. But for it to really stick and have the necessary global environmental impact, we'll need the rest of the world to follow suit. And that's going to be an even tougher battle, I'm afraid."

"Absolutely right," Blake agreed. "But this battle could be a turning point in the war. One step at a time. And as you know, Kat and I and the entire *Clean World Foundation* are in your corner. We want to do everything we can to support you. If you need anything, just reach out."

"Thanks guys. You have no idea how much that means to me." And it was clear Sonja meant it. Both Blake and Kat could hear the raw emotion in her voice.

Following the call with Sonja, they figured they should bring Rod up to speed on the latest developments.

Rod didn't exactly sound excited to hear from them. "What is it now? I don't suppose you're calling to tell me you've decided to mix it up with the Chinese navy, have you?"

Blake and Kat couldn't help but share a laugh before Blake responded with a wink in Kat's direction. "Kat really wanted to, but I managed to convince her it wasn't a good idea." That broke the tension, although Blake was positive the kick that Kat gave him under the table was going to leave a bruise the next day.

They quickly brought Rod up to speed on the current situation and their efforts to find out more about Cirillo Shipping Inc. "Kat has done some digging but hasn't really come up with anything definitive. If you could get the CIA and NSA working on it and maybe monitoring their communications, that could be helpful. In the meantime, we are going to continue to shadow them from a distance. *Zeus's* scheduled stop in Tartus, Syria, next week has really tweaked our curiosity," Blake concluded.

"Roger that guys," replied Rod. I'll put together a task force to look into it. We'll be in touch. Stay safe."

Chapter 18

Dauntless, East China Sea

As Blake had requested, Matt waited until sundown and then steered *Dauntless* in a wide loop around Zeus, overtaking and crossing about eight knots in front of her bow shortly after dawn. Mark launched a drone, swooped in for a closer look, and visually confirmed the ship's identity. Kat joined him in the war room and gave him the precise coordinates indicated by the GPS tracker attached to the radiocaesium crate. GPS signals are generally accurate to within about three meters, and by hovering over Zeus and matching the drone's location to the GPS tracker, they were able to determine that the shipping container containing the radiocaesium was located on the extreme stern of the ship, in the fourth column in from the starboard side.

"So, we're pretty sure our container is somewhere in that column, but there are nineteen containers in that stack. Can GPS tell us which of those is our baby?" Kat inquired.

"I'm not as confident about that. We've got a good GPS signal here, out on the open ocean, with at least eight satellites within view. The problem is, none of them are directly overhead, so I think the elevation reading we are getting is probably only accurate to within about fifty feet," Mark replied. "That narrows it down to one of the top four containers in that column. The smart money is on the top container because we know it was loaded at the most recent stop. But then again, a number of other containers were loaded and offloaded, so it's far from a sure thing."

"Right. Gotcha." Kat drummed her fingers on the table. "Can you swing around the bow and see if you can get a look into the bridge?"

Mark nodded. "Coming around now." Mark brought the drone in a climbing turn, passing the bridge at a high angle which accomplished two things. It minimized reflection off the windows to give them the best view in, and secondly, kept the drone above the normal sightline of the crew to decrease the chance of it being spotted. Suddenly, Kat stiffened, grabbed Mark's arm, and pointed to the screen.

"Stop!!" she demanded. "Can you zoom in for a closer look at that guy standing on the starboard side of the bridge?"

Mark panned his camera to where Kat was pointing and zoomed in as close as he could. "That's him, I'm sure of it!" she gasped.

Mark raised an eyebrow. "You know this guy?"

Kat nodded emphatically. "It's the man in charge of the Gangneung kidnapping operation. He's the same guy who tortured both Wei Lei and I with his stun gun. Not to mention leaving me with this souvenir shiner on my eye. I'll never forget that face. I thought we'd seen the last of him after we blew up his truck. Either he wasn't in it, or he has more lives than the average cat."

Both stared at the screen for a few more moments before Mark spoke up. "Well, that removes all doubt that someone at Cirillo is involved, and that someone is top management. No way that guy ends up on the bridge of *Zeus* otherwise. You ok?"

"Oh, I'm ok, all right," Kat retorted, her green eyes flashing. "That guy is going down and going down hard – if it's the last thing I do. We've seen enough. Bring that bird home."

Later that morning, *Zeus* entered the port of Taipei on the northwest corner of Taiwan while *Dauntless* continued past the island country, passing to the east and entering the South China Sea. After a brief four-hour stopover, *Zeus* was underway again, traveling south through the Taiwan Strait and into the South China Sea late that afternoon.

Over the next few days, *Zeus* continued its methodical crawl through the South China Sea, with a routine stop at the Port of Manilla in the Philippines and then west towards Malaysia, passing south of Singapore and then turning north into the Malacca Strait towards her next scheduled stop in Port Klang near the bustling metropolis of Kuala Lumpur. Kat checked the GPS tracker regularly, which continued to indicate the radiocaesium was still on the ship. *Dauntless* kept her distance, always staying below the horizon, especially now that they knew Song Hee was on board. The last thing any of them wanted was to spook their target or give them any reason to suspect they were being shadowed.

Shortly after they had spotted Song Hee on the bridge, Blake had an idea which he discussed with Kat, and together, the two of them had been thick as thieves for the next thirty-six hours working out the details. Once *Zeus* entered the Malacca Strait, Blake called the crew together. "I don't know about you guys, but Kat and I have decided we can make better use of our time than idly following *Zeus*. It seems the bad guys are stuck in the slow lane, moving this material along, and we just might be able to take advantage and get a step ahead of them."

"What's your idea, Blake?" Matt asked. "You think we haven't noticed you two acting all weird and mysterious the last couple days?"

Blake laughed. "Was it that obvious? What we're thinking is that Kat and I make tracks for Tartus while *Zeus* makes its planned 24-hour stop in Port Klang. We'll catch a commercial redeye tonight from Kuala Lumpur to Tripoli, which is just an hour's drive south of Tartus. We've booked a rental car which we'll use to cross into Syria and check out the warehouse that Cirillo Shipping rented. Kat has already obtained the necessary visitor visas using our Clean World Foundation credentials. We are supposedly researching the area for a potential project to desalinate seawater to provide clean drinking water and irrigation to coastal communities and farms. Rod has arranged for us to pick up some supplies from a CIA safe house located just outside Tartus."

Mark laughed. "And by 'supplies', I assume you mean weapons?"

"Naturally," Kat confirmed. "We learned a few lessons in Gangneung. These guys are playing hardball, and if that's how they want to play, we are happy to oblige. Included in Rod's gift bag is all the firepower we could possibly need, including a brand-spanking new Barrett Mk22 sniper rifle with the 7.62 mm NATO spec ammo – the latest and greatest only now being rolled out to the various special forces divisions in the US military."

Blake couldn't help but shoot his wife an admiring glance. *After what she's been through at the hands of these thugs, most people would have wanted nothing more to do with them. Intimidated. Terrified. Probably have nightmares or suffer PTSD. Not this girl. It's like they have poked a tiger in the eye with a blunt stick*, thought Blake. Green eyes flashing, Kat was chomping at the bit to take the fight to the enemy. Hungry to provide a little revenge, served up cold.

In their five years of preparation, transitioning from technology geeks to their new roles with the *Clean World Foundation*, they had both undertaken extensive physical and martial arts training. Just as *Dauntless* was designed to be able to take care of herself in pirate-infested waters, it was important to both of them that they be able to handle themselves physically in the rough and tumble areas of the world they hoped their Foundation could make a difference in.

For his part, Blake studied multiple martial arts disciplines, earning a black belt in several combat techniques, and honed his physical fitness to an incredible level. His clean-cut looks combined with an average height and build belied his ability to launch a ferocious, explosive, and devastating physical attack on an opponent. His philosophy was to avoid physical conflict if at all possible, but if it was inevitable, the element of surprise combined with all-out ferocity was his winning mantra. Hit first. Hit hard. Hit dirty. Exit quickly. There are no style points in a street fight. And there are no levels. If you commit to force, you commit fully. Blake didn't start fights, but if the other guy insisted on starting one, what happened after that was all on him.

Blake had also honed his expertise with multiple firearms. Handguns, rifles, automatic weapons... Blake had mastered them all. And, of course, he loved to fly and had acquired his pilot's license and various certifications on both fixed-wing and helicopter aircraft.

Kat also trained in various martial arts, although she had not achieved the same proficiency as Blake. Make no mistake, she was tough, strong, fit, and skilled. A couple of Song Hee's young toughs could attest - from their hospital beds - to her ability to handle herself. But Kat's love of disguise and chameleon-like aptitudes led her towards a different specialty. The time that Blake spent learning multiple weapons and flying, Kat spent on sniper training. A year earlier, her Navy Seal instructor had been granted special permission to enter her in an annual combined US Special Forces sniper contest, where she finished third against the best of the best that the US military had to offer. And that was solely judged on shooting precision. For disguise and concealment, which wasn't part of the competition, she would have had no peer.

Not one of them had any doubt whatsoever that Blake and Kat could handle the proposed mission. If there was any funny business going on at that warehouse in Tartus, it was hard to imagine they would be ready for the kind of incoming threat posed by a properly prepared and motivated Blake and Kat. Plan 'A' was to avoid confrontation. A quick in-and-out intelligence gathering exercise to determine what was being stored in that warehouse, but if the bad guys got wind of them and initiated a fight, Plan 'B' was to give them all they could handle and more. *Dauntless* would be thousands of miles away and unable to provide support, so that added a large element of risk. This time, there would be no rescue forthcoming should they be injured or captured on the mission.

Blake continued with a glance down at his watch. "Ok, so if we are going to get to Kuala Lumpur in time to catch our flight, we'll have to leave in two hours. Matt, you will give us a lift to the airport in the Bell 429 and then return to *Dauntless*. Scotty, you are temporarily in command until Matt gets back."

Both men nodded their assent. Scotty added a curt salute and an "Aye, aye, sir" in his distinctive brogue for good measure.

When Blake and Kat arrived at the Bell 429 for their flight to Kuala Lumpur, they found Matt already there with his pre-flight checks completed. "Welcome aboard folks," he said with a broad grin. "Please make yourselves comfortable and buckle up. We'll be underway shortly. Thank you for choosing *Dauntless* Airlines today." Moments later, the helicopter was raised to the launch pad, unfurled its rotors, and lifted off for the forty-five-minute flight to Kuala Lumpur International Airport.

They soon left *Dauntless* behind and proceeded north up the Malacca Strait. Matt gestured to his left as they caught and passed *Zeus*, looking huge even from three thousand feet overhead. As they turned inland, they flew directly over Port Klang, the largest commercial port in Malaysia. Kat stared intently out her window, trying to number the massive cranes lining the quay, but kept losing count in the massive tangle. 'Had to be at least fifty', she thought, and all of them in constant motion. Soon enough, they were on approach to the busy Kuala Lumpur airport, and Blake donned headphones to back up Matt as he followed instructions from the tower guiding him in.

Once safely on the ground, Matt gave each of them a quick hug, wished them luck, and was already lifting off for the return trip to *Dauntless* by the time Blake and Kat had walked to the nearby terminal. With only two hours to spare, they had no time to waste passing through customs, catching a shuttle to their terminal, and getting through security and on to the gate. All went smoothly, and soon enough, they were settling into their seats for the eight-hour direct flight to Tripoli, Lebanon. The sun had long set, and the lights of the bustling metropolis below twinkled merrily. Kat had booked them in first class, which was pricey, but came with pods that allowed them to stretch out comfortably and get some rest on the long flight. They would need it to be prepared for whatever awaited them. Of that, she was sure. Her sniper instructor was fond of saying, 'sleep is a weapon', by which he meant a warrior needed the kind of sharp mind and mental alertness that is impossible to achieve without proper rest.

The slight relaxation of the engine note as the jet settled into its approach to Tripoli woke Blake. He flicked up his window visor to find the sun was already well up. Reaching over, he nudged his sleeping wife, who stretched and yawned before her green eyes opened and took in the new day. They both agreed they had slept surprisingly well, all things considered. Upon landing, they quickly found the rental car counter and obtained the keys to an unassuming white Toyota Tundra, rugged enough to handle whatever trouble might come their way, but ubiquitous enough to blend unobtrusively into traffic.

The drive to Tartus was a straight shot north up the beautiful Mediterranean coast. At about the midpoint of the drive, they passed through the Aredah border checkpoint at the Al Kabir River that formed the border between Lebanon and Syria. The border guard spoke passable English and only briefly inspected their passports and visitor's visas before waving them through. Another short drive along the coast found them entering the picturesque town of Tartus. Blake followed the directions to the CIA safe house, using the numeric code Rod had given him to open the digital lock. Inside, he found two black duffle bags with the promised arms, ammunition, and equipment. After loading them into the locked box in the Tundra pickup bed, they proceeded directly to their hotel, the Royal Inn, located right on the waterfront. Check-in was straightforward, after which they took a short rest in their clean and tastefully decorated room.

Following a light lunch ordered in from room service, Blake and Kat donned casual 'tourist' attire and decided to walk the one-and-a-half miles to the commercial port north of their hotel to do some reconnaissance in preparation for the night's mission. They had two main objectives. The first was to scout the actual warehouse, determine what kind of security they were facing and refine the plan for Blake to break in. The warehouse itself was nothing to look at. Just a smallish cheap corrugated aluminum, boxy structure. More a shed than a warehouse, with a single garage door wide enough to accommodate a standard light truck, but not much more. They walked briskly by, making loud, idle conversation, as if they had not a care in the world and appearing to take little notice of their surroundings. There didn't appear to be anyone standing guard, and they saw just one security camera covering the front of the building and the garage door.

"Let's take a pass down the street behind it and see what we can see from there," suggested Blake. Coming down the street to the rear of the building, they could see another camera covering the back, where just one small window covered with a metal grate was visible. There didn't appear to be any windows or doors on either of the sides of the building and no obvious cameras either.

"I think we've seen what there is to see, dear," murmured Kat. "Let's figure out where I will set up." Glancing around, she nudged Blake and nodded her head in the general direction of a two-story brick building located about two hundred feet down the street. It was the only multi-level building on the block and had two large air-conditioning units mounted on the roof. "Good field of view," mused

Kat. "I can cover three sides of the warehouse from there and use the air conditioning units as cover. See how they are mounted about two feet above the roof? I can easily squeeze underneath and be essentially invisible."

Blake nodded. "Looks ideal. How are you going to get up there?"

"See the building next to it? The green one-story? I can get up on that roof easily enough using the window ledge. From there, I can use the collapsible ladder Rod thoughtfully provided us to get from that roof to the higher one next door. I can be up and down in thirty seconds or less."

"Ok then. Let's head back to the hotel. We'll come back after midnight, take a look at what's inside that shed, and be on our way out of town before anyone knows anything about it," Blake pronounced confidently. "Piece of cake."

Chapter 19

Tartus, Syria

Blake and Kat returned to the hotel, careful to stay in character as loud, brash, playful tourists. They even stopped at a large outdoor market bazaar, purchasing some of the local goods. "Doesn't hurt to support the local economy," Blake grinned, pointing down at the snazzy new leather belt he had purchased from the leather goods stall he had found.

"Did you pay full price?" Kat laughed.

Blake leaned in close, conspiratorially. "Just enough to stay in character," he winked. "What real tourist wouldn't haggle at least a little?"

Once in their hotel room, they hunkered down to plan their evening's reconnaissance. They were both surprised at the relative lack of security. If this storage shed was connected to the operation involving the North Korean radiocaesium, they would have expected a similar level of security they had encountered at the warehouse in Gangneung. Of course, as far as they were aware, no active kidnapping victims were being held at this location, but it was something that left them both a little uneasy.

Blake stroked his chin thoughtfully as he considered the issue. "Highly visible security might be a little too conspicuous for this location. Perhaps they've decided that, in this case, less is more. "

"Something like posted armed guards would definitely draw unwanted attention," agreed Kat. "But I think we have to assume they have eyes on the place somehow. And I don't like the fact that we still don't know the details. The best plan is to get in and out quickly before they have a chance to respond. We should have the element of surprise working in our favor, and we need to keep that advantage on our side."

Blake and Kat continued fine-tuning the plan for several more hours until there was simply nothing more they could do to prepare. After that came more waiting. Every true warrior knows that the toughest skill to master is the art of patience. The minutes and hours prior to action can be agonizing. Those who learn to use that time to their advantage, staying calm, relaxed, and rested, enter the battlefield with a significant advantage. This was a concept that was ingrained in them both during their extensive training throughout the past five years. Training and drills are one thing but can only go so far. There is simply no substitute for actual field experience, and in that respect, they were both rookies. Try as they might to remain calm and get some rest, they were both anxious to get going and found the next few hours dragged out painfully slow.

Finally, the clock hit the appointed time of 2:00 am, and it was time to go. They loaded their gear into the truck and eased out of the parking lot for the short drive to the storage shed. It was a still, quiet night. The heat of the day had long dissipated into the clear night sky, which made operating in their black night camouflage clothing much more comfortable. Whereas Blake had opted for a tight-fitting dark facemask, Kat had blacked out her face with makeup. The last thing a sniper wants is the fabric of a mask interfering with their sight at a critical moment.

Blake backed the truck into a narrow alley not far from Kat's chosen sniper perch. It served to hide the vehicle from plain sight and yet was positioned well for a speedy getaway, if necessary. They climbed out and met at the back of the truck to gear up for the mission. "Ready?" Kat asked.

"Now or never," Blake replied. They walked the short distance to the green one-story building, where Blake boosted Kat onto the window ledge. From there, she was able to grasp the roof and nimbly pulled herself up and over the edge. Shortly after, Blake heard two clicks in his ear, indicating she was in position on the two-story brick building next to it. Blake tapped his comms twice in response and then proceeded down the street toward the shed that was the object of tonight's mission. Halfway there, he turned around to study the roof where Kat was hiding. Despite knowing exactly where she should be, Blake could see nothing in the darkness. Nodding with satisfaction, he turned and continued towards the shed, pulling up his hood and keeping his head down. He had to expect other cameras to be around, and the last thing he wanted was a clear shot of his face. The single camera covering the front of the target shed was mounted on the near corner of the building, facing away from the direction of Blake's approach. As he neared the shed, he turned left and proceeded about halfway down its side, knelt down, unzipped the duffle bag he was carrying, and took out a small acetylene cutting torch.

"Hey Kat, how's the view?" he whispered.

"I have you in plain sight," came the reassuring response. "I have a perfect view of that whole side of the shed and can see most of the front and rear of the building too. If anyone approaches, I'll see them coming. And if they try any funny business, I can drop them before they'll know what hit them."

Blake acknowledged by clicking his microphone and got to work, cutting into the flimsy aluminum wall of the shed with his torch. Within a few minutes, he had cut out a sizable panel which he set aside and stepped inside. Pulling out a flashlight, he scanned the interior. "I've got three utility trailers parked in here," he reported. "They are covered with tarps, all strapped down tightly. Give me a sec... I'll need to cut through and see what we're dealing with."

Tucking the acetylene torch back into the bag, he pulled out his trusty SOG folding knife, snapped it open, and quickly sliced through the straps of the nearest trailer and pulled back the material. Kat could hear the material rustling through her earpiece as Blake pulled the tarp off the trailer. "Anything interesting, Blake?" She waited a beat and then heard Blake draw a sharp intake of breath. "What is it? What's on the trailer?" she demanded.

"There's a number of drums... maybe five-gallon drums. And boxes full of wires and electrical components. The labels on the drums appear Arabic, and I wasn't sure at first what I was looking at. I'm taking some pictures for Rod to analyze later, but I'm quite sure I know now what this stuff is. It has a distinctive odor. I'd bet my last dollar these drums are filled with high-explosives – given the location and the Arabic labels, probably homemade ISIS stuff. And the electrical components are what's needed to make it all go 'bang'— fuses, detonators, timers, relays, wiring... even casings and housings for bomb-making. There must be enough material in here to level an entire city! All I can say is I'm glad they didn't store this stuff up against the wall I cut through. I would have been vaporized, and maybe you too."

"Roger that, Blake. Good work, but I've got some breaking news. There's a Jeep screaming down the street, headed directly for you. Seeing as how it's 2:30 in the morning and it's the first vehicle we've seen, it must be the bad guys. And judging from the hurry they're in, they seem to know they have a problem."

Achmed was four miles away, sleeping peacefully, when his phone erupted with a loud alarm. Something had tripped the motion sensor in the warehouse where the explosives were stored! He was reluctant to station guards at the shed itself, knowing it would draw unwanted attention. Instead, he had divided his men into two groups of four that alternated twelve-hour shifts from a commercial property nearby that one of his friend's parents owned. He picked up the phone, switched off the alarm and was about to call the shift leader of the on-duty team, when it started ringing from an incoming call. He jabbed the screen. "Achmed here. What's going on?"

"Hey brother, the alarm went off at the shed. We are on our way to check it out now. Just calling to let you know and make sure it wasn't you that tripped it accidentally."

"No, it wasn't me. Get over there and report back as soon as you have something. As you know, the alarm is silent, and the intruder will almost certainly still be there. I want him apprehended quickly and quietly. Bring whoever you find back to the security station, and I will meet you there. We must know who it is and why they broke into our shed. It is imperative that the local authorities are not involved, so no shooting unless it is absolutely necessary. Besides, while the explosives are fairly stable, we can't risk firing bullets around them."

"Got it. We're in the Jeep and heading over now. I'll call you when we get there."

The connection was cut off. Achmed laid the phone down and immediately started getting dressed.

Blake was surprised but not shocked. "They must have had a motion sensor or something in here that tripped a silent alarm. My guess is they are monitoring it from close by. That would explain why we didn't see anyone on site. How many of them are there?"

"Just the one vehicle. Four guys. They are already at the shed and are getting out. All armed with handguns, drawn and at the ready. What do you want me to do?"

"Nothing for now. They will have to split up. My guess is two of them will stay outside, and the other two will enter. I can handle whoever comes inside, and then we'll deal with the outside posse afterwards. One thing is for sure, with all the explosives stored in here, no one will be anxious to start shooting. And they'll want to take care of this with minimal fuss. I doubt they'll want the local police involved. And neither do we, for that matter."

"Yeah, that makes sense," Kat agreed. "In the meantime, I'll be your eyes and ears. Two guys are staying out front. The other two have split up and are moving down opposite sides of the building. The guy on my side seems pretty interested in the big hole you cut and is waving one of his buddies out front to come join him."

"They should probably just sit back and wait for me to come out. They've got all the time in the world, and all the advantage sitting on my escape routes," Blake whispered back. "But they're probably not that smart. I bet curiosity will get the better of them, and they won't be able to help themselves."

"Looks like you're right," Kat shot back momentarily. "I think they are getting ready to come in via the garage door. One guy is getting set to throw the door open, another guy has his weapon trained on the hole you cut, and the other two look like they are going to storm through the garage door the moment it opens. You should be able to take out one or both when they are framed in the open door."

"I probably could. But where's the fun in that?" Blake replied. It probably wasn't the best time to tease his wife, but in all seriousness, there were at least three solid reasons not to shoot them immediately. First, even if he had a safe shot without risking blowing them all to kingdom come, he had better not miss because they would probably shoot back reflexively, and that would be the end of them all. Secondly, these guys were probably low-level security just being paid to do a job. They may have no idea what was being stored in there or for what purpose. He would only seriously harm or kill them if there was no other option. And finally, they might know something useful, and any information he could glean from them could come in handy. Dead men were singularly unhelpful in that regard.

"Fun?" Kat spluttered. "This is life and death here. You are facing four armed men at close range. Don't underestimate them. Get ready... here they come!!"

The garage door flew up with a screech, and it certainly appeared they knew what they were doing. Instead of framing themselves in the door, making easy targets, they dove in, one on each side, hitting the floor and rolling under the cover of the nearest trailer. Blake was set up on the opposite side of the shed, crouched behind the wheel of the furthest trailer. He flicked down his night vision goggles and risked a quick glance under the trailers but didn't see anyone. Unfortunately for him, it seemed Kat was right to worry about underestimating them.

"Hey fellas," he called out. "Whatever you do, don't shoot. These trailers are packed with powerful explosives. Firing bullets in here is not going to end well for any of us." Blake had decided that there was little to lose in speaking out. They already seemed to be well aware he was there. Besides, maybe they didn't know about the explosives. Best to make sure. Better for all concerned.

"We need you to step outside and come with us," came back the reply in surprisingly good English. "We have you completely surrounded and outnumbered. We just want to talk."

"Awesome. That's exactly what I wanted to do. Just a nice little chat with some friends I haven't met yet. But, you know, I'm rather comfortable right where I am. I think I'll stay put."

That made them think. Blake could faintly hear some whispering as they considered their next move. Evidently, they decided they had the advantage in numbers and would come to him. There was really no room inside for their victim to evade them. They had the outside covered. It was the only move they had. And it was exactly what Blake intended. He stood up and stretched his arms and legs as they approached, preparing his mind and body. "What are you doing,

Blake?" He ignored Kat's voice in his ear. Instead, he rehearsed his mantra. Hit first. Hit hard. Hit dirty. Exit quickly.

The lights flicked on, initially blinding Blake, who still had his night vision goggles on. He quickly flicked them up and stepped out from behind the trailer, his hands outstretched. He calmly appraised the two men as they approached. Both had their guns holstered. That was the good news. However, they were both armed with menacing-looking knives held expertly in front of them. Not such good news. "You need to come with us," the guy to his right said, waving his arm towards the open garage door."

"We've been over this already," Blake replied, putting on an air of exasperation for good effect. "I thought we decided I'd stay put." Both men continued to advance slowly towards him.

"You are American, are you not? You Americans always think you are in charge. You are not in America anymore. You will come with us."

"I might be an American, but I'm not expecting this to be a democracy. If that were the case, I'd be outvoted and have to leave with you clowns. I think I made myself clear. I'm not going anywhere," Blake answered, a steely tone creeping into his voice. *Come a little closer, said the spider to the fly,* he thought.

Blake's goading had the intended effect, angering the two Syrians and eroding their cautiousness. They both stiffened and began striding quickly towards their quarry, itching to teach the arrogant foreigner a lesson he would not soon forget. Blake stepped away from the trailer to gain space, letting his arms hang loosely, feet shoulder-width apart. The first guy stepped inside Blake's strike zone, fist cocked low, intending to deliver a powerful punch to Blake's midsection to soften up his victim. It was so broadly telegraphed Blake saw it coming a mile away. An instant before the man's fist started its motion, Blake sprang forward with all his might. The man's forward momentum as he closed to deliver the blow, combined with Blake's opposite momentum as he launched, gave maximum effect to the crushing head butt delivered to the man's chin. The forehead is the hardest and strongest point on the human body, and Blake used it to maximum effect. He literally felt the man's chin and nose implode with the force of the blow. The man crumpled to the ground, out cold, blood spurting profusely from his ruined face.

The second man was already reacting, shooting in, his knife in a slashing arc toward Blake's exposed neck. But Blake had anticipated the move and dropped to the ground, the blade passing harmlessly over his head. As he did so, he delivered a powerful sweeping kick to the man's pivot leg. The kick caught him perfectly on the front of the knee. The knee is a curious joint, perfectly designed to carry weight and enable a wide range of motion. Incredibly strong in some ways, but extremely vulnerable in others; bending backward is not its strong suit. Blake's kick to the front of the man's knee, combined with the fact that his foot was planted and bearing his entire weight on that leg, exploited the knee's inherent vulnerability in the worst way possible, hyper-extending it backward with such force that it literally snapped, viciously tearing the cartilage and severing all the major ligaments in one violent moment.

The man screamed and went down instantly, knife clattering across the concrete floor. He lay there writhing in pain, lower leg twisted at a grotesque and unnatural angle – cursing loudly in a language Blake didn't recognize. It was doubtful the man knew much that would be useful, and with two other armed men now on high alert outside, there was no time to conduct an interrogation. "Kat... the two inside with me are out of the fight. I need an exit plan."

Kat breathed a sigh of relief. "The hole you entered is being watched. Unless I take the guy out first, you will be shot the moment you stick your head out. I think your best bet is the garage door. The guy watching that has moved out of my sight. I think he may have gone around the far side. What did you do to the guy? I could hear him from here!"

"Let's just say he'll be operating on one leg for the foreseeable future. I kind of shattered his knee, I think. His buddy is out cold. I'm no judge of what ladies find attractive, but I suspect his days of charming them with his looks are behind him. They're both alive and will be fine… eventually. I'll probably have a sizable bruise on my forehead, but other than that, I'm unscathed."

"Ok. Looks good to make your exit. You ready? Give me a countdown, and hit the door when you reach zero. I've got the guy on my side covered. Watch to your left when you exit. That's the direction in which the other guy disappeared."

"Got it," Blake answered, glancing down at the shattered knee guy, who didn't seem the least bit interested in Blake's escape plans and was still rolling around and groaning. "Ok. Here goes. Five, four, three, two, one…" And with that, Blake stepped out into the night, glancing left as Kat had advised. The guard Kat had lost sight of had not left the front of the building. Instead, he was crouched at the far corner, just out of Kat's view, gun drawn, covering the entire front of the building, including the garage door. He had Blake dead to rights and fired immediately. The man aimed for center mass, and his shot was true. If Blake hadn't juked sideways simultaneously, it would most likely have been fatal. As it was, the bullet grazed his left shoulder leaving Blake gasping with the hot, searing pain. Before the shooter could get off a second shot, Blake immediately dropped to the ground and rolled, beginning to bring his own gun to bear. The shooter, however, was already rushing forward, gun aimed, ready to deliver the final kill shot. In desperation, Blake rolled again. Though, too little, too late!! Time seemed to stand still, and in a moment of singular clarity, Blake knew it was all over and felt unbearable sadness. Sadness at the pain his death would inflict on Kat. Sadness for all those he loved whom he would never get the chance to say goodbye to. Sadness that he had accomplished so little of what he had set out to do. He looked up and saw, in seeming slow motion, the barrel of the gun that would bring his death. In the strange freeze-frame reality he was experiencing, the gaping eye of the gun barrel trained at his head became his whole world. His own gun was moving into position as fast as he could make his arm move, but it just wasn't going to get there in time. It was that simple. He closed his eyes, waiting for the inevitable.

Kat heard the gunshot and saw Blake drop to the ground. She stifled a scream, thinking the worst, but was relieved to see Blake desperately rolling away. He was alive!! Shifting the barrel of her gun back up and slightly to the left, she caught the shooter in her scope as he stepped forward, with the gun aimed directly at her husband's head. She fired instinctively, the supersonic bullet finding its target a tenth of a second later, exploding the man's head like an overripe melon. Swinging the gun back to the side of the building facing her, she saw the second man begin to run towards the front of the building. He didn't get far. Three steps later, she squeezed the trigger a second time and watched his lifeless body hit the ground.

In that final moment, Blake had made peace with his inevitable fate. But instead of a gunshot snuffing out his life, the only thing he heard was the soft thump of a body collapsing on the ground. He opened his eyes only to find the gunman lying prostrate on the ground ten feet away, sightless gaze fixed in his direction. And then Kat's anxious voice in his ear. "Blake! Blake! Are you alright? Talk to me!!"

"I'm fine. At least I think so. Relatively speaking. He nicked my shoulder with his first shot, but I dodged the worst of it. Probably just a flesh wound, but it is bleeding a fair bit. What about the other guy around the side?"

"I had to put him down too," Kat answered. "He heard the first shot and was coming around front. I'm so sorry I didn't see that guy who shot you. He was out of my field of view, and if he hadn't stepped toward you, I wouldn't have had a shot."

"Nothing to be sorry about, dear. I honestly thought it was curtains for me. If you hadn't downed him when you did… well, let's just be thankful you came through. I'll meet you back at the truck. Time to move."

A minute later, they embraced quickly at the truck, threw their gear in, and took off with Kat at the wheel. Moments later, Achmed arrived on the scene to find two of his men dead, and the other two injured inside. And there was no sign of the intruder.

Blake and Kat didn't bother stopping back at the hotel. They were scheduled to check out that morning anyway and had settled the bill when they checked in. Once they were safely away, Kat pulled over and examined Blake's wound. He was right; it was a flesh wound, but a deep one that had taken a chunk of his deltoid muscle. It was painful and bloody, but he would heal. She dug out the first aid kit and cleaned and dressed his wound, before pulling back out on the road. Their flight from Tripoli to Sri Lanka was scheduled to depart in four hours. With just a brief stop at the CIA safe house to drop off the borrowed weapons, they had plenty of time.

Chapter 20

Tripoli, Lebanon

Blake and Kat made good time back to Tripoli, once again encountering no issues at the Lebanese border. Their paperwork was in good order, and their *Clean World Foundation* credentials and cover story were solid. Blake wore a baggy sweatshirt that concealed the bandages on his shoulder. Although it was stiff and painful, Kat had bandaged it well enough to staunch the blood flow. It could have been far worse, and Blake was just thankful he was alive to complain about the discomfort. He glanced over at Kat more than once and marveled at how lucky he was to have ended up with such an incredible woman.

The flight to Sri Lanka was uneventful. Once again, Kat had booked them in first class, where they were able to catch up on the sleep they had missed the night before. Matt was waiting for them when they landed. "Great to see you guys again," he smiled broadly as he slapped Blake on the back and briefly embraced Kat. Noticing Blake stiffen and wince, his brow furrowed. "Everything ok, boss?"

Blake nodded. "A little banged up, but I'll be ok. Kat took good care of me. We ran into a bit of trouble up in Tartus. We'll tell you all about it on the way. Right now, we need to get back to *Dauntless* as soon as possible. Based on what we've seen, there is big trouble brewing, and our window to shut it down is closing fast.

Indian Ocean, Bay of Bengal

Song Hee had decided the life of a sailor was not for him. He lived a life of action. Of danger. Of taking calculated risks and using his wits to survive. At sea, there was little to do but monitor activities on the bridge or return to his room to rest. The former he did mostly at night.

He figured if there was going to be trouble, it would find them late at night or in the wee hours of the morning. So, from 10:00 pm to 10:00 am, he would man the bridge, keeping a sharp eye on the ship's radar and demanding to know every possible detail about ship traffic in the vicinity. Then, for the next twelve hours, he would keep mainly to his stateroom, sleeping or surfing the internet. He didn't bother eating with the rest of the crew in the galley, choosing instead to eat alone in his room, but he had to admit the food wasn't bad. It might be the one thing about life at sea he could happily live with.

During port visits, Song Hee would closely monitor the two radiocaesium containers – ensuring he always knew their physical location. He had also demanded that they be moved as little as possible and kept on top at the extreme stern of the ship. That way, he figured, access to them should it become necessary, would be made quicker. Burying them deep in the center of the cluster of nearly twenty-thousand containers had its advantages too, but overall, he preferred keeping them in plain sight because of the flexibility that quick access provided. He found port visits more stressful than sea days, with all the moving pieces and the threat of inspections from customs officials. In his opinion, using a large, credentialed shipping company like Cirillo was a genius move. The sheer volume of goods moved required efficiency, and border security and customs folks rarely did much beyond ensuring all the paperwork was in order – something Cirillo prided itself in.

Song Hee also fielded a daily check-in call from Helle even though, to date, there was little to report. Yesterday morning, however, she mentioned her concern that *Dauntless* had apparently left the Sea of Japan at approximately the same time he boarded *Zeus* and was following a similar course heading. She asked if he had seen any sign of them, and he had told her that he was monitoring all shipping traffic they encountered and had seen no sign of *Dauntless*. But later that day, lying in his bunk, Song Hee couldn't shake an uneasy feeling that maybe he had seen something. Closing his eyes, he dug deep into his memory banks, reliving the previous forty-eight hours in as much detail as he could muster. And then it hit him. The day before, shortly after dawn, he remembered seeing the outline of what looked to be a large, dark luxury yacht crossing in front of them. It was maybe 10 miles away, dawdling along. He had thought nothing of it at the time. But as he continued to mull it over... *perhaps it was something. Could it have been Dauntless?* A coincidence like that was unlikely, in his opinion. Operating at the edge of the law and beyond it required sharp survival instincts. And now those finely-honed instincts were screaming that something was wrong. He had a hunch, and he had long ago learned it was not wise to ignore his hunches.

Once docked in Kuala Lumpur, Song Hee demanded that his two containers be unloaded and transferred to a secure location where he could inspect them in private. Using a forklift, he emptied the first container and scrutinized each of the wooden crates carefully. He found nothing. But about halfway through unloading the second container, something caught his eye. *What have we here?* he thought. A small, black, rectangular box was adhered to the bottom corner of one of the crates. He pried it off and turned it about in his hands before snapping a few pictures of it with his phone. Then, after thinking about it a bit more, he reloaded both shipping containers and reattached the device to the top of one of the shipping containers—fastening it securely against the underside of the outer lip. Calling the captain, he then directed the two containers be returned dockside and loaded back onto *Zeus* in their original position.

Song Hee was convinced the device was an electronic GPS tracker. He would send the photos to Helle to confirm his suspicions. In hindsight, it was a mistake to have brought those two women back to the warehouse where they were storing the *radiocaesium*. He had clearly underestimated them, particularly the troublesome blonde woman from *Dauntless*. Closing his eyes, he remembered the defiant, angry look that even the pain he inflicted on her could not erase. He remembered the insult suffered from her spitting in his face. Their paths would cross again someday; he was sure of it. And when that day came, he would have his revenge. She would meet a slow and painful end. He would make sure of that. Imagining all the cruelties he would inflict on her before finally allowing her the mercy of death helped calm the burning fires of rage within him.

In that moment, he never could have imagined that Kat was just as eager to meet him again. He was accustomed to being the hunter - the apex predator. It still hadn't sunk in that the tables had turned, even though finding the GPS tracker should have made that abundantly obvious. He was now the hunted, the vulnerable prey. As he reboarded *Zeus*, he decided it best to let Helle determine what came next.

Undisclosed location near Luxembourg, Belgium

For the third time in the last four weeks, the procession of limousines made their pilgrimage to the historic, imposing, European property - passing one-by-one through the sturdy wrought-iron gates and up the circular drive to the main door of the ancient mansion before disembarking a lone passenger. Each man and woman, in their own right, a powerful and influential person. Yet each summoned, like a puppet on a string, by the mysterious woman known only to them as Helle. They knew it was risky to physically convene, even though they took extreme precautions, and yet here they were. Meeting virtually carried its own risks. This was an unscheduled meeting. Something was afoot, and they all strongly suspected it was not good news.

As before, they passed through security, surrendering all phones and electronics. Even though Helle had not assigned seats, they each took the very same seat as they had from the beginning, the only difference being a slight gap marking the location the unfortunate Freyja had originally occupied. In an uncertain world where so much is uncontrollable – even for the wealthy and powerful - it is one of humanity's basic instincts to seek out the comfort of the familiar, even if it is something as simple as sitting in the same seat each time.

Once seated, the low murmur of small talk amongst the group faded to a hush as Helle's darkened form appeared on screen before them. "Thank you, once again, for meeting here today. As you all know, I would not have called you here if it wasn't critical. There have been several recent developments that threaten our operation."

Helle then brought them up to speed on all that had transpired since the last meeting when they had agreed to have Helle engage the North Koreans to hunt and destroy *Dauntless*.

"Since we last met, I was able to reach my contact in North Korea to pass on the intelligence that *Dauntless* was the perpetrator of the attack on their armed patrol vessel. That information was passed up their chain of command and, just as we intended, the order was given to track and sink her. Unfortunately, the submarine tasked with this mission failed miserably. *Dauntless* not only escaped without damage, she successfully counter-attacked - sinking the North Korean sub with the loss of all hands. Because the engagement took place in international waters, North Korea has not dared to make the loss of its submarine public."

A dark-haired, serious-looking woman about half-way down the table spoke up. "How is such a thing even possible? Are you absolutely sure?"

"I admit it is nearly inconceivable," acknowledged Helle. "And I was as shocked as all of you to learn of it. But I have personally confirmed that *Dauntless* is very much alive and well. In fact, she has recently left the Sea of Japan and is working her way west back to North America. We know they have been sniffing around our activities in the Koreas and have proven to be quite the nuisance to our operations there. At this point, we simply don't know how much they have learned of our operation, but they are still an active threat we need to keep a close eye on - especially after the call I received recently from Song Hee. He discovered what he believes to be an electronic GPS tracking device attached to one of the crates of *radiocaesium*. The photo he sent me confirms it, and the only outsiders who had access were the two kidnapped women who were briefly held in the Gangneung warehouse. That makes the timing of *Dauntless* leaving the Sea of Japan at the same time as *Zeus* extremely suspicious. I think we have to assume *Dauntless* is still on our tails, actively tracking those crates and the freighter, *Zeus*, transporting them."

While the council members digested this upsetting news, Helle hit them again.

"And that is not all. I received a disturbing report from Achmed, our man in Tartus. The utility shed where our explosives are stored was broken into, setting off the silent motion detector alarm. His men responded within minutes and attempted to apprehend the intruder who was still inside. It didn't go well. Achmed arrived on the scene to find the intruder had made a clean getaway. Even worse, he found two of his men outside the building dead. Both shot in the head with a single round from a high-powered rifle. Almost certainly a professional job, most likely by a sniper from a short distance away. He was able to retrieve the bullets and they have been identified as 7.62 mm NATO-spec ammunition – the kind of rounds favored by American special forces.

"The other two men were found alive inside the shed – one still unconscious with heavy damage to his nose and lower jaw. 'Like he was struck with a sledgehammer', according to Achmed. The other man was conscious but immobilized with a shattered knee. They reported that upon entering the shed, they found what they took to be an American man who had broken in by cutting through the wall and was inspecting the trailers stored inside. He was able to correctly identify the contents as explosives, going so far as to warn them not to discharge their firearms for fear of setting off a catastrophic explosion. When they attempted to move in to apprehend him, he surprised them with a pre-emptive attack. Neither of them could say for sure how the two men outside came to their end."

Helle paused and glanced around the room, as anxious murmurs arose from around the table. Nicos was the first to speak. "You say *Dauntless* was thousands of miles away, somewhere in East Asia, when this incident took place? So, who broke into the shed in Tartus? Achmed's men are highly trained and hardened ex-ISIS militants who can handle themselves. Clearly, this man they encountered was no amateur thief!"

"You're right, Nicos," Helle responded, nodding slowly. "This is definitely concerning. It shows we likely have at least two very sophisticated opponents, and this new one we know absolutely nothing about. How did they know to look in that shed? How were they able to identify so quickly what is stored there? And most concerning of all is the level of skill displayed. As you say, this was not a case of some local kids getting up to a bit of Friday night mischief. Based on the evidence at hand, these were highly-trained and focused special military forces, most likely American."

"If that's the case, and they got away to make their report, we can expect they will be back. Soon, and in force. This could spell disaster for our plan!" Nicos was literally wringing his hands as he spoke, his voice rising in panic.

"Thank-you, Nicos. I am well aware of what this could mean and have therefore instructed Achmed to immediately round up his remaining team and move the material. It was out of there before dawn and is now en route to Larnaca, Cyprus. Fortunately, Achmed knew a guy with access to a boat large enough to hold the material and make the trip. He's another former ISIS militant happy to earn some extra cash and knows to keep his mouth shut. Best of all, Larnaca has a commercial shipping port, so Achmed will have the goods placed in a shipping container where you will direct one of your Cirillo ships to pick it up."

Helle paused again and looked around the table. "The question before us is, how do we play the hand we've been dealt? We can assume, for now, the situation in Tartus is back under control. If we haven't thrown our adversaries off the track, we'll know very shortly. But *Dauntless* is no doubt tracking *Zeus* even as we speak, and we've learned the hard way that she and her crew are no joke."

As Helle continued, Nicos had calmed himself and was thinking hard. A slow smile spread across his face as he looked up. "I have a plan that will give *Dauntless* the slip once and for all."

"Go ahead Nicos. You have the floor," Helle replied.

Nicos explained his plan to the group, and they took another fifteen minutes discussing and refining it until all were satisfied it would work, and Helle had given it her seal of approval. With that business out of the way, Helle gestured for silence.

"Before we adjourn, I want to say a few words. In the last few weeks, we have made great strides toward our goal. We have obtained the necessary explosives and radioactive material to assemble a dozen massive 'dirty' bombs. These high-yield explosives will be assembled at a remote location on the south coast of the island of Newfoundland before being detonated simultaneously in the twelve largest commercial shipping ports on the eastern seaboard of the United States. Every major shipping port from Boston to Miami will be disabled. The blast itself will be massive - destroying or damaging key port facilities and infrastructure that would take months to rebuild, replace, or repair.

"The subsequent radioactive fallout, however, will take much, much longer to remedy and will keep these ports out of action for a decade or longer, radically impeding the import and export of fossil fuels from all major east coast refineries and forcing the United States to make a dramatic, unplanned turn towards green energy alternatives. The timing is critical as the European Union is on the cusp of adopting sweeping voluntary change of its own, reducing reliance on fossil fuels and curbing greenhouse gas emissions, while accelerating the adoption of green energy solutions. With both the EU and the United States moving away from fossil fuels and committed to lower greenhouse gas emissions, the rest of the world will fall in line, giving humanity its best chance for long-term survival. The glimmer of hope of environmental recovery we witnessed during the recent pandemic will be restored – this time permanently!"

The council members rose to their feet as one and applauded enthusiastically.

Chapter 21

Bay of Bengal, off the east coast of Sri Lanka

Matt, Blake and Kat hustled aboard the Bell 429 and forty-five minutes later, the helicopter set down gently on *Dauntless'* helipad at the ship's bow. On the trip back, Matt was dying to hear all about their adventure, but Blake preferred to wait until they had assembled the entire crew. First, it had been a close call and the fewer times he had to relive it, the better. Second, and more importantly, he needed time to think and put it all into perspective. It wasn't any less traumatic for Kat, and she was fully supportive of taking some time to decompress, to come to grips with nearly losing her husband and snuffing out two lives in cold blood. Glancing towards Matt, she could see the questions forming on his lips. Catching his eye, she gave him a slight shake of her head while holding up her index finger to her lips. Matt caught the hint, and his questions died on his lips.

Doc Watson was standing by as they disembarked, having been notified by Kat that Blake needed her attention. She strode up immediately and took him by the arm. Blake started to protest, but Kat quickly shut him down with a look that would have stopped a tiger in its tracks. Seeing that resistance was futile, he meekly allowed Emily to lead him away. Arriving at her sick bay, she promptly stripped away the dressings that Kat had applied, cleaned and inspected the wound before expertly redressing it. "It could have been a lot worse, but it looks like the bullet just creased you. Kat did a great job with the field dressing, by the way. No sign of infection, and it's already starting to heal over. You'll have a nice little scar as a souvenir, but other than that, you should be good as new in a couple weeks. In the meantime, I want you to report to me daily to clean and dress it. Take it easy with that arm; you don't want the wound to reopen. And take short showers to avoid the scab softening and coming off too early."

"Thanks Doc. Will do," responded Blake with a grin as he slipped off the examining table and headed out the door. "See you in thirty minutes in the war room? It's an all-hands-on-deck meeting."

When Blake and Kat stepped into the war room half an hour later, they found the entire crew already assembled. Eric's shirt of the day featured a scruffy-looking, snaggle-toothed character underlined with the caption, "Friday is Tooth-Brushin' Day". Emily scrunched up her nose in disgust. "Ewwww. Especially icky, seeing as today is Thursday."

Eric merely grinned. "Of course, Doc. I only wear it on Thursdays."

Biff had stocked the table with orange juice, coffee, and a generous selection of hors d'oeuvres, not knowing when Blake and Kat had last eaten. Both were famished and appreciated the thoughtfulness. Between bites, they filled in the crew on their adventures and findings in Tartus, acknowledging, but glossing over the details of Blake's close brush with death.

"We've just gotten off the phone with Rod to give him the same update," Blake continued. "The good news is that nothing about the incident seems to have come across the radar of the local authorities or news media. I guess the bad guys must have cleaned up their own mess, which they would obviously do, given half a chance. Based on what they are involved in, having the authorities involved would lead to some mighty uncomfortable questions."

"Interesting choice of words," Mark commented. Blake shot him a questioning look. "Based on what they are involved in…, I mean. The picture is becoming clearer now, isn't it? Radioactive material sourced from North Korea. Explosives and bomb-making components from Syria. It sounds like someone is making a massive radioactive 'dirty' bomb!"

"Or 'bombs'. As in plural. Multiple dirty bombs," commented Eric, who had been mulling it over. "Think about it. The amount of radioactive material Kat saw in Gangneung combined with what you guys found in that garage in Tartus...," his voice trailed off. "Tell me, Blake, from what you saw in terms of detonators, bomb casings and so on, would you say they are making a single bomb, or multiple ones?"

Blake didn't hesitate. "Definitely multiple bombs. Must be. There is no way everything we've seen could be combined into one explosive. There were enough detonators alone for at least 15-20 explosive devices."

"So now we know the 'what' of the plan, but until we know the 'why' the 'who' and the 'where', we are still largely in the dark," interjected Mark. "So, what's the next step?"

Kat took this question on. "For now, Rod has asked us to continue tracking the *radiocaesium* currently aboard *Zeus*. In the meantime, he is sending a team back to the warehouse in Tartus to surveil the shed. He's confident that we now have enough threads in play to gently pull at them and unravel this whole conspiracy. We've got eyes on everything they need to assemble the bombs. It should be a simple matter now to reel in the 'who' of the operation, as you put it. Once we have that, the 'why' and 'where' will be largely academic.

Port of Colombo, Sri Lanka

Song Hee could barely conceal his excitement as he monitored the berthing of the giant freighter in the Port of Colombo on the west side of the island nation of Sri Lanka. Helle had been lavish in her praise of his foresight to keep the tracker and reattach it, this time to the outside of the shipping container. Finding the tracker, without giving away the fact it had been discovered, was a huge momentum shift in their favor. What had been *Dauntless'* trump card had now become her Achilles heel, and he couldn't suppress the surge of smug satisfaction that coursed through him at the thought.

Arabian Sea

During *Zeus's* 18-hour scheduled stop in the Port of Colombo, Blake had decided to continue to push west around the southern tip of India and then slightly northwest into the southern reaches of the Arabian Sea. Having access to *Zeus's* schedule online made it easy to anticipate her next move, while Kat periodically cross-referenced Zeus's position with the GPS tracker. They booked *Dauntless'* passage through the Suez Canal twenty-four hours ahead of *Zeus's* reservation. The last thing they needed was for *Zeus* to get through in front of them, only to run into some type of delay that would allow their prey to escape. Besides, it would be much harder for the bad guys to pick up a tail that was running in front of them.

Blake and Kat retired early that evening, hoping for a good solid night's rest to recover from their Tartus adventure. But it was not to be. At 4:00 am, they were awoken to the sound of Scotty's thick brogue on the intercom in their stateroom. "Aye, Cap'n. Sorry to bother you at this ungodly hour. I know ye must be plumb knackered. But I've got a wee mystery here on the bridge you'll want to look into."

Blake stifled a groan as he stretched, having momentarily forgotten about his stiff shoulder. "Thanks Scotty. Be up shortly."

Kat stirred sleepily. "I'm coming too," she yawned.

A few minutes later, they both joined Scotty on the bridge. "What's the bee in your bonnet tonight, Scotty?" Blake wanted to know.

"It's *Zeus*, sir. She has departed the Port of Colombo."

"Uhhh…. yeah," Blake replied, somewhat annoyed, glancing down at his watch. "And right on schedule, by the looks of it."

"Yes sir. The time of her departure is not the issue."

Even Kat was beginning to lose her patience. "So what, pray tell, is the big mystery that required waking us up in the middle of the night, Scotty?"

Scotty merely pointed down at the digital display where *Zeus*'s current position and track were displayed. Both Blake and Kat followed his pointing finger, peering down at the screen, trying to make sense of what their eyes were seeing. Instead of heading west across the Arabian Sea towards the Gulf of Aden and her appointment with the Suez Canal, *Zeus* was rounding the southern coast of Sri Lanka and retracing her path **east**. Kat immediately punched up her laptop and confirmed that the GPS tracker was synced with *Zeus*'s position. Next, she pulled up *Zeus*'s online schedule and gasped. "The schedule has completely changed!! Over the next two weeks, *Zeus* will now be visiting a series of East Asian ports in Malaysia, Singapore, Indonesia, the Philippines, and Hong Kong!"

"What?!" Blake was stunned. "This makes no sense whatsoever!"

Looking up from her screen, Kat responded. "I think we need to give Rod a call and get his take on it."

Blake nodded and gestured towards the war room. "I agree."

Rod answered straight away, sounding cheerful. "Hello m'lady. Hello Blake. To what do I owe the pleasure this time? Although, I'm half afraid to ask. If you guys aren't on the verge of starting World War III, you are scaring me half to death with tall tales of your narrow escapes."

Kat chuckled. "Aww, c'mon Rod. Imagine how dull your life would be without us?"

Blake got down to business. "The reason for the call is that something unexpected has happened, and we need to discuss it with you." He went on to explain *Zeus*'s reversal of course and radical change in schedule. "It just seems extraordinarily odd—certainly not efficient business practice. I can't even begin to imagine the logistics nightmare of shuffling all that freight to make that kind of schedule change. Kat was just checking it out. Over twenty other *Cirillo* freighters have uploaded major schedule changes, all seemingly to accommodate the redirection of *Zeus's* freight. We need to get back home ourselves, so I'm reluctant to turn around and follow *Zeus* back east. I'm starting to feel like we're on a wild goose chase."

"Hang on. I need to think and check on something." Rod put them on hold for a few minutes before rejoining the call. "Ok. How about this? We had repositioned a US Navy task force in the area to provide support if needed. You've given us probable cause to board *Zeus* and intercept the contraband *radiocaesium*. Stay on course and head home. Uncle Sam will take it from here. You have served your country well. I wish we could thank you officially, but I think you know that your efforts can never be publicly acknowledged. I hope my heartfelt gratitude is enough."

Blake and Kat exchanged a meaningful look before Kat spoke for both of them. "We are thrilled to have had the good fortune to find ourselves in the right place at the right time to be of service. All we ask is that you keep us informed on any further developments. Speaking of which – has your team reached Tartus? Any word on that operation?"

"Not yet. We've had to shift some assets around, but we should have eyes on the place within 24 hours. Right around the time, we'll have a destroyer intercept *Zeus*. By this time tomorrow, I expect we'll have recovered both the explosives and the *radiocaesium*, which will hamstring the operation. We'll work our way up the chain from there to the head of the snake."

"Thanks Rod. We look forward to your call. In the meantime, Kat and I are heading back to bed. Over and out from *Dauntless*. Oh, and happy hunting."

Blake and Kat headed out onto the bridge, giving the Coles Notes version of their call to Scotty and directing him to maintain a westerly course towards the mouth of the Gulf of Aden. "You did the right thing waking us up, Scotty," Blake reassured him. "We're heading back to bed. See you in the morning. Well… later this morning."

Blake and Kat returned to their quarters and were soon asleep, allowing themselves the luxury of sleeping in a couple of extra hours. By the time they awoke, the rest of the crew were up and about, buzzing with anticipation. After fielding numerous inquiries, Blake had to assure them he would call them all to the war room to personally hear Rod's updates on the interception of *Zeus* and the raid on the shed in Tartus. The clock seemed frozen as the hours crept painfully by. Finally, late that evening, the crew were finally summoned to the war room for Rod's update.

It didn't take long before everyone was assembled, and Blake addressed the room. "Go ahead, Rod. The whole gang has arrived and is anxiously awaiting your big news." An expectant hush fell over the room.

Rod cleared his throat. "I've just heard back from the team in Tartus. They waited until dark before moving in. I'm sorry to say, they found nothing. The shed has been emptied and appears completely abandoned. They even searched it carefully for a motion detector and found nothing. No trailers. No explosives. No bomb components. They swabbed the place for explosive residue and that came back positive. Explosives were definitely stored there recently, but they have since been removed."

A collective groan echoed around the room. "What about *Zeus*?" Kat inquired. "Please tell us you've at least recovered the *radiocaesium* and detained Song Hee!"

Rod sounded despondent. "I'm afraid I have more bad news there. We found the tracker, all right. It was attached to a shipping container at the stern of the ship."

Kat was confused. "Did you say it was attached to a shipping container? I had it attached directly to one of the lead-lined wooden crates. It should have been found inside the shipping container."

"No. It was definitely attached to the exterior topside of a shipping container. Inside the container, we found nothing but ordinary textiles. The navy guys searched the entire ship and scanned it for radiation. Nothing. No one resembling Song Hee was found on board. In fact, the entire crew was new, having just boarded the ship in Sri Lanka. We found no paperwork out of place. No contraband. No reason to detain her any further."

Blake slammed his fist onto the table with such force that the rest of them jumped. "They found the tracker!!"

"But it was attached to a crate inside the container," Kat protested. "How could they?"

"I don't know, Kat, but they did. Perhaps they detected the signal it was emitting. I can't really say. But they discovered it at some point and have led us on a merry chase. Meanwhile, both the explosives and the radiocaesium have vanished into thin air, and we are back to square one."

"I have a theory," interjected Emily. "We know that *Zeus* did not change course and have her schedule altered until arriving at the Port of Colombo. What if the tracker was discovered there, and the radiocaesium was offloaded onto another Cirillo freighter, but the tracker was left on *Zeus* to throw us off?"

"Thanks Emily," answered Rod. "Exactly right, and something my team has checked into already. Unfortunately, we found that there were six different Cirillo freighters that had stops in the Port of Colombo that overlapped with the time *Zeus* was docked there. Even worse, five of them have already made it to their next port, where multiple Cirillo freighters have overlapping port visits. In total, we already have thirty-four Cirillo freighters who could potentially be carrying those two shipping containers we believe were originally on *Zeus*. We simply can't stop them all. We don't have the resources to do so, nor do we have probable cause for any single one of them. Or the material may still be in the Port of Colombo, where literally hundreds of thousands of shipping containers are constantly on the move. Or it could even have been transferred to a non-Cirillo-owned freighter. The bottom line is that we have no idea where it could be. It may have never even made it to the Port of Colombo. We simply don't know at what point the tracker was discovered and used to feed us false information. And one more thing. No Cirillo ship currently has a scheduled stop at Tartus."

Rod's words hit like a ton of bricks, the mood in the room crashing from hopeful anticipation to utter dejection. Just hours before, the whole operation seemed to be on the verge of being wound up. Instead, as Blake had just concluded, they were literally back to square one. And the clock was winding down.

The Arabian Sea

Song Hee had just gotten off the phone with Helle, who relayed the boarding and subsequent fruitless search of *Zeus* on the high seas shortly after leaving the Port of Colombo. Both *radiocaesium* shipping containers, along with Song Hee himself, were transferred at the Port of Colombo to this smaller Cirillo freighter, *Pluto*, which was now en route to Larnaca, Cyprus, to pick up the container of explosives. He would continue to keep a sharp eye out for trouble, but for now, it seemed like they were in the clear. His smug smile faded ever-so-slightly as his mind turned toward the one remaining cloud in his sky. He so badly wanted his revenge on the blonde woman from *Dauntless* and the rest of her crewmates. And now, that revenge seemed to be slipping through his fingers.

Chapter 22

Mediterranean Sea – north of Port Said

A week later, *Dauntless* exited the Suez Canal at Port Said and cruised back into the Mediterranean. Rod had pulled them off the case, but the threat was being taken extremely seriously through proper, official channels. The US had shared the intelligence that Blake, Kat, and the *Clean World Foundation* had helped to gather with Israel's Mossad, Interpol, and its Western European allies and intelligence agencies. Security at commercial shipping ports worldwide had been heightened, with authorities pulling out all the stops to detect contraband explosives and radiation. Specifically, Cirillo-owned ships were being closely scrutinized, and the US National Security Agency had been tasked with monitoring all communications from Cirillo offices and ships, including all top executives. Rod was convinced, as were Blake and Kat, that someone at or near the top of the company's executive team was actively participating in the plot to detonate one or more large radioactive explosives. The race was on to determine the target, or targets, and foil the plot before it came to fruition, but unless and until these efforts yielded an actionable lead, there was little anyone could do but wait.

The mood aboard *Dauntless* for the entire week was dour. Blake and Kat had taken pains to assure every member of the crew that they had performed above and beyond all expectations - having courageously thrown themselves in harm's way and willingly taken on grave risks beyond anything that could have been reasonably asked of them. They had shown remarkable professionalism, courage, and skill throughout. Blake and Kat were proud of every single one of them. But in the end, they had come up empty. The results spoke for themselves, and even Blake and Kat's well-deserved praise could not fully dispel the sense of failure. Blake and Kat felt it too.

It reminded Blake of a hard-fought hockey playoff series he was involved in as a teenager. His team had surpassed all expectations, making it to the final round of the Minnesota U-18 State championships. Local pundits were united in their prognostications that Blake's team would lose the best-of-seven final series handily. But they were tough and made up in determination and heart what they lacked in skill. Blake was hardly the largest or most skilled player on his team, but he was a natural leader and fierce competitor who kept himself in great condition. As the team captain, he logged more minutes than anyone on his team and in the pitched on-ice battles that took place in the corners and the front of the net, Blake's indomitable spirit and gritty style of play gave every member of the opposite team pause. The series came down to sudden death overtime in the decisive game seven. Mid-way through the first overtime period, their team's best scorer had a glorious opportunity to put the game away, but his normally reliable shot rattled off the crossbar of the net and stayed out. The other team picked up the puck and went the length of the rink, scoring the championship-winning goal just seconds later.

The feeling Blake had at that moment was one he would never forget, and one he never wanted to experience again. In that moment, it didn't matter that he had played valiantly, that his team had surpassed all expectations and were widely acclaimed for their accomplishments. They had much to be proud of. And yet... as they stood shoulder-to-shoulder on the blueline and received their silver medals, most of them were weeping openly. They had come agonizingly close to winning the championship but had come up short. *The results spoke for themselves.*

And that pretty much summed up how everyone aboard *Dauntless* felt about this mission. They felt the disappointment and shame of failure. It wasn't logical. It wasn't deserved. But they felt it all the same. And they needed no reminder that this was no sporting event of little consequence. This was a potential global catastrophe with countless human lives on the line. They had a chance to end it, but it slipped through their fingers. With the stakes so high, they simply could not afford to lose. And yet, they had been benched just as the other side seized all control and momentum.

And even when Blake tried to encourage the crew and commend them for their truly admirable service, his heart just wasn't in it. And he knew they could sense it and felt the same way. Even their return trip through the incredible engineering marvel that was the Suez Canal couldn't fully relieve the gloomy atmosphere. *Dauntless* completed its passage through the 120-mile canal in a relatively quick eleven hours, managing to weave her way past some slower traffic at Great Bitter Lake. Matt took care of most of the piloting duties during their passage, with Blake or Scotty providing occasional relief.

Blake and Kat talked it over and decided to book flights from Cairo back to St. John's to squeeze in the visit with Kat's family that had been cut short weeks earlier with Rod's surprise call. *Dauntless* would follow them across the Atlantic at a more leisurely pace, rejoining them in a week's time - time that they would be able to spend with family, recharge, and finalize the details of their upcoming fund-raising tour. Indeed, the date for the kick-off event in Boston was fast approaching.

Shortly after *Dauntless* exited the Suez Canal into the sparkling blue-green waters of the Mediterranean, Matt lifted the Bell 429 smoothly from the *Dauntless'* helipad and set down at the busy Cairo international airport just forty minutes later. With the luggage unloaded, Matt extended his hand to Blake. "We'll see you next week, Cap'n," he said with a smile, as the two men grasped hands firmly. "And yes, I'll take good care of your baby." He then exchanged a quick hug with Kat while leaning in close to her ear and quipping, "You know his first love is his ship, right?"

That broke the somber mood and Kat laughed outright. "Well, I'm the one who's taking him home tonight. So… take that, *Dauntless*!"

With a final wave back to Matt, they turned and headed towards the nearby terminal while Matt readied the Bell 429 for its return journey to *Dauntless*.

St. John's, Newfoundland

Blake and Kat finally touched down in St. John's, Newfoundland, an exhausting 14 hours later following layovers in London and Toronto. There was no direct flight from London to St. John's, so they had to overfly St. John's a full three and a half hours further west to Toronto. They literally flew directly over their destination, looking down longingly as Kat's hometown slipped past under the wings. Upon arrival in Toronto, they soon boarded another flight, retracing their steps back east again before finally touching down in St. John's, bleary-eyed, at 3:00 am local time.

Despite the ungodly hour, Kat's parents, Don and Brenda Mercer, were on hand at the airport to welcome them. With hugs and warm greetings all around, they soon collected their bags and were on the road to the Mercer family home in the nearby bedroom community of Conception Bay South. Don and Brenda had come to love Blake as the son they never had. While the extended family was quite large, Kat had just one sibling, her older sister, Joanne, who lived in Halifax with her husband and two boys.

Don Mercer was born and raised in a traditional large Newfoundland family in the small fishing village of Grates Cove. He moved to St. John's after finishing high school to attend university, where he eventually received his Bachelor of Arts in Education degree and then spent thirty years as an educator, eventually retiring as head of the Math Department at a local high school.

Brenda was born to the Green's 'around the bay' in the historic community of Bonavista, the location where most historians believe John Cabot became the first European to set foot in the New World. The Mercers, along with the other residents of Grates Cove - located at the northernmost tip of land across the bay to the east - strongly disagreed with this view of history, believing John Cabot landed first at the location of their community. Older residents of Grates Cove still recall a stone in the harbor engraved with the Italian version of Cabot's name, *Caboto*, believed to have been carved by John Cabot himself or one of his crewmembers. The fishermen of the 19th century cared little about such ancient history. They had more pressing concerns - struggling to eke out a subsistence living in the harsh conditions and extreme environment of the North Atlantic. A fishing stage was constructed over the rock with the curious engraving, such that it eventually became buried in offal and was essentially unapproachable. Things took an even stranger twist when a media van pulled into the community one fine summer's day in the mid-1960s, and two men hopped out and began chipping and hammering at the rock until they eventually removed and drove off with it. They told the curious locals they were taking it away for further study and validation. It hadn't been seen since.

To keep the family peace, Don and Brenda eventually agreed that Cabot probably visited both locations and who could really say, over five hundred years later, with any certainty in what order?

Brenda met Don at the Memorial University of Newfoundland and Labrador in St. John's, where she was doing her Bachelor of Nursing. They raised their girls in a comfortable split-level home overlooking scenic Conception Bay, just a short twenty-minute drive outside of St. John's. Now in their early sixties and retired, their girls grown, they continued to live in the family home, occupying their days with volunteer activities, gardening, and travel.

With both her parents having been born to large families, Kat had twenty-two aunts and uncles, forty-six first cousins, and too many other distant relatives to keep track of. Blake, having a small and distanced family circle by comparison, was endlessly fascinated and somewhat overwhelmed by Kat's large family. But he embraced their warmth, friendly nature, and strong sense of culture. He truly loved every minute he was able to spend with them, and in return, they welcomed this good-natured, hockey-playing American into their homes and hearts wholly and willingly.

"It's great to see you both again," Brenda said from the front seat as they drove home from the airport through the early morning darkness. "We were so disappointed when you cut your visit short a few weeks ago. What was the big emergency?"

With a cautious glance towards her husband in the semi-private darkness of the back seat, Kat answered. "As you know, the *Clean World Foundation's* first big project is underway, removing plastics and other debris from the Sea of Japan. Just as we were docking in St. John's a few weeks ago, we received a call that made it clear we needed to be onsite to address some serious issues that had come up. And given that we have some fundraising events coming up this fall in the States, we had to rush off to make sure we had time to squeeze it all in."

"And were you able to straighten things out?" asked Don.

"Yes, things are running smoothly now. But we still really wanted to get home for a bit and make up for the lost visit. Hence why we abandoned the ship to fly home. *Dauntless* will swing by to pick us up again before we head to Boston for our first fundraiser. But in the meantime, we have a whole week to spend at home.

"That's great to hear," beamed Don. "We've got fifty of our closest relatives coming Saturday evening for a good old-fashioned

Newfoundland shed party. They're all pretty excited to hear about your world adventures, and my guess is they are hoping you'll take them out for a spin in your fancy boat."

Blake grinned broadly and slapped his father-in-law on the shoulder. "That all sounds wonderful. But first… I'm looking forward to a nice comfortable bed and a long sleep."

On-board *Pluto*, somewhere in the Mediterranean Sea

Song Hee paced the bridge restlessly, frequently pausing to raise his binoculars and scan the surrounding sea. Even though the stop at Larnaca had gone smoothly, and the container with the explosives was safely onboard, it was clear that port security was on high alert. Extra scrutiny was given to the paperwork, and Song Hee noted that specially trained dogs were being employed to detect explosives. Placing a panicked call to Nicos, he described the situation. Nicos thanked him for the warning and assured Song Hee it would be 'taken care of'. And obviously, it had been. No dogs boarded *Pluto* to examine their cargo. Outside of the routine paperwork, there was no physical examination or radiation testing of any of their shipping containers on board, offloaded, or loaded while in port. Given the extreme level of scrutiny the other ships in port were subjected to, Song Hee knew for certain that Nicos had made someone at the Port of Larnaca significantly wealthier.

But now, as they sailed west towards the open Atlantic, Song Hee was keeping a sharp eye out for any sign of trouble. Coast guard ships and navy traffic of western countries were a concern. If they had reason to believe that *Pluto* was carrying illicit cargo, they would be boarded and searched without hesitation. But what he feared most of all was spotting the dark, menacing outline of *Dauntless*. So far, she had not shown her face. He just wished he knew if that was good or bad news.

Pluto had a few more commercial stops scheduled in the Mediterranean and then a final stop in Lisbon, Portugal, before heading west across the Atlantic to Boston; at least that was the official schedule that the captain and crew were aware of. Song Hee was, as yet, the only soul aboard that knew of a surreptitious planned diversion en route to Boston – to La Hune Bay, a large deep-water fjord located along the vast, uninhabited south coast of the island of Newfoundland.

Chapter 23

Francois, Newfoundland

"Let's hike up to the top of the next ridge and see what we can see," suggested Gary. His twenty-two-year-old son, Steven, knocked back another swig of cold water from his canteen, wiped a bead of sweat off his forehead, and nodded his agreement.

"Can't hurt." With a glance at his watch, he added, "We've got another few hours before the sun goes down, and we've seen precious little sign so far."

Gary and Steven Durnford, residents of the tiny, isolated community of Francois (pronounced 'Fran-Sway' by the locals) on the south coast of Newfoundland, were conducting the annual scouting trip that had preceded every moose-hunting season in their family for generations. Each year, around mid-September, the Durnford men would hike up to the high country behind their community and scour the surrounding countryside for signs of the abundant moose population found throughout all of Newfoundland. Early that morning, Gary and Steven had set out from their home to carry out the long-standing tradition, laboring up the steep hillside before working their way west across the high plateau, checking the numerous pockets of dense, stunted fir trees that the local moose population favored as sources of food and shelter. Now with the quickly shortening days upon them and the sun just starting to settle towards the western horizon, they had found scant evidence of recent moose activity at their traditional haunts.

The ridge that Gary was referring to overlooked La Hune Bay, a majestic, wild, uninhabited fjord that slashed a deep gash inland. The top of the eastern ridge overlooking the inlet was known to be prime moose habitat. If that was where the animals were hanging out this year, it was bad news as far as the Durnfords were concerned. An adult bull moose can weigh up to 1,500 lbs, and packing out an animal that size all the way back to Francois would be a Herculean chore. Still, it had been done before. And if they did bag a large moose this far from home, they might even be fortunate enough to find a safe route down to the pristine waters of La Hune Bay. From there, they could return with their longliner fishing boat to pick up the meat. All things considered, they had come this far and had enough daylight remaining to get up to the ridge and home again. Besides, it was a great early fall day to enjoy each other's company and the great outdoors.

Thirty minutes later, the two men reached the ridge overlooking the scenic fjord below. Steven immediately jabbed his dad's shoulder and pointed down to the far end of the fjord, where a large floating dock jutted out into the water. Tied up to the pier appeared to be a barge at least forty feet in length. Behind the dock, further up the beach, was a large recently-constructed shed. They could see a half dozen men scurrying about, all appearing to be wearing military-style camouflage fatigues. "L'ard tunderin'!!" exclaimed Gary. "What in 'tarnation is goin' on down d'ere? I ain't never seen a soul 'roundabouts there before. And now, sure, a small village has sprung up overnight. Strangest thing I've ever seen!"

Steven was equally dumbstruck. And very curious. "Wanna' head down there and see what they're doin? We've come this far. The by's back home'll give us da' gears for sure if we tells 'em we turned around without even askin'."

In their excitement, both men had lapsed into the traditional 'Newfie' dialect, which was a unique mixture of English, Irish, and Scottish accents that had fermented together over hundreds of years in the extreme environment of small, open boats on the frigid waters of the North Atlantic. In recent times, the influence of TV and the internet had softened the brogue, but when worked up, the inbred local dialect would spring to the surface.

They spent another thirty minutes picking their way carefully down to sea level, following a tumbling river down a steep gorge. They were still a half mile from their destination when two men stepped out of the trees and watched them approach. Both men wore the same military fatigues they had observed from on top of the ridge and were armed with semi-automatic rifles. As they approached, one of the soldiers held up his hand in the universal 'halt' gesture as he greeted them in a cordial but official manner. "Good day, gentlemen. I'm sorry to inform you that this area is currently a restricted military zone. We're with the Canadian Armed Forces, and we are conducting some military training and maneuvers for the next week or so that include some live-fire exercises. All civilians are being directed to keep their distance for their own safety."

"Ah. I see," Gary answered. "My name's Gary Durnford. This here is my son, Steven. We're from Francois out seeing where the moose are to. We spotted the new wharf and shed from the top of the ridge, and curiosity got the better of us. Hunting season starts the first of October, but I s'pose ye fellers will be out of here by then, eh?"

Both soldiers squinted in concentration, trying to get the gist of what Gary was saying through the thick Newfoundland dialect. "Yes, we should be gone in about a week. We like to leave things as we found them, so the temporary wharf and shed will be dismantled and shipped back out as well. When you come back in a couple weeks to get your moose, it'll be like we were never here."

After a few more minutes of friendly banter, the Durnfords turned around and headed home. It was a long hike back with just enough daylight to get home before dark if they hurried. Besides, they looked forward to sharing the interesting story of their encounter over a cold beverage or two. Word of mouth travels fast, and it wasn't long before most residents along the sparsely populated south coast had heard of the military training taking place in their backyard.

Two days following the Durnfords' encounter with the Canadian soldiers at La Hune Bay, a coastal ferry operated by the Province of Newfoundland, *MV-Marine Voyager*, was making its daily run along the south coast of the island between the isolated communities of Burgeo, Grey River, and Francois. The skipper of the vessel, Rusty Anderson, grunted in surprise as he approached Francois. For the third time now in 4 days, a large freighter loaded high with shipping containers was crossing his path. It wasn't that unusual to spot such a vessel in these waters. After all, the south coast of Newfoundland was a well-utilized international shipping lane, but he could not recall seeing so many in such a short time. And even stranger was that rather than traveling in the customary east-west direction of the shipping lane, these freighters were on a north-south course. And the one he noted the day before looked like it had just exited La Hune Bay, which Rusty knew to be nothing but pristine, uninhabited wilderness.

"What the dickens' is goin' on, Colin? I've sailed these waters for thirty years. I've never seen anything like it."

Colin, Rusty's first mate, had no answer. "Dunno, Skipper."

With a shrug, Rusty steered safely around the massive freighter. It would put him five minutes behind schedule, not that it mattered in the slightest. He did, however, make a note of the strange encounters in his logbook at the end of his shift.

St. John's, Newfoundland

Blake and Kat thoroughly enjoyed the week spent with Kat's parents. True to his word, Don and Brenda hosted a massive family gathering on the weekend. The estimated fifty guests turned out to be very conservative. Blake was sure the number was closer to a hundred, filling the house and spilling out into the backyard and shed. He stayed close to Kat and, together, they mingled with too many aunts, uncles, cousins, and friends for Blake to have any possible hope of keeping straight. Even Kat needed some occasional help to jog her memory. Everyone was interested to hear about the *Clean World Foundation* and the first big project taking place in the Sea of Japan. They had lots of questions about *Dauntless*, as well. The local paper had done a write-up on Blake, Kat, the *Clean World Foundation*, and of course, the magnificent yacht, *Dauntless*. As a result, Kat had become locally famous, and her many relatives were rightfully proud.

Blake was told he had met most of them at their wedding a few years ago, and he assumed that was probably true. But in truth, those days had been a blur, and his focus at that time was entirely on his bride. He loved the warmth of Kat's large family and was sure that, in time, he would get to know many of them. For now, he was glad he had the opportunity to mingle with them and begin to develop those relationships.

Near the height of the festivities, Kat stood on a chair from the back deck and banged on a pot for attention. Once the noise settled down to a dull roar, she announced with great excitement that *Dauntless* was expected to enter St. John's harbor in just three days, and all in attendance were invited to board her for an evening dinner cruise around the harbor, down the coast, and back. The invitation was received with a raucous roar of approval, and the party resumed with renewed vigor. As Kat hopped back down off the chair, Blake scooped her into his arms and led her in a spirited Newfie jig across the deck.

The downtime was a much-needed rest and distraction from the stress and ultimate disappointment they had experienced in recent weeks. They kept in daily touch with the crew of *Dauntless* as they proceeded at a leisurely pace back across the Atlantic. Matt reported that the trip was generally uneventful. There was no hurry, and so he was keeping up appearances by keeping speeds under twenty knots and emitting an appropriate radar signature to marine traffic. Blake promised the crew an additional five days of shore leave once they docked in St. John's, asking only that Biff give up one evening to assist with the pleasure cruise Kat had offered to her family. Biff was only too happy to oblige… after all, it was his greatest pleasure in life to cook for people and see them genuinely enjoy the fruits of his labors. Emily, who always had energy to spare, and was a good friend to Biff, also offered to stay and be his able kitchen assistant for the evening. That started a domino effect, and soon the entire crew was clamoring to be included and help in any way they could.

Blake, Kat, Don, and Brenda were all on hand to welcome *Dauntless* home. In fact, it seemed word had gotten out of her impending arrival, and crowds of people had taken to the sides of Signal Hill to witness the jet-black, majestic mega-yacht slip silently through the Narrows and into the harbor. The town had witnessed the odd visit from such yachts before - the ownership and distinguished guests of which always seemed to be a murky secret. It was something else altogether to see this one, the most impressive of any that had ever sailed through the Narrows, and to know there was a local connection. A hometown girl who had made it big. There was no jealousy or pettiness, as might be expected in some places—quite the contrary. There was a strong sense of communal pride. This was, in some way, their girl and their ship. Matt could hardly believe his eyes, looking up from the bridge at the crowds waving and welcoming them home. He obliged in kind, repeatedly blowing the ship's whistle while the crew traipsed out onto the deck, saluting and waving back to the adoring crowd. Kat had told them of the warmth and hospitality of her hometown, but they were still awestruck to witness it for themselves. It truly was a welcome lift to their collective spirit, and they sincerely appreciated it.

The friends and family cruise turned out to be a smash hit. While the weapons capabilities were kept under wraps, the guests had the full run of the boat, admiring the luxurious finishings, the well-appointed gym, and the onboard cinema. Biff and Emily were too busy preparing hors d'oeuvres to assist in giving tours of their respective areas, but the other crew members were only too happy to show off the galley and sick bay. Mark was in his glee, showing off all his 'toys' such as the drones, the RHIB, and the submersibles down at the moon pool. Scotty was only too happy to explain the sophisticated nuclear power plant and unique water-jet propulsion system, generously doling out his thick Scottish brogue and dry sense of humor to charm the guests. Certain aspects of *Dauntless'* capabilities, like her top speed and radar stealth, were not disclosed. When asked, Scotty would merely wink and say, "I 'low she's fast enough." Matt stationed himself at the helicopter, showing how its rotors could be neatly folded so the entire aircraft could be safely stored belowdecks and then raised on the elevator to the helipad above. Eric, wearing an impressively clean t-shirt emblazoned with the caption, *All The Grills Love Me*, manned the bridge with Blake, showing off the controls and sophisticated electronics. And all the while, the hired band belted out favorite local Irish tunes and folk songs of Newfoundland. The dancing, singing, and laughter extended well into the wee hours of the following morning before *Dauntless* returned to her berth and disgorged its tired but happy guests.

The days in port passed all too quickly, and soon it was time to depart for the planned autumn fundraising tour. Blake and Kat had completed the final arrangements, and their first event was a black-tie gala fundraising dinner to be held in four days' time in Boston. The departure from St. John's on a dull Wednesday morning was a much more subdued event than her arrival the previous Friday evening. Kat's parents waved a lonely, fond farewell from the dock as *Dauntless* slid effortlessly out into the harbor before turning on a dime and heading back out to sea. Blake and Kat had barely settled down in their stateroom when Blake's phone made the distinctive customized chirp indicating an incoming call from Rod Stringer's encrypted line. Both

Blake and Kat blinked in surprise as the phone continued to clamor for attention. "Well don't just stand there like an idiot," Kat playfully admonished her frozen husband. "Answer it!"

"Hello Rod. I hope you've got some good news for us," Blake said as he picked up the phone and put the call on speaker.

"Well, no, not really," Rod replied ruefully. "We've spent the last few weeks in a full spin but haven't been able to get a sniff. And when I say 'we', I mean the entire intelligence apparatus of the western hemisphere."

"Nothing at all?" Kat pressed, a hint of desperation in her voice.

Rod left the door slightly ajar. "Well, almost nothing."

Blake sensed the opening and countered immediately. "Almost nothing isn't the same as nothing. And I'm hoping that glimmer of a clue is why you're calling. Our entire crew has been in a funk since you pulled us off the case. I know for a fact that they are itching to get back in the fight. How can we help? Just say the word, Rod."

"You're right," Rod confessed. "There has been something strange that has come up you might be able to look into. Are you still docked in St. John's?

"As a matter of fact, we just departed an hour ago, headed to Boston for a fund-raising gala dinner," Kat answered quickly. "What is it you want us to chase down?"

"Right. Even better. I can't say for sure it's a lead on the case. But it might be. First, there are reports coming out of Newfoundland that a couple of locals were turned away from La Hune Bay by the Canadian military, who were supposedly conducting some sort of training in the area. I say 'supposedly' because we've checked, and there is no official or unofficial operation of the Canadian Armed Forces currently taking place in that area."

"La Hune Bay, huh?" As Kat spoke, she was consulting Google Maps on her laptop. "On the south coast, with the nearest community being Francois to the east?"

"That's the one," Rod confirmed. "And there's something else too, which really caught our attention and makes me think it may be connected to the dirty bomb terrorist plot. The captain of the ferry, the MV *Marine Voyager*, has reported seeing unusually high freighter traffic in the area in recent days. Shipping container freighters."

Blake stroked his chin thoughtfully as he answered. "Sure, Rod. But this is a well-traveled shipping lane. Surely, that can't be all that unusual, can it?"

"Not on the face of it, Blake. But normal freighter traffic flows east-west along the south coast of Newfoundland between Europe, St. John's, and ports further east in Nova Scotia, up the St. Lawrence River into Montreal, or turning south along the eastern seaboard of the United States. Captain Anderson's log is very clear. The unusual freighter traffic he has reported is traveling north-south. One freighter, in particular, appeared to have just exited La Hune Bay."

"La Hune Bay! Well now, isn't that a coincidence!" Kat gasped. "A fake Canadian military operation being visited by freighters never before seen in the area. Were these Cirillo-owned ships, by any chance?"

"We have no idea at the moment," Rod admitted. "There is nothing to suggest Cirillo ships have any business in the area, and we don't have any Cirillo ships, or any other freighters for that matter, showing in the area. Believe me, we've done a thorough check of all ship traffic based on their GPS transponders. But the captain saw what he saw, and his first mate backs him up one hundred percent. Something strange is going on, and seeing as how you guys are heading right past there on the way to Boston, I was hoping you could have a look and see what's up."

Smiling broadly at each other, Blake replied, his eyes dancing merrily. "We'll need to get the crew's consent first, of course, but I'm quite confident you can put us down as a resounding 'yes'. Score round one for the bad guys. But if this is the start of round two, we'll be coming out swinging!"

Chapter 24

European Union Headquarters, Brussels Belgium

The month that had passed since the European Commission adopted the resolution proposing steep cuts in greenhouse gas emissions – much more aggressive than that of the Paris Agreement – had proven to be a roller coaster of emotions for Sonja Larson, Commissioner of the Climate Action and Energy portfolio, and the resolution's proponent and strongest advocate. Her fellow commissioners supported the resolution, but as she had feared, selling it back home to their respective member states' governments had proven difficult. And now, most member states had rejected it outright in its current form. Sonja's phone had been ringing off the hook in the past week with various proposed amendments recommending smaller reduction targets, more extended time frames, or some combination of the two.

In private, off-the-record conversations with her colleagues, it was apparent to Sonja that the EU was reluctant to take this step unilaterally – particularly since there was no appetite in America to adopt a similar standard. The EU countries choosing to 'go it alone' would gift the Americans a substantial short-term economic advantage. And not just the Americans. The large Asian economies - particularly China – along with Russia, India, and all the developing nations would similarly be granted an economic edge that would have a significant impact over the next fifteen to twenty years. For Sonja, it was particularly galling to see the lack of leadership from the United States, which the world had come to rely on in the decades since World War II. She still felt strongly that if only she could, by sheer force of her will, influence the United States to support the proposed EU emission reduction targets, the rest of the world just might listen and fall in line.

Sonja steepled her head in thought and then pressed the intercom. "Maria, could you come by my office please?"

A short time later, Maria tapped on her boss's door and stepped inside. "Hello Maria. Thanks for coming. Please take a seat." Sonja gestured to the empty chair on the other side of her desk as she spoke.

Maria sat down and waited patiently until Sonja looked up and spoke again. "I've been thinking, Maria. The Commission is scheduled to take a final vote this afternoon on whether to adopt, on behalf of all the member countries, the draft resolution we passed a month ago. I know for a fact that we do not have the votes. Once Germany backed out last week, it was doomed. And the UK doesn't support it either, which matters because, even though it is no longer in the EU, it is still very influential, and its economy is still heavily integrated across Europe. Speaking with my colleagues from the member states, it has become obvious to me that their governments fear the economic repercussions of adopting these strong measures while the rest of the world continues to enjoy the short-term advantages of cheap fossil fuel energy."

Maria studied Sonja's face across the table, expecting to see weariness, if not outright defeat. And there was no doubt some of that, but there was also a firm set of the jaw and a flash in her eyes that spoke to something more. *Hope? Perhaps. Desperation? Maybe. Determination. Yes. Anger? Definitely!* Maria deduced. It seemed to Maria that this was the end of the road. And yet, it was clear that waving the white flag of surrender was not in the cards as far as Sonja was concerned.

"So, what are you going to do, Ms. Larsen? The vote this afternoon will effectively terminate the resolution, won't it?"

"Yes, Maria. And that is why we will not be taking a vote. At least not the vote everyone is expecting. Instead, I will be bringing forward a separate motion to delay the vote by a month." Sonja smiled faintly as she spoke.

"That will keep it alive for now, I guess," admitted Maria. "But what gives you any reason to believe things will be any different next month? Aren't you simply delaying the inevitable? And as you've said yourself many times, the time for delay and half measures has long passed. Delay is the equivalent of defeat."

Sonja sighed and nodded. "You're right, Maria. I suppose I have no reason to expect anything different with an additional month. But we've seen the world change before, unexpectedly and dramatically in a very short period of time. Think back to 9/11 or, more recently, to the worldwide pandemic. No one could have foreseen those events, and yet they radically changed our world in a proverbial instant. Perhaps it is too much to hope for, but keeping this resolution alive for another month at least keeps the possibility that something momentous might happen that will change the world again. It keeps hope alive. It's the only card left to play, and we're going to play it."

"Won't the Commission need a reason to delay the vote?" Maria asked, her brow furrowing.

"Of course. I have received numerous proposed amendments suggesting different approaches and less stringent emissions targets, etc. It's all garbage, of course, and will not address the existential threat our world faces. But I will smile nice for the cameras and say I need time to review them, negotiate with various parties, and present a revised resolution in a month's time that the Commission can fully support. Besides, it is basic human nature to put off major decisions. I expect my motion to delay will pass unanimously." With a smile and wink towards Maria, Sonja stood up. "Come on. Let's grab lunch before we head over to this afternoon's session. My treat."

Undisclosed location near Luxembourg, Belgium

Nervous anticipation had been building in Helle ever since she had given *Dauntless* - and whatever authorities had been shadowing her operation - the slip several weeks ago. *Pluto* had arrived safely at La Hune Bay, Newfoundland, ten days previous and safely unloaded her precious cargo of *radiocaesium*, explosives, and bomb-making materials. Song Hee had kept a careful eye on things and reported no disturbances of any kind. He had stayed on site and was providing daily updates on their progress. In a few minutes, she would be providing a final update to the Council – virtually this time. She had decided the risk of physically getting together at this late stage outweighed the risks of an encrypted virtual meeting, although, in truth, there was no risk-free way to meet or communicate. She did not underestimate the ability of agencies such as the National Security Agency of the United States to intercept supposedly private and encrypted calls, and so had taken every technological precaution possible. Still… there was no way to pull off an operation this complex without effective command and control, and so one had to roll the dice sometimes.

It was time. Helle donned her headphones and logged into the meeting. Most of the Council members were already present, and she waited a few minutes until everyone was present and accounted for. "Ladies and gentlemen. Welcome. This will be our final meeting. Our operation is now in its final stages, and the shutdown of every major shipping port on the eastern seaboard of the United States will take place in just four days. Even as I speak, several bombs are being delivered to their targets on Cirillo freighters crewed by specially selected, well-trained – and highly paid, I might add – Russian mercenaries." Pausing for a moment, she took note of the affirmative nods of the attendees as her words sank in.

"Nicos, would you explain where we are today and what lies ahead, please?"

"Certainly. Thank you Helle," Nicos began. "I am pleased to report that the Cirillo freighter, *Pluto*, successfully diverted to La Hune Bay in Newfoundland ten days ago, where she was met by a contingent already in place consisting of a small security detail, a construction crew and, of course, an expert bomb-maker and his team tasked with taking the raw materials delivered by *Pluto* and constructing twelve weaponized radioactive 'dirty bombs'. The construction team has been in place now for the last four weeks preparing for *Pluto's* arrival, building a barge large enough to offload a standard shipping container, a floating wharf, and a shed to store the material and assemble the bombs. All personnel on site are disguised as Canadian soldiers, and the security detail has been tasked with keeping the locals at a distance, telling them that they are on-site for a few weeks as part of a routine training exercise. They have reported minimal contacts and no issues arising from these contacts. The few locals that have ventured near have been friendly and supportive."

Nicos took a breath and a sip of water before continuing. "Although the bombs are constructed with conventional explosives, they weigh five thousand pounds each and are powerful enough to obliterate everything within a half-mile radius. But their real potency lies in the highly radioactive material dispersed in the explosion that will settle over the entire port city and render it uninhabitable for at least a decade. As of an hour ago, ten of the twelve bombs have been constructed and are fully operational. Eight of them have already been picked up by various Cirillo freighters and are en route to their respective target ports. As Helle explained, they are being picked up one at a time by Cirillo freighters in a tightly choreographed pattern based on distance and transit time to the target city to ensure that all bombs reach their targets and are detonated simultaneously. For example, the freighter bound for the furthest port from La Hune Bay – Houston, Texas – was the first to pick up its bomb. The seven additional freighters that have already picked up their bombs are respectively bound for New Orleans, Louisiana; Miami, Florida;

Jacksonville, Florida; Savannah, Georgia; Charleston, South Carolina; Norfolk, Virginia; and Baltimore, Maryland. The final four freighters currently en route to La Hune Bay will arrive in order of their port city targets, Philadelphia, Pennsylvania; Wilmington, Delaware; New Jersey, New York; and Boston, Massachusetts. Thus far, the operation has been carried out without a hitch."

"Excuse me, Nicos. May I ask a question?" Nicos paused and glanced at his screen to confirm who was speaking. "Of course, Demetrious. I always have time for a fellow Greek." Demetrious was a well-respected partner of a well-heeled corporate law firm based out of Athens that Nicos and Cirillo had worked with for years. They had developed a close friendship over many years of working together and bonding over shared environmental concerns. Nicos had personally recruited Demetrious for this operation.

"All your freighters have strict schedules and publicly posted live GPS tracking that monitors their current position, speed, and heading 24/7, correct? How then are we keeping these diversions to La Hune Bay a secret?"

"Thanks Demetrious. That is a great question. I was going to get to that, but since you asked, I will cover it now. Keep in mind that Cirillo operates hundreds of ships around the world, and it is not unusual for circumstances beyond our control to intervene and cause our ships to get behind. We work hard to stay on schedule, and Cirillo compares very favorably to industry benchmarks – something that our customers truly appreciate and respect us for. However, there remain many factors beyond our control that can, and do, impact schedules. Unpredictable weather, mechanical failures, cargo issues, and such are not uncommon. So, each of our ships, when it reaches the point at which it must alter course to La Hune Bay, is radioing headquarters with a made-up issue to explain the schedule delay and turning off its commercial GPS transponder for the duration of the diversion. We have invented various engine, electrical, steerage, and other mechanical issues as cover stories. One ship even reported a serious cargo shift after encountering a rogue wave that caused it to list and impaired its seaworthiness. Of course, the 14 hours required to rebalance the load was exactly the time needed to retrieve its bomb. In another case, I had HQ contact our ship to direct them to conduct an impromptu series of safety drills and checks – something we do routinely to keep our crews on their toes. In this case, however, it was just a ruse to cover for the delay. Any other questions?"

Dietrich, a top executive with Deutsche Bank, had one. "The Russian mercenaries crewing the ships... what is the extraction plan for them? I assume they are not interested in a suicide mission."

Nicos was about to answer when Helle intervened. "Once they pull into port and are dockside, they will open communications with the other eleven ships. Upon confirmation that all are in place and ready to execute the mission, they will arm the bombs simultaneously. Once armed, a timer will begin to count down from three hours, giving them plenty of time to get away. We have provided them Ukrainian passports and travel arrangements such that they will all be safely in the air en route to Kyiv by the time the bombs detonate."

Nicos kept his expression neutral. Helle was lying through her teeth, and he knew it for a fact. There was no timer. Once the arming sequence was entered, the bomb would detonate immediately. All on board and within a five-hundred-meter radius of the ship would be instantly vaporized. He had discussed this privately with Helle, who wanted no loose tongues or the possibility of any of the crew being picked up by the authorities trying to flee the country. What he did not know until this very moment was her plan to keep the rest of the conspirators in the dark on this point. He would have to be very careful. Helle's penchant for cleaning up 'loose ends' related to this operation made him wonder if she had plans to eliminate the entire Council, himself included!

Helle's answer seemed to satisfy Dietrich, and there were no more questions or comments. Helle concluded the call by reminding everyone why this was necessary. "I just heard on the news earlier today that the EU has postponed its vote on the kind of aggressive action against greenhouse gas emissions that we urgently need. My sources tell me the EU states understand the need to switch to green energy sources but cannot stomach ceding economic ground to the Americans, who are still hooked on cheap, domestically produced fossil fuel products. With their ports shut down for the next ten years and their major refineries unable to import raw material or ship out products, they will be shuttered, and the entire country will be forced to embark on a radical switch to alternate clean-energy sources. In so doing, it will allay concerns the EU currently has with doing the same, and I expect they will quickly adopt the resolution on the table. The world will have, once again, changed in an instant and be redirected down a new path that will halt destructive climate change in its tracks. The drastic but temporary environmental improvements we saw as a result of the Covid-19 pandemic will become a permanent shift that will give hope to all future generations. Ladies and gentlemen, our goal is finally within reach. Once again, I thank you all for your courage and sacrifice. In four days, together, we change the world."

With that, the meeting was adjourned. Helle laid down her headphones, shut down her laptop, leaned back and closed her eyes. She could visualize the eight freighters steaming relentlessly towards their unsuspecting targets, staggered in formation down the western Atlantic with four additional freighters steaming west towards La Hune Bay, like aircraft stacked in a landing pattern at a major airport. Four days! It was all but done. The fat lady was warming up her vocal cords. Nothing could stop them now!

Chapter 25

Somewhere off the South Coast of Newfoundland

Blake and Kat wasted no time calling the crew into the war room to update them on the latest news from Rod. As they confidently predicted, the entire crew was ecstatic to hear that they were being offered a second chance to participate in the investigation after weeks had gone by with no substantial new leads. Time was running short before Blake and Kat needed to be in Boston, but there was time for a quick pit-stop along the way to check out the odd activity being reported in the vicinity of La Hune Bay.

Waiting a beat for the excited babble to quiet down, Blake raised his hand for attention. "You don't need me to tell you how critical this mission is. Everyone is agreed that there is a massive quantity of explosives and radioactive material being illegally and surreptitiously shipped around the world. If this is allowed to become weaponized and unleashed on an unsuspecting civilian target, the toll in human death and suffering – not to mention infrastructure and economic damage – is almost unimaginable. We simply cannot let it happen."

At Blake's words, the mood around the table sobered quickly. Eric spoke for them all when he remarked, "We all feel terrible, boss. It just feels like we let everyone down."

Kat held up her hand. "I need to say this. Mistakes were made, there is no doubt. But they were not made by you guys. Blake and I made the final decisions, and we made some rookie blunders that we've learned from and won't repeat again. I was the one who got sloppy and got myself kidnapped. That provided a shortcut to finding the *radiocaesium* stash, but it tipped our hand to the bad guys that we were on to them and that ultimately played out in their favor. I was warned of the impending ambush, underestimated the enemy, and walked straight into their trap."

Blake reached out and wrapped his arm around her shoulder, giving her a tender squeeze. "Don't be too hard on yourself, Kat. I've beat myself up for triggering the motion alarm in Tartus, once again alerting the enemy to our presence and handing them a golden opportunity to cover their tracks. I should have been more careful. I almost paid for my error with my life. If it weren't for you, I would have…." His voice started to waver, and his eyes welled with tears from the emotional impact of the memory.

"The point is," Kat continued, as she grasped Blake's hand in both of hers, "we will learn from our mistakes, and we simply can't afford anymore. The stakes are too high."

"Thanks Kat. That's exactly right," agreed Blake as he steeled his emotions into check. "And that's why the number one priority of this next engagement at La Hune Bay is to remain undetected. We simply cannot afford to tip our hand to the enemy. Using a football analogy, the clock is winding down, and we are behind. We simply don't have the luxury of punting the ball and hoping to get it back in time to make the go-ahead score. It's do-or-die time." Blake glanced down at the Rolex Explorer watch he had chosen for the day. "I've asked Matt to slow us down so that we arrive on station after nightfall. We will use the extra time to comprehensively plan this mission to go ashore and conduct reconnaissance on the ground at La Hune Bay. By this time tomorrow, we need to know exactly what our adversaries are planning. But just as importantly, we can't let them know that we are on to them!"

Over the next few hours, the plan started to come together. Matt's military background came in handy as he stressed the importance of layered plans with multiple back-ups. "It's important to have a plan, but understand that things rarely go according to plan. We need not only 'a plan', but multiple contingency plans to anticipate as many 'what ifs' as we can. And even then, the agents on the ground must be able to adapt in real time to the situation at hand, keeping in mind the paramount objectives of the mission. As I see it… there are two co-equal mission objectives. The first is to gather the necessary intelligence to figure out exactly what these guys are up to. And the second objective is to remain undetected. Failure to achieve both objectives is a failure of the mission. With the mission achieved, we return all hands safely to base and put together a plan to stop them once and for all."

After two full hours, the meeting finally broke up, and everyone went their separate ways to prepare for the coming night's activities. Because stealth was a mission imperative, it was decided to keep the landing party to a minimum – just Blake and Kat. Matt would command the bridge of *Dauntless* and coordinate all communications, command, and control. Scotty would assist with the insertion and extraction. As usual, Mark would provide a bird's eye view with his drones, while Eric would assist Mark and be poised to bring *Dauntless'* array of offensive and defensive weaponry to bear, if required - and only as a last resort. Biff and Emily would assist Blake and Kat in gathering and packing all the gear they would require, and stand by to offer any support, as required, during the mission itself.

Initially, they looked at landing Blake and Kat at the end of Aviron Bay, a fjord located a short distance east of La Hune Bay, running parallel and separated by a headland only one-and-a-half miles wide. However, when they looked closer at relief maps of the area, they realized that the high cliffs surrounding both fjords would require a circuitous approach route into the interior and then following a treacherous river gorge down to La Hune Bay from the rear. It was deemed too time-consuming and risky to be feasible, particularly in the dark, for two people unfamiliar with the terrain.

Instead, they decided to launch their largest submersible from the waters outside La Hune Bay - approximately six miles from the target site. It was large enough to accommodate three persons and was equipped with a water-tight entry/exit hatch. Scotty would pilot the submersible to a point about five hundred feet offshore where Blake and Kat would exit underwater through the hatch, one at a time.

Meanwhile, Mark would keep a drone in position overhead, equipped with infrared sensors designed to detect the location of human heat signatures and provide intelligence on how many security personnel were onsite and their precise location - invaluable knowledge for Blake and Kat to be able to operate undetected. Plan A was to simply avoid detection, but there was a Plan B to neutralize one or more guards if absolutely necessary – one that everyone hoped would keep their intrusion covert.

Dauntless arrived on station shortly after 11:00 pm, after trawling along all day at an uncharacteristically slow pace for the sleek yacht. While Matt stayed on the bridge, the rest of the crew made their way down to the moon pool chamber belowdecks to see Scotty, Blake, and Kat off. Blake and Kat had already donned their sophisticated rebreather diving gear, as the cramped quarters of the submersible would make it difficult to suit up en route. Once all three were inside with the main hatch sealed, Scotty gave the thumbs-up signal to Mark, who swung the vessel, dubbed *The Big Dipper*, out into the middle of the pool and detached the connection. With a final jaunty salute from Blake, Scotty manned the controls, and *The Big Dipper* slowly descended into the inky waters below.

Scotty eased down to a depth of about forty feet, shut off all exterior lights and dimmed the interior lighting to just a faint glow from the digital display panel. At *The Big Dipper's* cruising speed of four knots, it would take roughly an hour and a half to reach the extreme end of La Hune Bay, where Blake and Kat would exit. Meanwhile, Mark had flown a drone ahead of them and reported six guards stationed at equidistant points around the perimeter at a radius of approximately 750 feet. They were unlikely to be a concern given the plan to penetrate underwater and well inside the guards' perimeter. The heavily wooded terrain in between would do the rest. Of more pressing concern were the two guards Mark had spotted on site. One stationed on the wharf, and another on the roof of the shed, conducting regular rounds around the perimeter of the roof. The risk of covering the open ground between the water and the shed without being detected was too high!

"We're going to have to switch to Plan B," Blake concluded. "Kat, you sure you are up to the task?"

Patting the large watertight bag next to her that contained their gear, Kat nodded her assent. "I got this, Blake."

A short time later, Scotty slowed the submersible to a stop. "This is where ye get off. We are at a depth of 40 feet, 500 feet offshore from the wharf. I can remain on station for a maximum of two hours if we are going to conserve enough battery power to make it back to *Dauntless*."

Blake went first, wedging himself into the escape hatch, pulling on his regulator, and sealing the door behind him. Scotty punched the display panel, and the hatch filled with seawater. A moment later, Blake opened the outer hatch and floated out into the sea beyond. Kat followed suit, and finally, Scotty placed the watertight bag with their gear in the hatch, which was retrieved on the other side a moment later by Blake. With a final wave and thumbs-up gesture, Blake and Kat gave one kick with their fins and were instantly gone from Scotty's view, swallowed by the blackness of the water.

Rather than surfacing next to the wharf, Blake and Kat took a compass bearing from their dive watches and headed for a point a couple of hundred feet down the shore, which was concealed from the view of the guards by a small rocky point. As the bottom rose and the water grew shallow, they surfaced cautiously and swam the final ten feet. Emerging from the water, they took off their dive gear and transitioned into the night camouflage clothing they had packed into their gear bag. Kat removed a long rifle and loaded it with specially designed tranquilizer darts. Supposedly, one dart would put a man down for two hours – taking effect within fifteen seconds. Even better, the darts had been manufactured to Blake's precise specifications and were laced with Versed – a drug known to cause short-term memory loss – so the victim would have no memory of the few minutes prior to losing consciousness. He would simply wake up and find himself lying on the ground, most likely assuming he had fallen asleep on duty and in no hurry to report the slip-up to his superiors. At least, that was the hope.

Blake put their dive gear into the dive pouch, tied it to a tree with a thin, black rope and submerged it a few feet from shore. "Ready," he whispered to Kat. They carefully crawled up the hill from shore until they had a good vantage point of both the wharf and shed. Blake pressed his comm, "Mark… can you see us? What's the situation?"

"I got you, boss," Mark replied immediately. "There's no movement from the perimeter guards. Nearest one is two hundred and fifty feet from your location. The roof guard is still active, and the shore guard is moving up and down the wharf in a regular pattern. Neither have given any indication that they have seen anything amiss. Plan B?"

"Plan B," Blake confirmed while scanning the area with his night vision goggles. "Kat is getting set up now. We have a clear sight of them both. I'll let you know once she's tagged them."

Kat was laying down on her stomach, the gun resting on a log in front of her for stability. She swung the barrel back and forth between the two targets a few times to get a feel for the maneuver. She wanted to make sure that once she tagged the first guard, there would be no delay in knocking down the second one before the alarm was raised. After a couple of minutes, she took a deep breath. "I'm ready."

"You got this, Kat. Just like you have done a thousand times on the range. Just relax and let your instincts take over. Green light whenever you're ready."

Kat closed her eyes briefly and calmed herself, controlling her breathing and slowing her heart rate. She lined up the roof guard and swung her sights back to the wharf guard for one final practice. Swinging back to the roof guard, she flicked on the laser, pinpointed his exposed neck, exhaled, and pulled the trigger. The gun coughed softly. Swinging the rifle barrel immediately back to the wharf, she lined up the laser and fired a second time. Blake could see the first guard reach for his neck – looking like he was swatting at some irritant, possibly thinking it was a mosquito. Swinging around to the wharf guy, he was alarmed to see he had dropped to a crouch and was staring intently in their direction. "I think he must have heard the first shot and dropped to his knees just as you fired the second!" he whispered breathlessly to Kat.

Kat had noticed the same thing, and the gun coughed a third time. This time, the man clearly flinched slightly and slapped at his neck.

The next fifteen seconds seemed more like fifteen minutes. They were both really beginning to doubt Kat's aim or possibly the efficacy of the powerful tranquilizer drug, but then both men wobbled and sat down woozily. Seconds after that, they were stretched out, prone and motionless. Mark's excited voice came through their earpiece. "They are both down! Great shooting, Kat."

Blake and Kat immediately began making their way back down the wooded embankment towards the wharf, still exercising extreme caution. They stopped at the edge of the clearing and confirmed with Mark that he was picking up no other heat signatures nearby before proceeding to the large shed. "In the back right corner of the shed, I've got what appears to be six motionless heat signatures. Almost certainly the remainder of the on-site contingent who are peacefully asleep in their bunks."

"Roger that, Mark. We are proceeding to recover the darts from the downed guards," Kat answered.

Blake pointed to the prone guard on the wharf. "I'll retrieve the dart from his neck while you make your way onto the roof of the shed and retrieve the dart from the other guard."

"No problem. We'll meet up on the near side of the shed," Kat responded.

Blake crept out onto the floating wharf and retrieved the dart from the stretched-out guard. Pocketing the empty cartridge, he checked the man's pulse, which was regular and strong. Straightening up, he then made his way over to the side of the shed as quietly as he could, careful to avoid jostling any loose stones. Moments later, Kat joined him with a quick thumbs-up gesture, showing him the empty dart cartridge she had retrieved before quickly tucking it into a zippered pocket. Blake nodded and pressed his ear to the side of the wall but heard nothing.

"What now?" asked Kat.

"Let's move around and check the door at the front. I'm really hoping that, given the isolated nature of the operation, we will find it unlocked. After all, it's not like they are expecting any unauthorized personnel on site. I'm guessing all their eggs are in the security detail basket designed to keep any potential trespassers far away."

"Makes sense," Kat nodded. "Motion sensors? Remember, they got us in a heap of trouble back in Tartus."

Blake shook his head. "I doubt it. Not here. Once again, it's not like this is located on a busy city street where you might be concerned about a break-in. Plus, in Tartus, they didn't have on-site security. The motion detector was their security."

"And if you're wrong?" Kat pressed.

"In that case, the perimeter guards will start closing in, and the sleepyheads will start moving. Mark will give us a warning, and we will hightail it out of here and back into the woods. If we can avoid detection, they'll have to assume it was tripped accidentally."

Kat laughed at that and slapped him on the shoulder. "What's so funny?" demanded Blake suspiciously.

"I think you are forgetting about the two guards who are lights out. A tripped motion alarm might be explained away, but two drugged guards is a dead giveaway."

Blake grinned ruefully. "Well, that's what I have you along for, I guess. Two heads are better than one. Regardless, we need to see what's in the shed. Let's be as careful as we can. Before entering, we can do a full visual scan for any security cameras or motion detectors. It's the best we can do."

With that, they proceeded to the main door and turned the latch. It was unlocked! Blake carefully pulled it open, wincing at the squeaky hinges. All remained quiet and still. With their night vision goggles pulled down, they carefully scanned the entire open space looking for any blinking lights or other evidence of additional layers of security. Seeing nothing, Blake signaled that he was entering and for Kat to follow. They crept forward single file, heads on a swivel. Blake was the first to see something. Pulling back a tarp, he saw dozens of empty drums – drums he recognized as the same ones he saw in Tartus filled with high explosives manufactured by ISIS.

Kat was next to inhale sharply. Tugging at Blake's arm, she pointed to a stack of large wooden crates on the far wall. Making their way over to them, they could see that, like the drums of explosives, the lead-lined wooden crates were empty. A large forklift fitted with oversize off-road-type tires was parked nearby.

The center of the main room was occupied by commercial-sized work benches, liberally strewn with tools, wiring, and other electrical components. Blake knew immediately what he was looking at. "Time to go, Kat. We've seen what we needed to see. This is where the explosives and *radiocaesium* have been combined into a weapon. Or, more likely, weapons. I expect that both the explosives and the *radiocaesium* were delivered by freighter in shipping containers, offloaded onto the barge we saw tied up to the wharf, and maneuvered into this shed using the forklift. I think we are looking at a sophisticated bomb-making operation here."

"But... I don't see any bombs. Do you?" Kat countered, looking around and gesturing broadly with her hands for emphasis. "If you're right, that can only mean one thing. They have already been picked up for delivery to their target. Or targets. That must be what the parade of freighters in and out of the bay was all about. I'm thinking we have multiple bombs, multiple freighters as delivery vehicles, and multiple targets."

Blake nodded. "Bingo. Exactly what I was thinking. And that's not the worst of it."

"Nope," agreed Kat. "The worst of it is that all of those bombs are steaming towards their targets, and we're sitting here dead in the water in La Hune Bay, with no idea how many bombs there are, what ships those bombs are on, or where they are headed. We might already be too late."

They quickly made their way to the door, let themselves out, and closed the door behind them. Checking with Mark to ensure the coast was clear, they followed the shoreline back to where their dive gear was stashed, quickly geared up and swam back to rejoin Scotty in the submersible.

"Aye, it's good to see ye. I was gettin' a wee bit worried." Scotty greeted them once they had both re-entered *The Big Dipper* via the escape hatch. We are getting tight on battery reserve. Might have to reposition *Dauntless* closer if we run out of juice, but I'll get ye home. Dinnae fret about that!"

En route back to *Dauntless*, they heard from Mark one more time. "Both guards are awake. From what I can tell, neither looks to have any idea what happened to them, and everyone is maintaining their position. No general alarm has been raised, that I am sure of! Looks like a successful mission!"

Chapter 26

Just outside La Hune Bay, south coast of Newfoundland

The return trip to *Dauntless* in the dark, cramped confines of the submersible seemed interminable to her impatient passengers, especially knowing that with each passing minute, multiple radioactive 'dirty' bombs were getting closer to their targets. But the more they willed the submersible to pick up the pace, the slower it seemed to move. Blake had wasted no time in contacting Matt, bringing him up to date on the mission, what they had found, and their suspicions. He also had him put *Dauntless* in full stealth mode and reposition her to meet them halfway – saving precious time and addressing Scotty's concern with respect to *The Big Dipper*'s batteries. There were still three hours until sunrise, and Blake and Kat were confident *Dauntless* would not be detected by the security detail far down at the end of the bay. "Tell the crew to get some rest. I have a feeling they are going to need it. We're going to call Rod as soon as we get back on board to relay what we've found and figure out what comes next."

"Roger that, sir. I'll send Mark to his bunk and stand by to winch you back on board myself. Don't worry about me. I'll stay on station and be ready for whatever comes."

"Thanks Matt. I know you will." And Blake meant every word. He and Kat often discussed the crew they had recruited, and each one of them was outstanding. But Matt occupied a special place in their estimation. Always reliable. Always cool under pressure. Always quick to recognize what needed to be done and equipped with the skills necessary to do it. Blake would not hesitate to trust him with his life, and he knew Kat felt the same.

The Big Dipper had scarcely settled onto the deck of *Dauntless* before Blake and Kat were out and headed up to the war room to raise Rod, leaving Scotty and Matt to secure the submersible. "Hey Scotty. Great job tonight. Captain's orders are for you to head to your bunk for some shut-eye. I'll stay on watch the remainder of the night, and you can relieve me in six hours."

Scotty stifled a yawn and nodded. "Aye sir. Ye dinnae need to tell me twice. G'night lad. I'll see ye in the morning." With that, Scotty gave Matt a pat on the shoulder and left.

Up in the war room, Blake dialed Rod's number with a glance at his watch and a wink at Kat. "If we keep calling Rod in the middle of the night, Mary is going to suspect that he is having an affair!"

A moment later, Rod answered, his voice thick with sleep. "Hello. This better be bloody important."

Blake and Kat quickly brought him up to speed, describing exactly what they had found at La Hune Bay, concluding with their suspicions that their worst fears were being realized.

"We are convinced we have multiple radioactive 'dirty' bombs headed for multiple targets aboard commercial freighters with access to large ports all over the world. But based on the direction of travel, we believe the targets are located along the eastern seaboard of the United States. Or possibly Canada as well. If we can't quickly locate all of them and stop them, we will have a terrorist attack inflicted on us that will make 9/11 seem like child's play," Blake concluded.

There was a sharp intake of breath as Rod, now fully alert, absorbed their report. "This is indeed our worst-case scenario, and they are even further ahead than we feared," he finally managed. "I think you're right that we don't have much time. But I do have a couple more pieces of the puzzle. First of all, we have been monitoring the communications of Cirillo's Chief Executive Office, Nicos Papadakis. Ninety-nine percent of it is boring business and domestic stuff. But every now and then, he makes or receives a call using sophisticated encryption software. Those calls have all been to the same number – one which we haven't been able to identify as it appears to be a burner phone. So, while we haven't been able to decipher what was said, the location of the burner phone he connects with seems to be most often located on the outskirts of Luxembourg, and we have narrowed down the location to somewhere within a two-mile diameter."

"Hey, can you send me a list of the calls you have intercepted, along with the time stamps and coordinates of the location where the burner phone was located?" Kat requested.

"Of course. Give me a second…. Ok, just sent to your phone."

"Thanks Rod. Kat will have a look at that, run it through her computer, and see if anything jumps out," Blake said. "In the meantime, you mentioned there was something else?"

"Yes… we've trained a satellite over La Hune Bay and have been analyzing the images. We've noted at least eight separate freighters making an appearance in and out of the bay, sometimes only hours apart."

"At least eight…" Blake repeated. "You mean there could be more?"

"Yes. There were times the cloud cover was too thick to get a clear picture, but we've had a team working on it, and we now think there have been a total of twelve freighters dropping by. This is based on a sophisticated analysis of all the satellite data relating to ship traffic and factoring in variables such as their speed and course direction. Furthermore, all eight we had a clear view of have been positively identified as Cirillo ships."

"And let me guess," Blake added. None of them were broadcasting their GPS location or appeared to have any commercial reason to be there."

"Bingo!" Rod confirmed. "In fact, the last of the freighters exited La Hune Bay just hours ago. Did you happen to see it?"

"We didn't get a visual, Rod," Blake replied. "We approached well after dark. There was a radar contact south of our position and moving away that could be the ship you describe, but we can't be sure."

While the two men were speaking, Kat had popped open her laptop and was scrutinizing the call log that Rod had sent. She suddenly slapped the table and looked up. "Blake... what date did we meet with Sonja in Seville last month?"

"Ahhh... August 26th, I believe. Why?"

"One second. Rod? The time stamps on this list you sent me. Are they GMT time?"

"Yes," confirmed Rod.

"Give me a second..." Kat busied herself for a few more moments with her laptop before pushing it away and looking up with a dazed look on her face. "You're never going to believe this. One of those encrypted calls that Nicos made to that burner phone terminated in Seville at the very same time we were meeting with Sonja. I just had to take a minute to calculate the time zone difference between Seville time and GMT. And that's not all. The GPS coordinates, based on the nearest cell tower, place that phone at or very close to the Barcelo Sevilla Renacimiento Hotel, where we met with her."

The color drained from Blake's face. "Towards the end of our meeting, Sonja excused herself to take a call. Remember?"

"I remember. And Sonja is residing at some old estate south of Brussels near Luxembourg while she serves on the European Union Commission?" Kat added.

"You're right, Kat," Blake confirmed with a slow nod.

Rod was having trouble keeping up. It was the middle of his night, after all. "What are you guys saying?"

Blake answered for them both. "Sonja Larsen, our good friend, our trusted partner in *Operation Ocean Renewal*, and Denmark's widely respected representative to the European Union Commission and head of its Climate Action and Energy Portfolio, is up to her neck in this plot. She could even be the head of the snake."

None of them wanted to believe it, and long seconds passed as they each pondered the facts, looking for a hole in the theory. Kat broke the silence. "The evidence is circumstantial, at best. It wouldn't hold up in court. It's probably not even enough to convince a judge to sign a search warrant, but I feel in my gut that it's true. And if we're right, she is about to unleash holy hell."

Rod had been around long enough to see promising theories based on circumstantial evidence evaporate under disciplined scrutiny, and when it did, valuable time was lost, reputations damaged, and crucial trust and credibility that had taken years to develop stripped away in a moment. "It's a possibility. Not yet a working theory," he cautioned. "But I think what's missing here is motive. Sonja is a committed climate change activist and generally advocates for a variety eco-friendly causes. Both her strong work with the EU Commission over the past few months, as well as her partnership with you guys in *Operation Ocean Renewal*, speak strongly to that. I just can't see her being that twisted person hell-bent on inflicting death, destruction, and environmental havoc on this scale."

That put a damper on things for a moment before Blake countered. "Sometimes people get so focused on the ends, they can justify whatever the means to get there, no matter how terrible. History is replete with examples of this. We all know Sonja is consumed with climate change and the threat it poses to our way of life. Sonja sees it as an existential threat to human life, itself. If she somehow made a connection in her mind between the detonation of these bombs as a means towards preserving human life on the planet, then it's just possible she would be motivated enough to try it."

That made sense to Kat, who was nodding along in agreement. "Well, we can discuss it for the remainder of the night, or we can find out for sure," she declared. "Let's just feed her some false information and see if she acts on it. I just realized if she's in on this, she probably knows our secret identity as well. My true face was revealed back in Gangneung when I was kidnapped, and if she is truly the head of the snake, as Blake put it, then she saw me. But now that trump card has switched hands because she doesn't know that we have uncovered her true identity!"

"What do you have in mind, Kat?" inquired Rod.

"Let's call her up on the pretense of getting an update on *Operation Ocean Renewal*. I'm willing to bet she'll ask where we are and what we're doing, and when she does, we'll tell her we were on our way to Boston but got sidetracked after being asked to investigate a large farmed-salmon die-off near Francois."

"But there is no major farmed salmon die-off in the vicinity," protested Blake.

"Of course not," Kat continued, undeterred. "That's the whole point. She'll attempt to verify that story the minute she's off the phone, and when she does, she'll know we are lying. If she knows we are involved in investigating this operation and are making up a story about why we are currently hanging out suspiciously near her operation in La Hune Bay, she will move immediately to conceal her tracks. If we're right, that burner phone of hers will make an encrypted call very shortly to a satellite phone in La Hune Bay, and that place will turn into a beehive of activity in a rush to make it disappear. Mark will confirm it for us, one way or another, with his drones while we get underway for Boston."

Blake gave his wife an admiring look. "What do you think, Rod? Sounds like a solid plan to me."

"Yep. Sure. Give me ten minutes to coordinate things on my end and then make the call. As soon as you hang up, let me know, and we'll see if that burner phone goes active soon after. We'll also see if the NSA boys can locate a corresponding satellite phone signal from the La Hune Bay site. If that all falls into place and you guys can confirm they commence an emergency dismantling of their camp in the middle of the night, then I think the circumstantial evidence becomes quite compelling."

Ten minutes later, Kat texted Rod, "Ready?" Moments later, he texted back, "Make the call."

Kat dialed Sonja's number and put the phone on speaker.

After a few rings, Sonja picked up. "Hello Kat. Good to hear from you again. How are things?"

"Great, Sonja. Blake is with me as well. We just thought we'd give you a call to get an update on *Operation Ocean Renewal*."

"I see," Sonja replied. "Well, although my workday is just underway, I thought you guys were back in North America where it must still be the middle of the night. You keep some strange hours, that's for sure."

Blake and Kat exchanged a look of alarm. In their haste, they hadn't thought of that.

Blake recovered quickly. "Oh. Uh... yeah. We just left St. John's at midnight on our way to Boston now for our first major fall fundraiser. We were just getting ready to hit the sack when Kat noticed we had received an email from the Newfoundland and Labrador Department of Environment and Conservation. Apparently, there's been a major die-off of farmed salmon here on the south coast of Newfoundland, and they wondered if we could assist in the investigation. We've been up ever since gathering information and developing a plan of attack so we can get right on it in the morning. We're hoping to have a look around, collect some water samples, etc., and continue on our way without much delay."

"That's interesting," Sonja responded. I had not heard of this incident. Where did you say the die-off occurred? I have heard that warming oceans have been a major factor in such die-offs. Just another symptom of the threat climate change imposes on us all."

"The closest community to the die-off is Francois," Kat clarified. There's not much of a population in the vicinity, but the deep, sheltered fjords in the area are conducive to aquaculture. But enough about us. How are things with you, and what's the latest you've heard on *Operation Ocean Renewal*?"

Sonja proceeded to give them a brief update on *Operation Ocean Renewal* – which was now wrapping up very successfully. She also shared with them her disappointment with the EU's reluctance to adopt the kind of greenhouse gas reduction targets she thought necessary.

As soon as the call ended, Kat texted Rod to let him know. Blake meanwhile paged Mark to ask him to launch a drone and return to the La Hune Bay work site. Rod called back within five minutes.

"The burner phone placed a call only seconds after you hung up with Sonja. We traced the signal to the European Union Commission headquarters in Brussels. The NSA is still working to confirm, but preliminary data indicates she reached out to a satellite phone located at La Hune Bay. Do you have eyes on the place?"

"Launching a drone right now. We'll have eyes on the place in twenty minutes. Stay on the line."

Blake flicked on a large screen on the wall and pulled up the drone camera view. Sunrise was only thirty minutes away, and the darkness of the night had given way to a pinky dusk. As the drone closed the distance to the far end of the fjord and zoomed its powerful camera lens in, it quickly became apparent that the sleepy outpost from a few hours before had been transformed. At least a dozen men now swarmed the site in a flurry of activity. It looked like full panic had set in.

"Sonja's our girl, Rod," stated Blake. "No doubt about it. She took the bait hook, line, and sinker. Looks like every available hand has been roused out of bed and put to work. My guess is by nightfall, the shed will be torn down, and every bit of material will be floated out to sea on that barge and sunk."

"Hard to disagree, Blake," Rod answered. "Send me that footage. I'll see if I can get Interpol to round up Sonja and Nicos for questioning. We need to locate the bombs and intercept them!"

"We'll keep working on that on our end too, Rod," Kat added. "I've got some ideas. Keep in touch. We'll do the same."

Chapter 27

Undisclosed location near Luxembourg, Belgium

Sonja poured herself a gin and tonic and folded herself into her favorite stuffed leather chair. It was all but over now. Twelve bombs on twelve commercial container ships soon to arrive at twelve major shipping ports on the Atlantic coast of the United States. In approximately forty-eight hours, they would be detonated and, once again, the world would be changed in an instant. The Americans would undoubtedly be infuriated, desperate for someone, something, anything to focus their collective fury on. And that was putting it mildly. If 9/11 occurred a week after this event, it would have trouble cracking the headlines. The media would still be preoccupied with the destruction and more-or-less permanent disablement of every major commercial seaport on the Atlantic coast. Oh… New York just lost a couple buildings, and another 2,000 people died? In the context of a tragedy the magnitude of Helle's creation, it would seem like a minor aftershock following major earthquake.

Now that events were inexorably rushing towards their conclusion, it was high time to ensure her own survival. The Americans would not be knocked off balance for long and would demand to know who was responsible and bring them to swift justice. She did not doubt their considerable resources, skill, and determination that would be brought to bear on this investigation. No stone would be left unturned, and Sonja knew that inevitably one or more of the Council members would be implicated. She didn't know exactly how, or even how long, but there had been too many levers pulled. Too many people involved. Too much money changing hands. There was evidence there to find, and a chain is only as strong as its weakest link. And once the Americans inevitably captured a link in the chain of evidence, they would quickly begin following those links, eventually working their way to the top.

Yet, it would take some time, and she had taken every precaution to maximize that time. Nicos was a good man in many ways - smart, loyal, and resourceful. But he was a fool in one respect, seeming to think the operation would end with the 'big bang' and that he could then return to his normal life. He assumed that all the precautions, security, and secrecy were implemented to make this return to normalcy possible. Sonja had no such illusion. Helle would have to disappear forever. A wisp. A phantom. Here for a time, and then gone without a trace. Vanished forever like she never existed.

That thought stabbed home. She had rather enjoyed her Helle persona and, knowing that it too must be sacrificed for the greater good, brought her no pleasure. However, there were certain elements of Helle that she would take with her. Maybe these traits had been there all along, hidden in the dark recesses of her soul, just waiting to make their presence known. Her cold, calculating mind. Her ability to focus on the ends and be as ruthless as necessary to achieve them. Her determination. Her ambition. These traits had surged to the fore and, while Sonja would cover them up with the veneer of polite civility, they would remain just under the surface, powering her lofty ambitions and ensuring the world remained on the course she had set it on; a world where future generations would build on the ashes of the destruction she had caused. She didn't need their thanks or acknowledgment. She would know, and that would be enough.

Sonja took a sip of her drink and forced her mind back to the present and the thorny issue of the multiple loose ends represented by the Council. There was really only one answer. They needed to be eliminated, even Nicos. She had known it from the start, and the planning for their demise was the most intricate and secretive part of the entire plot.

The problem with loose ends is that in attempting to eliminate them, you create even more. The more you try and stamp them out, the more they multiply. More and more tendrils of evidence waving about for the Americans to find and follow back to their source. This was exactly why she had to be so careful.

To solve this complex issue, Sonja had turned to organized crime; Bratva, the Russian mob, to be precise. Bratva had its origins in the former Soviet Union and is widely acknowledged to be the largest organized crime group in the world, active not just in the Eastern Bloc countries, but throughout Western Europe and North America. They had a robust presence - through thousands of linked criminal elements - in every illicit activity known to mankind: drugs, prostitution, gambling, human trafficking, loansharking, counterfeiting, hacking, and ransomware schemes. Of more interest to Sonja was their thriving and sophisticated business of murder-for-hire. You could even specify what kind of death you wanted for your victim. A painful and slow death meant to exact revenge or convey a message to a broader audience. A quick execution-style death – crisp, efficient, business-like. Or... the most expensive choice on the expansive menu – the 'accidental' death where the target appears to be the unlucky victim of an unfortunate, but random, set of circumstances. A traffic accident, perhaps. A heart attack. A drowning. An innocent victim caught in the crossfire of a rival gang shoot-up. Even a horrific mass shooting with multiple victims carried out by a seemingly deranged individual... except, one of the victims was not random at all, and the others sacrificed to conceal the truth that the whole event was an elaborate targeted assassination.

Helle didn't know and didn't care how it was done as long as each death appeared random and accidental. She had simply transferred the cyber currency payment via an ultra-secure encrypted Bratva network, along with the names and a seventy-two-hour time frame beginning - Sonja consulted her watch – in exactly one hour. There would be no loose ends, of that, she was confident. The cover-up of Freyja's death two months earlier had been a good trial run and had gone flawlessly. The Americans' investigation might well come to suspect that the deaths were anything but accidental. But penetrating the notorious Bratva network and finding any link back to Sonja would be inconceivable. This was where all the loose ends would come to die.

Sonja shook her head to clear her thoughts, focusing next on Blake and Katherine Zane. In many respects, their concerns and interests were aligned. It was no coincidence that they had become partners in *Operation Ocean Renewal*. Where they parted ways, philosophically speaking, was the extent to which they were willing to go to achieve their goals. In Sonja's opinion, Blake and Kat lacked the fortitude to really do what was necessary. To see the world as it was and not as they wished it to be. It was unfortunate, indeed, that they had somehow tripped onto Helle and the Council's plans and very nearly foiled them. In truth, she admired their tenacity. They were resourceful and courageous, and it was a miracle that they had even survived the North Korean submarine's attempt to take them out. Sonja was still unclear exactly how they had wriggled out of that trap. As clever and skilled as they were, however, they had come up short. But barely. Their discovery of the La Hune Bay operation had been a close call. Had they been even a day earlier, they might have spoiled the whole thing.

Very soon now, it would be all over. Helle and the Council would be no more, and no doubt Sonja's bond with the Zanes' would grow even stronger as they worked together to pick up the pieces in the new world. The delicious irony of the whole situation turned the corners of her mouth into the beginnings of a smile.

With a second glance at her watch, Sonja realized it was time for her final check-in with Song Hee. She picked up her phone, launched the encryption app, and punched in his number. Song Hee picked up on the first ring.

"Hello boss," he answered.

"Status report, please," Helle demanded. She had no interest in small talk.

"As you know, I boarded the final freighter, *Neptune*, and we departed La Hune Bay yesterday evening, bound for Boston. Our current position is about 25 miles south of Halifax, Nova Scotia – so nearly halfway to our destination. We encountered a strong early fall storm with gale-force winds and waves of fifteen feet. The rough sea state has forced us to reduce our speed; however, the captain assures me we will arrive in port tomorrow night on schedule at 1:00 am." As usual, Song Hee was succinct and kept to the pertinent facts. The fact that the heaving ship had caused him to puke his guts didn't seem like something Helle would be interested in hearing about. "Anything I should know about from your end?" Song Hee queried.

Helle had carefully considered whether she should tell him about her strong suspicion that *Dauntless* was in the vicinity of La Hune Bay mere hours after the departure of *Neptune* and was also likely now en route to Boston. In the end, she decided it was likely irrelevant at this point and didn't want to distract him. She wanted his focus to be on the mission ahead and not looking over his shoulder at ghosts.

"All clear," answered Helle. "The La Hune Bay site has now been completely dismantled, and all evidence we were ever there was floated out to sea on the barge and sunk."

"And *Dauntless?*"

"I'm keeping a close eye on *Dauntless*. Nothing to worry about there. She is keeping to her prearranged schedule. After a brief stop in her home port in St. John's, she has recently departed for a series of fundraising stops this fall in the United States."

Song Hee had mixed emotions. On one hand, he was anxious to complete the mission and celebrate the huge payday he had been promised. On the other hand, he desperately wanted some payback. *And I will get it,* he promised himself. *When this is all over, at a time and place of my choosing, I will have my revenge. Particularly with the blonde woman. I will take my time with her. She will die slowly, indeed.* His thoughts were interrupted by Helle's disembodied voice in his ear.

"Run through the plan. One more time."

Song Hee shook his head. "I've got this, Helle, or whoever you are. *Neptune* will arrive at the Paul W. Conley Container Terminal at the Port of Boston at 1:00 am tomorrow night. All the paperwork is in order. It is a routine, scheduled stop where we are to unload eight hundred shipping containers and reload an additional six hundred and fifty containers over a twenty-four-hour period before departing for Norfolk, Virginia. I am to maintain hourly contact with the other eleven freighters to ensure we all arrive at our respective ports simultaneously. Once everyone is moored, I will give the signal to arm the bombs, at which point we will use the three-hour timed delay to disembark and make our way to the airport for a scheduled direct flight to London. We will be cruising at 35,000 feet over the Atlantic when the bombs go off."

Pretty accurate, Helle thought, *except for the part about making a clean getaway.* It was regrettable, really. Song Hee had proven himself to be a valuable resource – perhaps even a loose end she might consider allowing to exist to be used in the future. Still, there was no way she could allow the rest of the mercenary crew to scatter, so he would have to be sacrificed for the cause, just like so many others. Playing her part to the bitter end, Helle feigned interest in whether the crew leaving the ship unattended would raise an alarm.

"Won't the Port Authority be suspicious when the entire crew abandons ship?" Helle queried.

"No. We've scheduled cargo operations to commence at 5:00 am. Fairly standard stuff for late arrivals, as I understand it. We'll be discreet. No one will realize the ship has been abandoned until it is too late. The other eleven freighters have made similar arrangements."

"OK, Mr. Hee. It sounds like everything is under control. This will be our final communication until the operation is concluded. Once the bombs have been successfully detonated, I will transfer the agreed payment for your services to your Bitcoin account. Godspeed."

"Thank you Helle. I will expect to hear from you upon my arrival in London. It's been a pleasure," Song Hee responded, and the connection was cut off.

Dauntless, 30 miles east of Cape Breton Island, Nova Scotia

Mark had no sooner confirmed that the drone had been recovered when Blake instructed Matt to put *Dauntless* back on course for Boston. Blake returned to his suite for a hot shower and short rest, but Kat was nowhere to be seen. Instead of climbing into bed as planned, he pulled on a fresh change of clothes and returned to the bridge where Matt was still on duty. Dawn was just breaking to reveal a dull, gray sea under a leaden sky; waves tipped with frothy whitecaps whipped up by a freshening breeze that had backed around to the east. Blake didn't need the latest marine forecast to tell him there was a storm on the way. Nevertheless, a quick check with Environment Canada confirmed that there was a gale warning in effect with winds forecast up to forty knots and seas of up to 15 feet. Summer was clearly in rapid decline, and early autumn gales were common in this area as hurricanes raced up from the south, transitioning into powerful extratropical cyclones as they entered the North Atlantic. Nothing that *Dauntless* wasn't designed to handle, but it promised to be a rough ride, nonetheless. "Hey Matt, have you seen Kat?" he asked. Matt pointed at the door behind him.

Stifling a yawn, Blake stepped off the bridge into the adjoining war room, where he found Kat working intently on her laptop. Sliding up behind her, he reached out and gently massaged her neck and shoulders. "Hey Kat, it's been a long night, and who knows what lies ahead? Maybe we should grab a bit of sleep while we can. Besides, it looks like we're heading into the teeth of a gale which may make getting some rest later next to impossible. Besides, Rod has the entire US intelligence apparatus digging in on this. We've got to believe they will crack this in time."

Kat leaned back into Blake's hands, clearly enjoying his ministrations. "Oh... that *does* feel good. You're right, we both need some rest if we are going to be any good to anybody."

"So why are you here on your computer and not back in our suite getting a head start on your beauty rest?" Blake asked.

"I know you're right, but I just can't drop it. Not yet. Who's closer to this than us? I've been trying to work out which of Cirillo's ships are carrying the bombs. Figuring that out is the key to heading off this attack. I can't rest until then. There's too much at stake!"

"Fair enough," Blake replied as he pulled out a chair and sat down next to her. "Put it up on screen, and we'll work on it together. What have you got so far?"

"Thanks, dear." Kat tapped on her keyboard, and the display transferred to the large wall-mounted screen.

Blake studied it for a moment. "So, I'm guessing all those red dots with yellow tails represent the current positions and track of all Cirillo freighters currently operating in the Eastern Atlantic? There must be a hundred of them!"

"Eighty-nine, to be exact," Kat nodded. "I was just about to layer in another line from each ship to their next port of call."

While Kat worked on that, Blake was thinking. "We know that all twelve freighters had to interrupt their regular route to swing by La Hune Bay to pick up a bomb. Can you pull up a list of all Cirillo freighters who reported a schedule delay and then cross-reference it with the eighty-nine ships currently operating in the eastern Atlantic?"

"Good thinking, dear," Kat nodded enthusiastically. "Give me a sec."

It took some time, but thirty minutes later, seventeen ships on the screen switched from red triangles to purple triangles. "Those are the ships that had delays?" Blake asked.

Kat nodded. "I think you're on to something. Cirillo prides itself on its record for punctuality. Having seventeen of eighty-nine ships behind schedule is very unlike them.

Kat glanced at the data on her screen again, noticing something else. She sorted the list of ships in ascending order by time of next port of call… and gasped.

"What is it, Kat?"

Kat simply pointed at the display on the big screen. Blake studied it briefly and saw almost immediately what Kat had seen. Twelve ships had identical port arrival times. Twelve different ports, but the same scheduled arrival time - 1:00 am, September 22nd. "I see it," Blake said slowly. "And you know what else? Each of those ships are purple dots, meaning they reported schedule delays that could have been used as a cover for a side trip to La Hune Bay. I think we have our delivery vehicles, targets, and timeline."

"Yep," Kat agreed. "Let's get Rod back on the line."

Chapter 28

Dauntless, 25 miles south of Peggy's Cove, Nova Scotia

Rod answered at the first ring, sounding much more chipper than he had an hour previously. "Hello Blake and Kat. Doesn't sound like you guys went back to bed, either."

"Not a chance," Kat responded. "We're on the final countdown to an 'end of days' level event. This is no time to be asleep."

"Damn straight," Rod grunted in assent. "We've got every intelligence asset in the country on full alert running this down, though I'm not too proud or foolish to refuse any and all help offered. We're making progress, but I'm hoping this call means you've got a lead of your own?"

"We do," Blake confirmed. "Kat deserves most of the credit, though. We think we have identified all twelve ships carrying the bombs!"

With that, Blake walked Rod through their analysis of Cirillo freighters operating in the Atlantic that had reported schedule delays, culminating in discovering twelve of those same ships scheduled for arrival at their respective ports at the identical time.

"Fantastic work, you guys!! It does seem likely that they would want the detonations to happen simultaneously, and the best way to do that is to coordinate the port arrivals. Cross-referencing that with ships that reported scheduling delays long enough to account for a side trip to La Hune Bay to pick up a bomb is pure genius. Our guys are good, but no one has thought of that yet. Any way I can convince you to come back and work full-time for Uncle Sam? We sure could use good people like you!!"

Kat laughed at that. "You've already got us working for free, Rod – risking our lives and pulling all-nighters. Putting us on the payroll will not only cost you a lot more but, even worse, turn us into boring desk jockeys just like the rest of the bureaucratic clock-punchers you already have on the payroll." The words were delivered with twinkle in her eyes and voice that made it clear she meant no disrespect.

"You mentioned you had made some progress as well?" Blake probed.

"Yes, and your intelligence corroborates a report I had just received prior to your call. As you know, we are monitoring what we believe to be Sonja's phone. Not long ago, she placed a call to someone on board the Cirillo freighter, *Neptune,* and they spoke for seven minutes. We're trying to crack the encryption to see what was said, but I'm told that could take days, even with our best supercomputers on the job."

Blake jabbed Kat, raised his eyebrows, and mouthed, "The guy from Gangneung??"

"I would bet my life on it!!" Kat whispered excitedly in reply, nodding her head vigorously.

Rod continued. "Of course, we immediately started tracking the phone from the recipient of the call, and shortly afterwards, eleven brief calls of less than thirty seconds were placed – each to burner phones located on eleven different Cirillo freighters. They correspond exactly to the ships you identified!!"

"So, putting this all together, I think we have established a strong enough case to intercept, board, and search these ships prior to allowing them to come anywhere near a commercial port. What's the plan for that?" Kat wanted to know.

"This is a job for the US Coast Guard. I will put them on alert immediately and have them dispatch the necessary resources to get the job done," Rod assured them. "Once again, your assistance is greatly appreciated."

"We're especially concerned about *Neptune,*" Blake cautioned. "The person Sonja called is on that ship and, based on the calls issued from there, it seems that the other ships' activities are being coordinated by that same person. If it's the guy that Kat ran into in Gangneung and we later witnessed on the bridge of *Zeus*, then he has proven to be a force to be reckoned with."

"I'll let the Coast Guard know. I have full confidence in them. If *Neptune* wants to get anywhere near Boston, she'll have to go through them first," Rod said confidently. But that reminds me... we have reason to believe that the man behind Kat's kidnapping is a local thug named Song Hee who runs a drug smuggling operation in Gangneung. The men who were in the truck you guys blew up on your way out of town were members of his gang. If Song Hee was in the vehicle at the time, he must have escaped relatively unscathed."

"What would a local drug lord and gangbanger be doing mixed up in collecting radioactive material for Sonja's terrorist operation?" Kat wanted to know.

"No way of knowing at this point," Rod responded. "We don't even know what Sonja's motivation is. My personal view is Sonja has some ideological motivation – although, for the life of me, I can't think of what it might be. Song Hee is probably just a paid actor."

"It's nice to put a name to the face, Rod. I know we'll be happy to see that man brought to justice. And as you know, we are also currently headed for Boston, although well behind *Neptune*. If there is any assistance we can provide, just say the word. I mean it, Rod." There was no mistaking the sincerity in Blake's voice.

"Thanks Blake. Thanks Kat. I think you've done all that is necessary. We've got it from here—"

"One more thing," Kat interjected. "Has Sonja been rounded up?"

"Not yet," Rod replied. We are working with the Interpol and the local authorities, but they haven't been able to convince a judge to issue a warrant for her arrest. You must remember that Sonja is a powerful and well-respected diplomat. There is no way any judge is going to stick their neck out and authorize a public arrest without ironclad evidence. It was touch-and-go to even get authorization for full physical and electronic surveillance, but we now have all of her communications monitored, as well as a professional team on the ground to monitor her physical movements."

A few minutes later, they said their goodbyes and hung up. Blake and Kat just sat and looked at each other for a long moment.

"I don't like it," Kat said finally. "I can't put my finger on it, but if Song Hee is on board *Neptune*, he isn't going down without a fight. What was it Rod said? 'He would have to go through the US Coast Guard to get at Boston.' Well… what if he does just that?"

"Then we are going to be there ready to step in," Blake answered. "It's a no-brainer. We're on our way there anyway. We'll just step on the gas and see if we can catch up."

Kat smiled. "Have I told you lately how much I love you? The rational side of my brain says to trust the authorities and go to bed, but I would feel a whole lot better if we were positioned close enough to join the fight, if necessary."

"I couldn't agree more. Why don't you head back to our suite? I'll just stay on the bridge for a minute to let Matt know that we need to put *Dauntless* into 'invisible mode' and put the pedal to the metal to catch *Neptune*. Later this morning, we'll hold an all-hands-on-deck meeting to bring everyone up to speed and get to work on a plan should we be called upon."

Kat stood up and headed towards the door before turning with a thoughtful look on her face. "We've known Sonja for a long time. We are partners and friends. I know neither of us has had a lot of time to process this, but why is she doing this? I just can't fathom it!"

Blake just shook his head. "It's driving me nuts too. She's dedicated her life to making the world a better place, supporting good environmental causes with everything at her disposal. Why she would go to such lengths to plan and carry out a terrorist attack on this scale – wreaking death, destruction, and terrible environmental damage with the radioactive fallout this will cause – is beyond my pay grade. I want answers as much as you. But for now, we have to put that out of our minds and be ready to do whatever is necessary to ensure we put a stop to it."

Even as he spoke, *Dauntless* lurched violently, pitching downward and to starboard as she careened down a large wave, before coming up solid in the trough with a resounding thud. Kat wobbled before grabbing the door frame to steady herself. "What's going on?" she exclaimed.

"It's the remnants of Hurricane Matilda that brushed North Carolina yesterday," Blake explained. It has transitioned into a powerful extratropical cyclone that will make our lives miserable today."

"And slow us down," Kat muttered. "Can we still catch *Neptune?*"

Blake took a long glance at his watch. "It's going to be close, but I will ensure Matt and Scotty know the stakes and ensure they drive as hard they dare. We designed this ship to take a pounding. Today we will find out if she's up to the task. *Neptune* will be slowed somewhat by the conditions as well, but this storm is a big equalizer."

Over the next few hours, the storm intensified dramatically. The wind picked up to a steady gale force of thirty-five knots with even stronger gusts up to forty-five knots, and *Dauntless* was routinely encountering wave heights of 20 feet or more, despite the official marine forecast of 15-foot waves. First Matt, and then Scotty, who relieved him, gave no quarter to the storm nor mercy to either the ship or her crew. They needed to maintain an average speed of twenty-five knots to reach Boston by the midnight deadline Blake had imposed, and in normal circumstances, the seas were not conducive to anything more than fifteen. Nevertheless, the men grimly shoved the throttles forward, crashing the bow of *Dauntless* through the towering waves, the entire ship thrashing violently and shuddering from stem to stern.

For the crew, now up and about, it was the worst conditions they had experienced so far, and all were suffering various degrees of seasickness, except for Emily, who was entirely unfazed by it all. She seemed surprised that breakfast wasn't being served as usual, grabbing a muffin from the galley as she passed by. Biff managed to secure everything in his station, between trips to the lavatory, but soon retreated, green-faced, to his bunk. Mark and Eric weren't faring much better and soon retreated to their respective quarters as well.

Pure exhaustion eventually caught up with Blake and Kat, and they slept fitfully for several hours as the storm raged on and *Dauntless* battled relentlessly against the elements, clawing frantically forward, slowly closing the gap to *Neptune* with every passing hour. Blake thought that if ever his ship was earning her name, it was now. He couldn't help but feel a surge of pride over his creation with every heart-stopping lurch.

Shortly after noon, they got up and called everyone to the war room – everyone except for Scotty, who was needed on the bridge to navigate the ship safely through the raging seas and wring every ounce of speed out of the hard-charging *Dauntless*. As usual, Biff brought in a tray of snacks and some bottles of water, but only the irrepressible Doc

Watson partook. Eric's shirt of the day, which read, 'This is what AWESOME looks like', contrasted sharply with his grim expression and pale, greenish pallor.

Once everyone had straggled in and secured themselves to a chair around the table, Blake filled them in on everything they had learned and why they were now racing desperately through the remnants of Matilda to catch *Neptune*.

Matt had managed to squeeze a few hours of sleep in and, with his Navy background, was faring better than most. He fired the first question. "Hey boss, you said the US Coast Guard is on full alert and would be intercepting all the ships, including *Neptune*. Why, then, are we pushing so hard to catch her?"

"I'll take that one," Kat jumped in. "We have reason to believe that the man who had me kidnapped in Gangneung, and who we later identified on board *Zeus,* is running this operation from aboard *Neptune*. Rod tells us they have identified him as Song Hee, a local Korean drug lord and gangbanger. While we are fully prepared to let the Coast Guard take the lead and do their job, we know this guy is a dangerous foe. We want to be on station and prepared to step in if anything goes wrong."

"So... it has nothing to do with not losing an opportunity to dish out a little personal revenge?" Mark asked with a wink and smile.

Kat took the bait. "I'm not going to lie. That would be sweet. I would like nothing better than to meet up with that scumbag again and dish out some justice of my own."

Blake suppressed a smile, reaching out to pat her hand. "That's right dear, but hopefully it doesn't come to that, and we can let the proper authorities handle it."

Kat shot him an inscrutable look, as Blake continued. "I share Kat's concern that Song Hee and the *Neptune* may not go down without a fight. The *Neptune* is a very large ship – nearly as large as *Zeus*, far outweighing any Coast Guard vessel sent out to intercept her. As far as we are aware, she isn't armed, but still… if Song Hee forces the issue by refusing to stop and be boarded, the Coast Guard vessel will need to be prepared to use lethal force. And if they attempt the interdiction too close to shore, even that may not be enough to prevent *Neptune* from getting into the port or close enough to do major damage."

"So, we need a two-pronged plan," Matt suggested. "First of all, if the attempted interdiction takes place well out to sea, *Neptune* refuses the Coast Guard's demands to stop and be boarded, and they delay for whatever reason to sink her, we will do it ourselves."

"My pleasure," Eric said immediately, perking up noticeably at the thought. "A couple well-placed torpedoes, a handful of missiles, and some 30mm close-range cannon fire ought to do the trick. What do we need a second prong for?"

Blake chuckled. "I think Matt is worried the Coast Guard will intercept *Neptune* too close to shore. Even combining our firepower with the Coast Guard's, *Neptune's* momentum will take her even closer to shore, and they could detonate the bomb before we can sink her. The explosives probably won't have much impact from outside the harbor, but the resulting radioactive cloud could drift onshore, inflict massive casualties, and put the port out of commission for years. We can't take that chance."

"Exactly, captain," Matt confirmed.

"I'm confused," admitted Emily. "If the Coast Guard can't stop *Neptune*, and she's already in close enough to do some major damage with that bomb, what can we possibly do?"

Kat had it figured out. "The only play we have at that point is boarding her, seizing control, and ensuring the bomb is never detonated."

Matt was nodding. "Exactly what I was thinking. But does anyone have any idea how we can manage to board a mammoth ship like *Neptune*? Ideally, we'll need to do it covertly to maintain the advantage of surprise and avoid having them set off the bomb before we can gain control. The only thought I had was using the helicopter, but that would be about as stealthy as a stampede of elephants. If they have any weapons at all, they won't hesitate to open fire. It would be a suicide mission all around."

Matt's words had a quieting effect as everyone pondered the challenge. But then, a slow smile spread across Blake's face. "Hey Mark. How many hang-gliders do we have on board?"

Mark's face lit up. "Three of them. We still have them from when you, Kat, and Matt took hang-gliding lessons last spring. Are you thinking what I'm thinking?"

"I think so," Blake smiled. "We'll have the cover of darkness to our advantage, and the storm will have abated. *Dauntless* will be invisible to anyone on *Neptune*. We'll position ourselves a half mile behind our quarry and let *Dauntless* tow us up into the sky. From there, we'll cut the lines and coast down onto the top of an unsuspecting *Neptune*. We have the rest of the day and evening to figure it out from there, but three of us with the element of surprise against whoever they have? I like our odds!"

Chapter 29

Neptune, **10 miles east of Boston Harbor**

It had all come down to this. Song Hee nervously paced the bridge, pausing occasionally to bring up his binoculars to scan the distant lights that marked the entrance to Boston Harbor. The sweeping beams of the Boston Light were clearly visible dead ahead, marking both the deadly rocks of Little Brewster Island, on which it was located, as well as the start of the main shipping channel into Boston Harbor and the Conley Container Terminal. This would serve as ground zero for the powerful radioactive bomb he planned to detonate.

History mattered little to Song Hee, particularly the history of a foreign nation in a part of the world he knew only by what he had gleaned from a handful of American movies he had seen years ago. The Russian mercenary captain, however, had a far greater fascination with the United States and had apparently read up on this historic area. In heavily accented English, he was nattering on about the history of the Boston Light, currently guiding their approach. Originally built by the British in 1716, it remained in British hands throughout the American Revolution. Upon their final retreat, and under heavy American fire, the British dispatched a small crew to set a charge, blowing the top clear off the lighthouse. It was subsequently rebuilt by the Americans in 1783 with sturdy walls seven-and-a-half feet thick. Robust enough, apparently, to withstand nearly two-hundred-and-fifty years of the worst the stormy North Atlantic could throw at it. Still standing this very night, a silent witness to what Song Hee expected would be a key event in future history books.

The raging storm they had weathered over the past twenty-four hours had finally abated, the wild winds and sheets of rain having given way to scattered clouds scudding across a dark, moonless sky. The waves, still somewhat restless at four to six feet in height, were not having much effect on the giant freighter, producing just a casual roll under Song Hee's feet. Despite Helle's assurances, he was taking no chances and routinely grilled the captain on any radar contacts within 20 miles of their position. *So far, so good. No sign of Dauntless*, he thought. Moments later, however, his optimism vanished as the ship's radio crackled to life.

"This is Captain Tom Hartman of the United States Coast Guard on board the *USCGC Seneca* with an urgent message to the captain of the MV *Neptune*. You are ordered, forthwith, to come to an immediate halt and prepare for a routine boarding and inspection."

Song Hee whirled and snapped at the captain, who was already reaching for the handheld transceiver to respond. "Touch that and die," he snarled. "You are not to give any indication we have received the message. Proceed, at full speed, on our course."

The captain's first instinct was to ignore him but, glancing up, he caught sight of Song Hee's Glock 17 aimed directly at his head. He slowly placed the transceiver back in its cradle, nudged the throttles forward, and scowled back at Song Hee. "Remember, this is not our fight. We are paid well to do our jobs, but money is no good to dead men."

"If it's your life you are worried about, then you will do as I say. I'm currently the biggest threat to your meaningless life," Song Hee leered. "Where is *Seneca*, anyway? You are supposed to be keeping an eye out for all threats. Why haven't I heard of this Coast Guard nuisance before now?"

The Russian captain's face darkened into a mask of fury, but he managed to keep his voice level as he answered. "The Coast Guard routinely patrols the entrances to the channel, but it is unheard of to request to board a legitimate commercial freighter on the high seas. Boardings and inspections, if necessary, are normally conducted dockside. There was no reason, until now, to think her presence was a threat to our mission."

"No reason to suspect the Coast Guard is a threat to our mission!?" Song Hee repeated slowly, derision dripping from his voice. "What about the massive radioactive bomb we are carrying!! Is that not a reason to worry about armed law enforcement? You are a fool!! Where is that ship?"

The captain gave no reply, merely pointing dead ahead. Song Hee brought his binoculars to bear in the direction the captain was pointing and could clearly make out the running lights and outline of the Coast Guard cutter. "What's the range, and is she moving in our direction?" he demanded.

The captain glanced down at his radar display. "She's currently just over 3 miles from our position and appears to be holding steady. At our current speed, we will be on top of her in thirteen minutes."

The ship's radio crackled to life once more. "This is Captain Tom Hartman of the *USCGC Seneca*. I repeat. Stand by to be boarded. Acknowledge immediately. This is an order!" The words were followed by the sudden appearance of a strong searchlight, which shot out from *Seneca* and painted *Neptune* starkly against the dark waters and sky, illuminating the bridge as if it was broad daylight.

The Russian captain looked to Song Hee for his orders. There was no hesitation. "Maintain radio silence. Full steam ahead. Steer directly towards that cutter. If she moves off our path, adjust your course accordingly."

***Dauntless*, 11 miles east of Boston Harbor**

Dauntless had managed to close the gap to her quarry, but it had been a tough slog, enduring long hours of relentless abuse courtesy of the elements stirred into a frenzy by Matilda's fury. As far as Scotty could tell, the ship was relatively unscathed, but he would need to give her a thorough inspection when this was all over. By 9:00 pm, the worst of it was behind them, and the wind and waves began to ease. As the lights of Boston revealed themselves over the horizon, twinkling merrily against the clearing skies, they had closed within a mile of *Neptune*, her vast, dark outline clearly visible dead ahead. Running in complete darkness and with her full suite of radar stealth technologies deployed, *Dauntless* was effectively invisible to the numerous vessels operating in the surrounding waters. Cognizant of the risks this entailed, Blake had taken over the helm, with Matt and Scotty both assisting in keeping a careful watch and helping him steer around any potential collision threats.

It had been a long day battling Matilda, sleep deprivation, and seasickness - with most of the afternoon spent preparing for a potential boarding mission. Planning they all hoped - with the possible exception of Kat – would not become necessary. With the endgame rapidly approaching, the entire crew gathered on the bridge. The easing of the storm had revived their appetites, and they gratefully consumed the strong coffee and ham sandwiches that Biff had brought. Fatigue gave way to renewed energy and nervous tension as the caffeine, calories, and adrenaline took effect. There was only one question on everyone's mind. *"Where was the Coast Guard?"*

That question was finally answered when they picked up Captain Hartman's challenge issued from the bridge of *Seneca*. "Kat, can you look up *Seneca's* technical specifications?" Blake asked. "Specifically, her tonnage and armaments. We need to know if she's capable of putting *Neptune* down, if it comes to that. And, Matt, what is her position?"

Matt had just located her. "She's positioned about 7 miles out from the entrance to the harbor in the main shipping channel just south of Little Brewster Island, covering the only approach *Neptune* has available. There are too many small islands and shoals scattered about to gain entrance to the harbor any other way."

Blake shook his head. "Blocking the channel would be a good tactical move in any other situation; however, given we are potentially dealing with a large cloud of deadly radioactive material, I wish they would have conducted the interception further out from shore. With the prevailing onshore winds tonight, even if the bomb were detonated at a range of 5-10 miles, it would be disastrous. What can you tell us about *Seneca*, Kat?"

"She's a *Famous*-class cutter with a length of 270 feet and displacing 1,800 metric tonnes. Her armaments consist of a single MK 75 62-caliber naval gun and two 50-caliber machine guns," Kat replied, reading off the screen of her laptop.

Matt scowled in disgust and shook his head, which Blake picked up on immediately. "You don't look impressed, Matt. What are you thinking?" he asked.

"They've sent a scrappy terrier out to confront a raging rhino! Just look at the size discrepancy. You've got the 1,800-tonne *Seneca* going up against the 175,000-tonne *Neptune*?! Give me a break. That's nearly a one-hundred-fold size difference!"

"Yes, but our little terrier *Seneca* has teeth to back up its bark," Emily pointed out. "And no doubt, it is much faster and more agile."

"I'll give you faster and more agile, but that is a limited advantage given the narrow channel they've chosen in which to stage the confrontation," Matt replied. "And also, those teeth aren't what you might think. Those guns are primarily defensive weapons and, paired with a top-notch fire control radar like *Seneca*'s MK 92, their accuracy and high rate of fire make them a formidable anti-missile or anti-aircraft system. Even used against the small, fast surface ships favored by drug smugglers, they can be very effective. But to try and slow or sink a massive, fully loaded freighter like *Neptune*... they might as well be peppering it with a pellet gun. It's just the wrong tool for the job. This mission calls for a full-on naval destroyer equipped with some real stopping power."

Scotty had been alternately studying the radar screen and using a pair of night-vision binoculars to keep an eye on *Neptune* in front of them. "Aye, it doesn't look like our man, Song Hee, is paying any heed whatsoever to Captain Hartman. *Neptune* is continuing on course and, if anything, has increased its forward speed."

As he finished speaking, they picked up Captain Hartman's second, sterner broadcast. They waited in vain for any response from *Neptune*. Instead, she continued to barrel ahead in silence, closing quickly on Little Brewster Island and the Boston Light.

"I have a really bad feeling about this," Blake said grimly. "We need to be ready to act immediately if *Neptune* somehow gets past *Seneca*. Kat, Matt... you guys are with me. It's time to gear up. Mark, get two drones in the air. I need you and Eric to be our eyes and ears, and be ready to provide some additional fire support, if needed. But this is, first and foremost, a stealth mission. Our best hope to prevent the detonation of that bomb, not to mention secure our own survival, is to seize control and disable the crew before they know we are on to them.

USCGC Seneca, five miles east of Boston Harbor

Captain Tom Hartman was losing patience. Neither of his warnings had elicited any discernable response from *Neptune*, and even worse, she was bearing down quickly on the position he had established, facing north broadside to *Neptune*'s angle of approach, directly in the center of the channel. There was not enough room on either side of him for *Neptune* to squeeze by without going aground. *A foolproof plan*, he thought grimly. But despite her apparent lack of options,

Neptune's imposing bulk continued to bear down on them, undeterred and silent.

He raised the transceiver to his lips a third time and depressed the 'transmit' button. "This is Captain Tom Hartman, *USCGC Seneca*, with your third and final warning. You are on a direct collision course with my vessel and must immediately run your engines full astern, come to a full stop, and stand by for boarding and inspection. You have thirty seconds to comply, or we will open fire. Govern yourself accordingly!"

Turning to his Chief Weapons Officer, Alvin Bailey, he barked, "Mark thirty seconds. If there is no response, be ready to fire a warning burst over the bridge on my command."

Lieutenant Commander Wilson, at the helm, was looking nervous. "Captain, *Neptune* has just closed to less than a mile and is still making twelve knots. She will be on top of us within minutes. What do we do?"

"Steady Lieutenant Commander. Hold our current position. Be ready to go full ahead, on my command, in case we need to take evasive action." If *Neptune's* captain wished to play a dangerous game of chicken on the open seas, he would find a foe equal to the task. The United States Coast Guard did not stand down!

But neither, apparently, did *Neptune*. Hartman timed thirty seconds, and still on, she came, her hulking shadow looming ever larger. "Ready Mr. Bailey? On my mark... Fire!!"

All three guns roared to life, sending a triple stream of tracers arcing towards the oncoming freighter. One stream just cleared the top of the bridge, another streaked down the starboard side, while the third brushed the port side. *It's an impressive display of firepower,* Captain

Hartman thought to himself. *They'll think twice before messing with the United States Coast Guard in the future!*

Moments later, the guns fell silent, but still *Neptune* rushed toward them. Captain Hartman grabbed his transceiver. "Full Stop. Now!!" he screamed. "This is your final warning. Prepare to be fired upon!!"

No answer was apparently forthcoming. *Neptune* continued to close on a direct collision, her hulking outline dwarfing his much smaller vessel. "Fire at will," Hartman yelled to his Chief Weapons Officer. "Full ahead. Come around thirty degrees to starboard as we come up to speed!" Hartman intended to move his ship out of the path of the oncoming freighter and then turn sharply to stay in the channel, all the while spraying *Neptune* with deadly fire.

***Neptune*, six miles offshore, on final approach to Boston Harbor.**

The Russian captain threw the throttles in full reverse as the warning shots from *Seneca* arced overhead and down both sides of the freighter. Song Hee's handgun was still pointed at the captain's head, and without a moment's hesitation, he pulled the trigger from point-blank range, splattering the captain's brains messily onto the large window in front of them. Song Hee quickly stepped over the lifeless body and shoved the throttles forward once again, simultaneously taking the helm and keeping the bow of *Neptune* pointed dead-center at the Coast Guard cutter's silhouette. Grabbing the ship's intercom, he broadcast an urgent message to the remainder of the crew. "This is your captain, Song Hee. We are under attack from the US Coast Guard. Every man to his station and brace for imminent impact. This mission is still a go."

He had no sooner finished speaking when *Seneca*'s guns opened fire again, except this time they meant business, the heavy slugs tearing into the steel hull, the shipping containers, and the superstructure of *Neptune*. By good fortune, only a handful of slugs tore through the bridge as Song Hee ducked low and hung on grimly. Straightening briefly, he made out *Seneca's* late movement to get out of *Neptune's* path, and adjusted his steering input accordingly, doing his best to keep *Neptune's* bow pointed directly amidships of the Coast Guard vessel. Gritting his teeth with determination, he jammed the throttles to their stops and kept steering into *Seneca's* turn, all the while ignoring the hundreds of shells tearing into his ship. Eventually, he knew they would take their toll, but not soon enough to do his quarry any good. It was all but over now, the giant freighter's colossal mass and forward momentum sealing the much smaller cutter's fate.

With a grinding crunch and ear-splitting shriek of steel tearing into steel, *Neptune's* bow smashed into *Seneca* broadside, just forward of amidships, approximately level with the bridge. The collision barely broke *Neptune's* momentum, as her sharp bow literally tore the cutter in two, before rolling both sections of the doomed ship down the length of her massive hull. Glancing up at the screen displaying the view aft of the ship, Song Hee could briefly see two sections of hull surface briefly, only to slip beneath the waves just moments later. He suspected his ship was mortally wounded too, but the engines were still pounding away, and the steerage was intact. It would either stay afloat long enough for him to position it in the harbor, arm the bomb, and slip away… or it wouldn't. He would find out soon enough.

Dauntless, Five miles outside Boston Harbor

Matt, Scotty, Biff, and Emily stared in horror from the bridge of *Dauntless* as the stunning events unfolded in front of them. The drone Mark had launched just moments before had given them a bird's eye view of the entire scene. As Matt had predicted, the small naval cannon and 50-caliber machine guns were no match for 175,000 tonnes of freighter and cargo under full steam. They saw *Seneca* gun her engines at the last minute in a desperate attempt to evade the giant freighter. But it was too late, and there was not enough room to utilize her greater speed and maneuverability effectively in the tight channel.

With every fiber of their being, they willed the cutter forward, out of the path of *Neptune*, but it was not to be. With the soundtrack of a thunderous boom and the screaming of tearing metal playing across the water, *Neptune* ended *Seneca*'s existence. It was all over in seconds, the drone camera seconding from a better angle what *Neptune*'s camera had also witnessed and transmitted to Song Hee. Two large sections of *Seneca*'s hull briefly bobbed in *Neptune*'s wake before plummeting to the bottom of the channel, and *Neptune*, with her deadly radioactive bomb on board, surged forward towards the entrance to the harbor with nothing in her path to stop her.

Blake, Kat, and Matt were positioned out on the stern of *Dauntless*, jet-black hang gliders strapped to their backs and ready to launch. They had heard *Seneca*'s guns firing, followed by the awful sounds of the collision and feared the worst.

"Report!" came Blake's urgent voice through the speaker on the bridge.

"*Neptune* has just rammed *Seneca* and is proceeding on course to Boston Harbor. The Coast Guard cutter was rolled under *Neptune's* hull, came up in two sections, and sank immediately," Scotty reported matter-of-factly. "It looks like it is a good thing we arrived as backup. We're the only thing standing in the way of that bomb now."

"Listen carefully," came Blake's response, loud and clear. "Contact Rod and tell him what happened and that we are covertly boarding *Neptune* to gain control of the ship and thwart the attack. He is, by no means, to call in an airstrike on it. First, it will obviously put us in harm's way, and he doesn't want that on his conscience, but more importantly, the bomb is too close to a heavily populated urban center to risk unleashing all that *radiocaesium*. Secondly, I want Biff and Emily to launch the RHIB and conduct a search for survivors of *Seneca*. If, by some miracle, someone got off that ship, I want them picked up and brought on board *Dauntless*. May God have mercy on their souls. Mark is on drones. Eric is on weapons. Scotty, you have command of *Dauntless*. Wish us luck. We are launching now."

With that, Blake gave a curt nod towards Kat, who unclipped from the cable anchoring her to the deck. Her hang glider, taut in the breeze created by Dauntless' forward momentum, whisked her instantly off the deck, the one-thousand-foot tow cable uncoiling rapidly behind her. Seconds later, Matt unclipped and was whisked into the air, with Blake following close behind. Moments later, all three were yanked to a halt as their tow lines played out, towed aloft by *Dauntless*, now closing quickly on *Neptune*, still churning gamely towards the harbor entrance four miles distant.

Chapter 30

4 miles east of Boston Harbor

From their position high above and to the rear of *Neptune*, the three-person assault team surveyed their target. The plan had four straightforward objectives. The first was to board the ship undetected. Should they be spotted on approach, they would be sitting ducks to enemy fire. Even worse, it could trigger a decision to detonate the bomb early. Having boarded the ship without raising any alarms, they planned to split up to accomplish the second and third objectives. Kat and Matt's mission was to seize control of the bridge, bring *Neptune* to a halt, and open communications with the authorities. Blake's objective would be to locate the bomb and secure it. The fourth and final objective was to kill or capture all individuals on board *Neptune*, not named Blake, Kat, or Matt. The most recent update from Rod had confirmed that the entire crew were Russian mercenaries hired specifically for the mission, and were therefore considered terrorists posing a clear and present danger to the security of the United States. They were to be stopped by any means necessary – up to and including lethal force.

Mark's voice crackled in their ears. "We have a problem. They have stationed a sentry on top of the containers at the stern of the ship. There is no indication he has seen anything amiss yet, but you will almost certainly be spotted as you make your approach."

"Roger that Mark," Blake replied. "Kat, you're going to have to take him out on approach."

Kat had an M24 sniper rifle strapped to her back, equipped with an AN/PVS-10 Sniper Night Sight scope. Together, and when paired with the 175-grain 7.62 x 51mm Hollow Point Boat Tail projectiles, the rifle had an effective range of 2,600 feet. Kat had one round preloaded in the firing chamber, with five additional rounds loaded in the magazine—six shots to take out the target. In broad daylight, with the barrel stabilized on terra firma, it was child's play for a person of Kat's skill. Though shooting at night from a hang glider at a moving target atop a heaving ship and never even having practiced or trained for such a scenario? Kat had no idea if she was up to the task. But no choice, either. She would have to approach as close as they dared, let go of the control bar, and reach behind to grasp her weapon. It would have to be quick and smooth. Grasp the weapon, aim, and shoot. Swallowing hard, she replied with as much confidence as she could muster, "Understood. And Mark... keep your eyes peeled on the target. Let me know the instant he appears to have spotted us. That will be my cue to take the shot."

The onshore breeze was working to their advantage as, together with the stored gravitational energy that eight-hundred feet of altitude provided, it would enable them to catch *Neptune* before they hit the water. It was go-time, and Blake gave the command. "OK then. On my mark, detach from the towrope, and we'll begin our approach. Kat, obviously, will take the lead. Matt and I will follow single-file behind. Ready everyone? Five, four, three, two, one, release!"

Kat went first, releasing the tow cable and pushing forward on her tow bar to begin her descent and increase her speed. Matt counted to three and did the same, followed a beat later by Blake. Kat couldn't help but feel the immense pressure of the situation. With limited hang-gliding experience, she now had to use every ounce of her concentration to select her landing point and maintain the proper angle of descent. Too steep, and they would hit the water behind their target. Too shallow, and they wouldn't have the necessary speed to catch *Neptune,* which would also result in cold, wet failure. Putting all her trust in Mark to watch the sentry, she concentrated entirely on the task at hand, aiming at a landing spot approximately amidships and then doing her best to match the rate she was approaching *Neptune* with the rate she was losing altitude.

Blake and Matt were putting their trust in Kat to guide them in, following close on her heels. Keeping in single file also reduced their visual profile from the perspective of the sentry at the stern of *Neptune,* which they all hoped would allow them to get close enough for Kat to successfully neutralize the sentry before he could raise the alarm. And though Blake was fully committed to following Kat – succeeding together or failing together – he was also carefully gauging their angle of descent and closing speed. As best he could tell, if the wind held and *Neptune* maintained her current speed, they appeared to be on target to land smack dab in the middle of the vast expanse of the stacked shipping containers laid out in front of them like a giant runway. "Atta' girl, Kat," he thought proudly. Taking a glance behind, he could barely make out a smear of white in the water, marking the wake of *Dauntless,* now falling back a bit as planned. Other than that, she was invisible against the dark water, and he was confident would remain invisible to the crew of *Neptune*.

As they closed to within four-hundred feet from the stern of Neptune, Mark's excited voice crackled in their ear once again. "Now, Kat!! I think our guy may have spotted you. He is definitely looking up in your direction." Kat could make out the target clearly; his silhouette was framed sharply against the lights of *Neptune*. Taking a deep breath to settle her nerves, she steadied the hang-glider, released the control bar, and grasped her weapon. Pulling it free, she lined up her target as best she could and squeezed the trigger. The rifle cracked sharply, but a slight gust of wind caused the hang glider to jerk upwards just as she fired, and the bullet sailed harmlessly above the man's head. The man reacted by dropping to a crouch and reaching for his radio. With one hand, she grabbed the control bar to steady her hang glider. Releasing it again, she reloaded, aimed, and fired. This time, the round found its mark, as against all odds, the man keeled over and lay still. Quickly sheathing her rifle and regaining control of the hang-glider once more, Kat couldn't believe her luck. She was certain she couldn't hit that shot more than once in ten tries. Mark quickly confirmed the kill. "He's down. He's down. Way to go, Kat! That was incredible!!"

Kat's mouth was dry. "Beginner's luck," she managed. "We've still got a lot to do before we can celebrate, starting with landing safely."

"Atta' go girl!!" Blake exclaimed. "Now, take us in." In single file, the trio of dark shadows closed quickly on the large freighter, passing over the stern at a height of approximately thirty feet. Kat touched down first, flaring gently to scrub off speed, and landing lightly on both feet at a trot, quickly collapsing the wings to avoid being swept back up. Matt landed next, catching a late side wind that caused him to land a bit awkwardly. After a slight stumble, he regained control and hobbled to a halt. "I twisted my ankle on the landing, but I think I can still get around okay," he assured them. Blake came in hot, overflew the other two before executing a perfect flare and landing softly.

They quickly folded and secured the hang-gliders, finding a crevice between the shipping containers large enough to wedge them into. Mark broke in once again on the coms, "Nice landing, guys. The Russian judge gives you a perfect ten! Even better, I don't see any signs of you having been spotted, although you need to move quickly to get off the top of those containers. Despite your dark clothing, your silhouettes are visible against the horizon."

"Roger that, Mark. We're on our way." To the others, he gestured towards the hulking superstructure at the bow of the ship. "Let's hustle directly to the base of the superstructure. We only have about ten minutes before this ship enters the harbor, and they could blow that device at any time – but as long as they think they are in the clear, I think they will wait until at least then."

The other two nodded in agreement. "We're all betting our lives on that assessment, but the bottom line is, the sooner that bomb is secured or disabled, the better," Matt observed dryly.

"Well then, no time to lose," Blake responded. "Time to split up. You and Kat make your way to the bridge and seize control of the ship while I find and secure the bomb. If you can't respond verbally on comms, one click means 'I'm ok, I just can't speak right now.' Two clicks mean, 'I'm in trouble and need help.'" With that, Blake gave Kat a quick kiss and quickly scurried off, heading towards the starboard side of the superstructure, where he quickly disappeared out of sight.

Matt nudged Kat. "Let's go. I'll lead. You watch our six."

On the bridge, Song Hee was grimly set on finishing the mission. There was nothing else left for him. His criminal organization back home, his only means of livelihood, was wiped out. He had bet everything on this venture. Without success and the large payday Helle had dangled in front of him, he was convinced his life was over. Now that he had slammed into, and destroyed, that Coast Guard cutter, he was doubly committed. As a mass murderer of duly appointed law enforcement officers, he would be shown no mercy. The best he could hope for, if caught, was a life behind bars. The only thing left was to bring the freighter into the harbor, arm the bomb, and attempt to escape in the mass confusion that followed. The money he received from Helle would enable him to start a new life with a new identity far from US authorities.

He knew his cover was blown the moment the Coast Guard attempted to apprehend his ship. It did not surprise him in the least when, one by one, reports came in from the other freighter captains that they had been apprehended and boarded, their missions ending in failure. Glancing at the screen showing the video feed from the rear-facing camera, he froze. Toggling a switch, he zoomed in closer and could make out three dark figures moving towards the bridge across the top of the shipping containers, which was odd considering he had only posted a single sentry in that area. Grabbing his radio, he barked, "I've got eyes on three men moving across the top of the cargo towards the superstructure. Report in immediately and confirm your positions." One by one, except for the sentry, his men reported in. None of them were currently atop the ship. Somehow, as impossible as it seemed, *Neptune* had been boarded! He depressed his mic again. "We at least three unknown intruders last seen approaching the superstructure from the stern. They are to be stopped by any means necessary!" With that, he made a snap decision. Switching control from manual to autopilot, which he had preprogrammed to follow the shipping channel into the middle of the harbor, he quickly made his way to the port stairwell and headed down – keeping his trusty Glock aimed in front of him. It was time to arm the bomb and make his getaway!

Mat began cautiously edging his way in the direction Blake had disappeared moments before, limping a bit on his injured ankle. Kat followed close behind, watching their backs. Both kept their handguns out and at the ready. At the far end, they found an unlocked door and cautiously eased it open, finding a deserted metal stairwell that wound its way up seven levels, past the crew quarters, to the bridge above. Matt held up his hand, halting. "Hey boss, we have just entered the starboard stairwell on our way to the bridge. Where are you?"

"I came in the same door and exited the stairwell on Deck Two. I heard some voices, and I plan to try and capture one or more crew members. It might require a little friendly persuasion, but I think they'll be happy to tell me where the bomb is located," came Blake's whispered response.

"Roger that boss. We are proceeding up to the bridge."

With that, Matt and Kat began climbing up the stairwell, moving quicker now. They paused again at the top, just outside the door to the bridge. "Ready?" Matt whispered. Kat nodded and mouthed, "Go!" She was convinced that Song Hee was on the other side of that door, and every fiber in her being was electrified with anticipation. Matt turned and flung the door open, gun out in front of him, sweeping the bridge. It was empty, save for a prone figure, clearly dead, his blood and brains splattered all over the window in front of his body.

Kat rushed over, taking a quick glance at the man's face. "It's not Song Hee. Take control of the ship and bring it to a halt. I'm heading back down to assist Blake. Lock both doors behind me and radio the authorities to let them know that we have control and are in the process of securing the bomb." With that, she whirled and ran out the door they had entered moments before.

Kat had no sooner entered the stairwell when she noted the abrupt change in the note of *Neptune*'s engines, as they reversed and began to slow her forward speed, inducing considerable vibrations throughout the ship that made the entire metal stairwell chatter noisily. At that moment, Mark's voice sounded through her headset once again. "I've got a runner exiting the port stairwell at the rear of the superstructure and sprinting toward the stern. He could be going for the bomb!"

Blake heard him too. Abandoning his plan to capture a crewmember, he whirled and ran back to the stairwell at full speed, leaping down the eight-step sets in a single bound, and charging back outside onto the tops of the shipping containers. He immediately spotted his target running hard towards the stern and making a beeline towards a single shipping container, sitting by itself atop the others. He had noted it on the way in, positioned as it was nearly directly amidships, isolated, and easily accessible. 'It had to be the location of the bomb!!', he thought grimly. The man had to be stopped at all costs. Blake aimed and fired three shots in quick succession. Expert marksman that he was, no handgun had reliable accuracy at that range. Holstering his gun for the moment, Blake began sprinting after the man, hollering into his headset, "I'm in pursuit of the runner. I think he is headed towards the bomb to set it off. We can't let him get to that container!"

He was relieved to hear Kat responding, "We have secured the bridge. Matt has taken over the helm and is calling in reinforcements. I'm on my way down to back you up."

Song Hee heard the shots from behind him and felt the three bullets whiz past him. Glancing behind, he saw Blake sprinting after him and redoubled his efforts, weaving to make himself a more difficult target. Reaching the container, he was forced to pause to undo the latches, making himself a stationary target for his pursuer. Indeed, two more bullets clanged against the metal only inches from his head, forcing him to abandon his position before he could get the door open. He cursed under his breath and quickly dove around the right side of the container, which offered temporary cover from the angle of Blake's pursuit. He proceeded to the opposite end of the container and crouched low. Peering around the other side, he squeezed off a few rounds at his pursuer, but missed his quickly closing target, who fired back, causing Song Hee to pull back under cover. "I'm pinned down behind the bomb container taking fire from one of the intruders!" he barked on his radio. "Where is everyone? Get out here immediately and take him out!!"

Kat had made her way down five of the seven decks on the starboard stairwell when two crewmen suddenly burst into the stairwell from the deck below. She fired instinctively and nailed one of them in the shoulder. The man screamed and went down hard. His partner whirled and managed a hasty shot in Kat's direction. The bullet sailed wide, struck the metal landing above Kat's head and ricocheted back down, narrowly missing her a second time. The first man, though injured and losing blood, was still able to draw his weapon. Kat aimed and fired before he could get a shot off, and this time her aim was true, drilling him in the forehead, his lifeless body slumping back down to the steel landing. The second man jumped back through the door into the corridor behind him, safely undercover for the moment. Kat's predicament was that she had no time for a prolonged stand-off. She needed to get past him in order to render assistance to Blake. All their lives depended on ensuring that the bomb didn't go off. She had an idea. She began to gasp and whimper, leaning down to scrape her gun across the metal landing. Seeing no movement, she intensified her acting efforts, moaning loudly as if in great pain. It was working. She observed the man's gun slowly poke out of the doorway, followed by his arm. Continuing to moan and gasp, she got into position and steadied her aim. The instant the man's upturned face appeared in her sights, she squeezed the trigger, ending his life.

Jumping up, she charged down the remaining two levels, levered open the door, and peered out.

Blake covered the last fifty feet to the cargo container and took cover. He noted the doors were still safely latched. "Mark, do you have eyes on the guy I was chasing?"

"Yes sir," Mark replied immediately. He is on the opposite end of the container. I'd say you guys are in a stalemate."

"OK. Let me know if he attempts to come around one of the sides. In the meantime, and this is important, is there a set of doors on his end?"

"Hang on…" After a brief pause, Mark confirmed, "No sir. Looks like the only access doors are on your end. And our guy is doing much the same as you for the moment. Just sitting there trying to figure out his next move."

Blake breathed a huge sigh of relief. He felt sure that the bomb was located inside this container, and for the moment, he took great comfort in the risks the guy was taking to get to the bomb. It likely meant that it wasn't on a timer, capable of being armed remotely, or had a geolocation arming device that would cause it to detonate once it reached a preprogrammed set of coordinates. No... it seemed like it required someone to manually arm it. And that gave them time and options.

Just then, he heard Kat through his headset. "Blake, I'm back outside. Is that you I see taking cover behind that shipping container?"

Blake looked back and waved in the direction of the superstructure. "OK. I see you waving. I understand the guy you're chasing is on the other side?"

"Indeed," Blake replied. "I've got an idea. With Mark's help, I'll keep him pinned down while you come join me." Blake spoke again... "Scotty, are you listening in?"

"Aye, sir," Scotty replied immediately.

"Bring *Dauntless* alongside. I want Eric covering the entire length of *Neptune* with his 30mm machine guns. If any other enemies pop up, he will be able to take them out quickly.

"We are nearly in position," Scotty confirmed.

"Ok Kat, you ready?"

Kat took a deep breath. "Cover me." And with that, she took off running.

Blake saw her coming and kept careful watch to ensure no one else appeared behind her while Mark kept his drone's camera glued on Song Hee. "Our guy is taking a peek down the port side of the container," he warned. Blake calmly took a couple of steps, reached around the side, and squeezed off a warning round. "Ok. That worked. He's backed away from the side again," Mark confirmed.

Moments later, Kat joined him. "What now?" she asked.

"I was thinking I'd boost you onto the top of the container, and you could take him out from above,"

"Ok. Sounds good. Let's do it," Kat agreed readily.

Song Hee was getting impatient. "Where are you guys? I need the man guarding the doors of the bomb container taken out! He's got me pinned on the far side! We are running out of time!"

"We're coming boss. We were on our way up to the bridge when we heard gunshots in the starboard stairwell and couldn't raise two of our guys who were using it to come to your assistance. They are both dead, sir!!"

"Get out here, now!!" came Song Hee's terse reply.

Blake leaned down and laced his fingers together, making a pocket for Kat to place her foot. With a single quick motion, he boosted her high enough to grasp the top of the container and pull herself up and over. While Kat made her way quickly and quietly to the opposite side, Blake fired a single shot down each side of the container to distract their foe. Pausing momentarily to focus, Kat took a breath, gun at the ready, and leaned over the top. Suddenly there was a commotion at the far end as two more crewmen exited the superstructure and began firing wildly at her and Blake.

Song Hee was cursing the ineptitude of the Russian gangsters hired for the job. It felt like he had been waiting forever for backup to arrive even though, in reality, it had been only a few short minutes. But in that time, it had become obvious that his enemies were in control of the ship, as the engines were now running in full reverse, slowing *Neptune* dramatically. No doubt, the full cavalry would be arriving shortly and his time window to arm the bomb and make his getaway was closing fast. Just then, a voice screamed in his ear, "Look out above!!!" Song Hee glanced up just in time to see a gun extending in his direction, followed by a face that had haunted his dreams for weeks. He dove instinctively to his right just in time, Kat's shot just grazing his head.

Kat instantly recognized the upturned face as her tormentor from Gangneung, Song Hee himself. The shock and blinding rage surging through her delayed her reactions just enough to allow the man to avoid her shot aimed directly at his head. With the hail of gunfire that had erupted behind her and bullets flying, she was out of time. As Song Hee rolled, she instinctively leaped, crashing into him and bringing her gun hand down hard on his in a desperate attempt to knock the weapon out of his hand. It worked!! Song Hee's gun clattered to the deck, just out of his reach. But in doing so, she lost the grip on her own gun as it, too, hit the deck and skittered away.

Blake dropped prone to the deck to minimize his profile, quickly reloaded with a fresh magazine, and began firing back gallantly at the new attackers, slowing their approach. The attackers were still out of reliable handgun range; however, it was only a matter of time before someone got lucky. Blake didn't like the two-against-one odds stacked against him and needed to quickly tilt the table in his favor. "Scotty!! Eric!! I'm taking fire from two men advancing towards my position from the superstructure. Are you in position to lend assistance?"

"Just got here, Captain," came Eric's calm voice. "Sit tight. I've got 'em."

A moment later, machine-gun fire from *Dauntless* raked the deck, causing the two gunmen to quickly scramble back inside.

"I'll keep an eye on them, boss. They won't cause you any more trouble."

"Thanks Eric. Hey guys, Kat went over the top of the container to take out the goon on the other side. What's her status?"

Mark answered. "You need to get over there, Blake. Kat jumped down and is in the fight of her life. We don't have a clean shot."

Kat dropped onto Song Hee like a ton of bricks, slamming him to the rough metal container tops with such force that the air was expelled from his lungs with an audible grunt. She didn't allow him any time to recover, following it up by slamming her elbow into his face with all her might. It stunned him briefly, but he recovered quickly, grabbing the first thing he could see - Kat's long blonde ponytail – yanking down brutally and snapping her head back. Kat responded by delivering a hard back kick aimed at Song Hee's crotch, but it missed its mark. The fight then quickly devolved into a chaotic grapple, both of them scratching and clawing desperately to gain the advantage. Kat's martial arts training did her little good in this type of combat, and Song Hee's superior size and strength began to win out.

He finally managed to tie her up from behind, wrapping his legs around her lower body and locking his feet together. He then squeezed his forearm under her tightly wedged chin and began to apply pressure against her carotid artery while simultaneously jerking their bodies towards his gun. Kat continued to writhe and buck frantically, even as darkness began to cloud her peripheral vision as her oxygen supply was inexorably squeezed off. Just when she thought she could hold out no longer, the pressure eased, and her head began to clear… and she felt the cold dread of a gun barrel pressed against her temple.

"Drop it!!" Blake screamed as he burst around the corner, his gun aimed in the direction of Song Hee's head. He dared not shoot immediately for fear of hitting Kat. "It's all over."

Song Hee kept his gun barrel locked on Kat's head while carefully levering them both into a standing position, facing Blake, and keeping his head and body shielded behind Kat. "You drop it," he leered. "You have three seconds before I blow this pretty little lady's head off."

"Don't do it, Blake!" Kat pleaded. "It's Song Hee! You have to stop him and secure the bomb!"

Blake locked eyes with Kat, giving her a calm but determined look. He would comply with Song Hee's order. But they were not giving up. Blake held both hands up, gun facing up and away, before slowly crouching down and laying the gun on the deck. He did not take his eyes off Kat and Song Hee for a moment.

"Kick your gun over to me," Song Hee barked.

Blake did as he was commanded, and his gun clattered across the deck and came to a stop at Song Hee's feet. Song Hee glanced down, undecided whether he should pick it up. In that moment, Blake and Kat locked eyes once again, both knowing instinctively that this was their one chance. With Song Hee momentarily distracted, Kat executed a lightning-quick *Harai Goshi* – a classic Judo throw. Sweeping her right foot across the front of Song Hee's legs, she ducked low, twisted to her left, and rotated Song Hee's mass over her right hip and hard onto his back. It was textbook perfect. She followed it up with a chopping heel stomp to his throat, crushing his trachea. That wasn't any particular martial arts technique that she was aware of. It just felt right in the moment.

Blake scooted over, retrieved his gun, and aimed it directly at Song Hee's head while Kat stepped clear. Somehow the man still retained a grip on his own weapon even though the hard fall and blow to the throat had robbed him of his breath and most of his senses. But he just could not admit defeat. Could not bring himself to surrender.

With a demonic grin, he willed his arm to move, the gun slowly rising off the deck. From six feet away, Blake could only shake his head sadly. His weapon cracked one more time, a small round hole materializing between Song Hee's eyes as his lifeless body slumped to the deck.

Blake and Kat wrapped their arms around each other, and for a long moment, it was as if they were the only two people in the world - savoring the preciousness and fragility of life and the joy of sharing it with each other. It was over far too soon, their reverie broken by the sound of approaching helicopters and a searchlight waving back and forth across the top of the ship that had now come to a complete stop.

Matt's voice sounded in their ears. "Two National Guard CH-47 Chinook helicopters are inbound, carrying a total of 75 troops, including an *Explosive Ordnance Disposal* (*EOD*) team. What's your status?"

Before answering, Blake unlatched and threw open the container doors. Inside, as they suspected, was the unmistakable outline of a large bomb with a digital control panel open and facing them. "We have located and secured the bomb. It's inside a shipping container sitting approximately amidships on top of the load. There are at least two bad guys still holed up inside. Four others have been killed."

"That's five down altogether, including the dead guy we found on the bridge," Kat corrected. "Keep the doors locked until we confirm the other two at large are secured. Blake and I will meet the reinforcements."

The two Chinooks settled down, and Blake and Kat quickly briefed the commander on the situation. Moments later, the remaining two Russian crewmen exited the superstructure, approaching slowly with their hands on their heads before laying face-down on the deck. They were quickly surrounded, handcuffed, and taken into custody. Kat guided the six-person *EOD* team to the container with the bomb, where they quickly got down to business rendering it harmless.

"That's a wrap, folks," Blake announced over the radio. "The authorities can take it from here. Matt, you can leave the bridge and meet us down here. We'll be back on board *Dauntless* shortly for a well-earned champagne shower. Over and out."

Chapter 31

Epilogue

An hour later, a weary Blake, Kat, and Matt were ferried back to *Dauntless* in one of *Neptune*'s lifeboats. Plans for the celebratory champagne shower were shelved in light of the grim news from Biff and Emily, who were relieved of duty following an all-out response from the Coast Guard's local search and rescue detachment that included twelve surface vessels supported by both helicopter and fixed-wing aircraft. Of the ninety-eight men and women on board *USCGC Seneca* that night, Biff and Emily managed to pull just eight survivors from the dark waters, one of whom was badly injured and, despite Emily's valiant efforts, died shortly after he was extracted from the sea. They later learned that an additional five crew members were rescued by the Coast Guard, but in the coming days, the rescue operations inevitably transitioned to recovery efforts. Of the eight-six souls that gave their lives in service for their country, all but two of the bodies were eventually recovered and returned to their loved ones. Among the fatalities were Captain Tom Hartman, Chief Weapons Officer Alvin Bailey, and Lieutenant Commander Justin Wilson, who were all posthumously awarded the Coast Guard Distinguished Service Medal for exceptionally meritorious service in a duty of great responsibility.

While the *Dauntless* crew retired to their cabins for a well-earned rest, Scotty stayed on the bridge long enough to pilot *Dauntless* into Boston Harbor, where she was guided directly to the United States Coast Guard Base in the very berth that *USCGC Seneca* had vacated the previous evening. It was the Coast Guard's way of showing respect and honor to the valiant crew of *Dauntless*. The gesture was accepted with humility and acknowledged with gratefulness.

Blake and Kat finally hit the hay around 4:00 am and slept soundly until noon. Blake was up, showered, and dressed first and wandered out, finding no one else up and about save for Biff, who was in the galley cooking up a hearty brunch along with Doc 'Energizer Bunny' Watson helping out, chatting away, and appearing none the worse for the wear following the previous night's harrowing activities. "'Energizer Bunny', indeed!" mused Blake to himself, a small smile turning up the corners of his mouth.

Later, following a hearty meal shared with the rest of the crew, Blake and Kat retired to their quarters once more for a follow-up call with Rod Stringer.

After exchanging warm greetings, Rod turned serious, his voice sounding a little strained and tired. It had been a sleepless night for him, and rest was still many hours away. "I'm so glad you folks are all ok. I've been briefed by the Coast Guard on the events of last night, and I can't tell you enough how grateful I am and, heck, how grateful your country is. Despite the tragic loss of *USCGC Seneca* with most of her crew, had that device detonated, it would have been so much worse. You and your courageous crew deserve all the credit for that. It's a debt that can never be repaid."

"We had a feeling that we might be needed as backup," Blake responded. "We didn't think twice about it and are grateful we were at the right place and time to offer assistance. While we agree our efforts were not in vain and the prevention of the ultimate ends of the terrorists were foiled, we just aren't in a mood to celebrate in light of the horrendous loss of innocent life with the sinking of *Seneca*."

"Yes," Rod agreed. "I take your point, but I understand two of your crew, Biff and Emily, were out in the immediate aftermath, pulling eight crewmen from the water - seven of which survived. Again, on behalf of the families and loved ones of those you rescued and the entire United States government, I thank you and salute you."

"Anyone in our shoes would have done the same, and you know it," Kat replied softly, her eyes glistening. "Like Blake, I really don't feel like a hero this afternoon - just incredibly sad at the needless loss of life. But I am grateful that there was something we could do to prevent an even greater tragedy."

"You are heroes, even if you don't feel like it," Rod insisted. "And I haven't forgotten your critical efforts and risks undertaken over the past few months in uncovering the entirety of the terrorist plot. Let's not overlook the other eleven freighters that were successfully intercepted by the Coast Guard, boarded, their dirty bombs neutralized, and terrorist crews arrested and detained. We can't marginalize the value of the human lives lost last night, but the scale of the tragedy averted is almost beyond comprehension. It may feel like a defeat in some respects, but make no mistake, this is truly a great victory."

"That's great to hear," Blake answered. "The National Guard commander gave us the Coles Notes last night, and we've been monitoring the news media this morning. It really is a proud moment for the Coast Guard, all things considered. We just had a bad feeling that Song Hee was calling the shots on *Neptune* and might just have been cunning and desperate enough to do exactly what he did. We witnessed the entire thing, and I will be the first to testify that Captain Tom Hartman was exemplary in the fulfillment of his duties. He, his officers, and the crew all deserve the highest accolades for their bravery in the line of duty."

"Thank you, Blake. That is very kind of you. I truly wish I could publicly acknowledge the role the Clean World Foundation, *Dauntless*, and her faithful crew played in averting this disaster. But as I'm sure you already know and fully appreciate, that will have to remain classified. What I can do, and I have already placed the request through official channels, is to fund a large donation courtesy of Uncle Sam to the Clean World Foundation. No amount of money could ever repay the debt owed, but I sincerely hope you will accept it as a token of our appreciation."

Blake and Kat glanced at each other and nodded before Kat responded on behalf of them both. "We would be happy to accept whatever you wish to donate. It will be put to good use, I assure you. Not to mention a great way to kick off our autumn fundraising tour!"

Blake and Kat had many other questions for Rod, and the conversation continued for the better part of an hour. While the investigation was still in its early stages, Rod conveyed that interrogations with the captured crews of the various freighters made it clear that they were under the impression that once the arming code had been entered on the devices, a three-hour timer would begin to count down, allowing them time to get to the nearest airport and make their escape. They were no idealogues - in it solely for the money and had been promised plenty of it. In fact, the expert demolition teams found no evidence of timers on any of the devices. Initiating the arming sequence would have resulted in an immediate detonation and loss of life for all on board – something they suspected that Song Hee, himself, was likely unaware of.

Sonja had made a break for it immediately after learning that her scheme was unraveling. She didn't get far. Her vehicle was intercepted on the way to the airport, and she was arrested, charged, and taken into custody. Three-hundred thousand dollars in US currency was found in the vehicle, along with three false identities that included what appeared to be top-quality fake passports for Switzerland, South Africa, and Turkey. She was not cooperating with authorities and quickly lawyered up.

Nicos Papadakis had made a run for it twenty-four hours prior to Sonja. The surveillance team that had been assigned to him called it in, and he was apprehended shortly thereafter at Athens International Airport in the process of boarding a flight bound for London - his first scheduled stop en route to his chosen haven country of Chile. Like Sonja, he had several aliases in his possession, complete with passports, credit cards, and supporting ID. Unlike Sonja, he had already agreed to a plea deal and was cooperating. He only knew the ringleader by her code name, Helle, but authorities were confident that Helle and Sonja were one and the same. Nicos had also provided valuable insight into the motivation and rationale for the attacks. Blake and Kat could only shake their heads sadly at the warped, twisted mentality of their trusted friend and partner, Sonja Larsen, for whom the ends seemingly justified any means whatsoever, no matter the horrific toll on human lives and livelihoods. Destroying the world was not the way to save it.

Nicos had also passed on the identities of eleven other wealthy, influential people across Western Europe involved in the planning and funding of the mission. The authorities had spent the last twelve hours trying to arrest them, only to find that they had all met recent, untimely deaths due to accidents or sudden natural medical events. Any one of the deaths would not have raised suspicion of homicide, but all at once and, in combination with Nicos' testimony, the deaths would be investigated further. Further questioning of Nicos revealed his suspicion that Helle had arranged sophisticated hits on all Council members, including himself - which was why he had decided to go into hiding prior to the attacks.

The call eventually wound to a close, as Rod had other duties to attend to. "You two love birds take care now. I'll be sure to be in touch with updates as the investigation continues. When is your first fundraiser? Have you had to postpone or cancel any of them in light of what's happened?"

Blake chuckled ruefully. "The show must go on, Rod. I'm sure you understand. There's been a lot of planning gone into this and, despite the adventure we've been on these past couple of months, Sonja was right about one thing. The world needs to find a new path and find it quickly. We're just going to do it our way. The right way. Kat and I will be hosting our first event tomorrow night at the Ritz-Carlton right here in Boston. We'll give you half price on the $1,000 per plate fee if you can find your way here in time."

Rod hadn't had many laughs in the past few weeks, but that earned Blake a genuine guffaw. "Still too rich for my blood. But tell you what... once I get my promised federal government donation arranged, why don't I present it at one of your later stops on the planned tour? And if I come bearing a big cheque, I'm getting my fancy dinner for free!"

"Deal!!" Blake and Kat chimed in together.

8 weeks later, the Cayman Islands

Kat leaned back in her beach lounger, and dangled her toes in the soft, white sand, savoring the sensation of the sun's radiant heat penetrating her bronzed skin. Blake was sitting up next to her, nursing a refreshing, slushy Strawberry Daiquiri, keeping tabs on the ebb and flow of the impromptu beach volleyball game that had commenced just up the beach. It was Emily, of course, that had initiated the fun - pleading with and cajoling strangers in the vicinity to take part. Biff had been relaxing in the warm surf but reluctantly allowed Emily to drag him out of the water and over to the court. The giant man was currently standing at the net, effortlessly swatting down every ball that came his way while Emily squealed in delight. It wasn't really fair for the competition. "Hey Kat. Don't you think Emily and Biff are spending a lot of time together lately? Is there something going on between them?"

Kat groaned and rolled her eyes behind her large, mirrored shades. "Seriously, Blake? You're just noticing now? There's been something going on between them for weeks. Maybe longer."

Following the hugely successful fundraising tour that concluded in early December in Miami, Blake and Kat insisted on treating everyone to a week's stay at a private resort in the Cayman Islands. It had been eagerly anticipated by the crew now for weeks, especially when Blake and Kat promised them that, in addition to paying all expenses, they would also be collecting their full salary during the stay, even if they opted out to rest and recharge in a manner of their own choosing. All were present and accounted for.

After pondering Kat's words for a few minutes, Blake had another question. "How do we feel about intra-crew relationships? Does that create any issues for us? Maybe we need to set some ground rules… or something." Blake's voice faded away in uncertainty.

Kat laughed and patted Blake's arm. "Now dear, don't you think that might be a tad hypocritical? Leave them be. If an issue develops, we'll deal with it. In the meantime, aren't they the cutest? It just shows there is truth to that old cliché about opposites attracting."

Blake had to admit she had a point. Putting it out of his mind, he slid his sunglasses back down and picked up his book. "Fine. Let's get everyone together at dinner tonight and see what they think about Rod's proposal."

That evening, in a private dinner that Kat had arranged, Blake and Kat informed the crew that Rod had been in touch and had offered to formalize an arrangement with The Clean World Foundation. In return for a large annual donation to the Foundation, the United States government would reserve the right to engage *Dauntless* to assist in intelligence-gathering missions under mutually agreeable terms. The unique capabilities of the ship and crew, combined with their impeccable cover as an international environmental charity, gave it a unique ability to operate globally, including places where conventional military and intelligence assets of the United States could not. Blake and Kat were willing to participate but would only sign on if the crew was in unanimous support. A secret ballot was taken and given to Matt to tabulate. A few moments later, he returned and announced with a large grin, "It's unanimous. Looks like we'll be saving the world in more ways the one."

Blake raised his glass in a toast. "To the finest crew on the finest ship that has ever sailed the seven seas. May the wind be ever in her favor."

Manufactured by Amazon.ca
Bolton, ON